About the Author

Andi Josephine Jordan is a young mum to three beautiful boys, living in South Wales. She loves to read, watch films and spend time with friends and family. Although life has not been easy, she has worked hard to make sure she is in the best place she can be; overcoming the traumas of her past and pushing forward to the best possible future. She is a glass-half-full kind of person, a Hufflepuff, but most importantly she loves nothing more than to be helping people in any way she can.

The Human Luna

Andi Josephine Jordan

The Human Luna

Olympia Publishers
London

www.olympiapublishers.com
OLYMPIA PAPERBACK EDITION

A CIP catalogue record for this title is available from the British Library.

ISBN: 978-1-80074-625-1

This is a work of fiction.
Names, characters, places and incidents originate from the writer's imagination. Any resemblance to actual persons, living or dead, is purely coincidental.

First Published in 2023

Olympia Publishers
Tallis House
2 Tallis Street
London
EC4Y 0AB

Printed in Great Britain

Dedication

I would like to dedicate this book to my beautiful nan, Geraldine Jordan, who passed away in January 2021.

Acknowledgements

I'd like to thank my friends and family for their encouragement when writing this book, their positive comments when I had my doubts and for pushing me when I didn't think I was good enough. I'd also like to thank my children for helping celebrate with me and being my biggest fans even when I wasn't sure what was happening. I love you, boys.

Prologue

I was never the most popular girl growing up, in fact, I only really had two friends throughout high school. Meygan and Josh, without them I wouldn't have survived. Some days, they were the only reason I went to school, sure the break was nice but no one would notice if I wasn't there. My own dad didn't want to know me so why would anyone else? He spends more time at work than he ever does at home, it's always up to me to take care of everything and it's been this way since I was nine years old.

My dad blames me for my mother leaving, he always has and he likely always will. Shortly after my mother left he moved all of my stuff up to the attic, he couldn't bear to look at me, I looked too much like my mother.

Every morning I would get up, let the dogs out, wake my sisters up who ALWAYS argued it but if I didn't wake them who else would? Our "mother" abandoned us nearly two years ago, our "father" would get up at the crack of dawn to work all day; only to come home when we were in bed. That's if he came home at all.

Sometimes I wondered whether he even loved us or whether he just put up with us because he had to, maybe he liked the image of the single dad with three daughters, raising them after being abandoned by the love of his life. A great example of how you don't know everything that goes on behind closed doors; I was the one that learned to cook at nine years old because if I didn't, we wouldn't eat, I was the one that figured out how the washing machine worked because I was fed up of me and my sisters being bullied for our clothes always being smelly.

That doesn't include all the other household chores; hoovering, washing up, feeding the dogs (we had four; Jenkins, Bailey, Charlie and Tyson – Dad said only males because he was fed up of being surrounded by women). Luckily my sisters were old enough to help a bit but how much could an eight and six-year-old really do? I didn't want their childhood destroyed like mine had been; they will not know the things that I have had to.

I often think about my future; whether our mother will ever come back, whether our dad will ever change or even if I will ever feel happy again. I've only known exhaustion for the past year; between the cleaning, the cooking, the school runs and the homework I don't get much of a break. My aunt is coming to visit next month! We haven't seen her in months; she met someone and moved to England with her, building their own life together, I wish I could just up and leave like she did but it's never going to happen I will always be stuck here cleaning up after everyone else.

I was snapped out of my thoughts by the sound of Emily coming up the ladder to my bedroom; my father made me move to the attic shortly after my mother left, he said it was my fault – that I drove her away, that I was a monster, he still says that I'm the reason he doesn't come home – blames me for him missing out on time with Emily and Clara.

Sometimes I believe it – I really do – but ultimately, I know it's not my fault. I can't comment on my mother's reasons for leaving because I don't know why she left. What I do know is that I'll get through this. We all will.

"Come on, Sanny! You said we could go to the lake todayyy!" Emily was trying to pull me out of bed as hard as she could, I had completely forgotten about the picnic at the lake. I still had to pack it.

"Well, I tell you what; if you can make your bed and put all your toys away whilst I pack the picnic we can go. Okay?" I was trying to buy myself some time hoping it would rain before we had to leave.

"You're no fun! I want to go now!" Emily stormed downstairs to do her chores whilst I just laughed at her grumpiness, looking at the clock I realised it was only 7.16 a.m. Why couldn't she ever sleep in? Honestly why people have kids I'll never understand!

I walked down to the bathroom to have a quick shower before heading back upstairs and chucking on my favourite bikini, observing myself in the mirror I realised that I've always disliked my appearance; if it wasn't for my long near white hair, long eyelashes and plump lips I'm sure people would think I was a boy. Honestly, I had a rectangle figure. Which I guess was normal for most girls my age but I hid under hoodies and baggy bottoms; it's probably the reason I had no friends but what could I do? My dad wouldn't buy me clothes and when he did, he just grabbed whatever was cheapest whether it's boys' clothes or girls', my best friend Meygan would sneak me some of her old clothes; it wasn't often but I appreciated it all the same! It's the only time I had clothes that fit.

Satisfied with my outfit of choice I headed downstairs to wait for the girls to show up so we could head to the lake; luckily it was only a ten minute walk otherwise I don't think we would do anything on nice days like today unfortunately.

"Ready!" the girls shouted in unison so we could leave. The walk was fairly quick today, we enjoyed getting out of the house together when we could. It meant that we could have fun and act like siblings rather than me being their temporary mam, we were there for a few hours before we sat down for our picnic and a few kids from school showed up. I never knew how to interact with the kids in my year, nobody could understand what I was going through, why I couldn't hang out after school or go out on the weekends. It was the first time I'd seen any of them outside of school if I'm honest.

Chapter One
The Woods

"Oh, look, it's Shannon!" one of the girls shouted pointing over at me, I wasn't sure who she was. The only person I actually knew was Josh; that's because his mam and mine were best friends so we grew up together, he was the other person I liked to hang out with when Meygan wasn't around but honestly since he'd been hanging around with the "popular" crowd he didn't acknowledge me much. Once again, I was dragged away from my thoughts by the crowd coming over and sitting with us.

I smiled politely and kept an eye on my sisters who were playing catch on the field, trying not to let the group know how irritated I was that they had shown up.

"We were starting to think you were allergic to anything normal," one of them said in a sarcastic tone.

"Yeah, I thought you only left your cave for school," another retorted, putting their arm around me as I tried to wriggle away from them. Another moved closer and put her arm around me.

"Aww, come on, we want to spend time with you. I don't think we've ever seen you outside of school."

"You know most people don't wear bikinis unless they can fill them, right?" the girl who acknowledged me first said.

"Come on, Gem, leave her alone," Josh said, I managed to break free from the two people that were holding me when I realised, I couldn't see the girls any more.

"Emily? Clara?" I shouted as I ran to where they were playing previously, I couldn't see or hear them anywhere; I kept shouting until Emily appeared out of the woods running. What were they doing in there? Nobody goes into those woods, there are wolves in there! I ran towards her when I heard the last thing I wanted to.

"Bear! Clara! Bear!" she screamed as I got close, I stopped only to tell her to run to Josh who was thankfully already chasing after us, there must have been a wolf, there are no bears in Wales.

"Stay with Josh, get him to take you home now!"

I did something that I never thought I would and I ran to the woods without a second thought; Clara was in danger. I had to.

In the woods it was silent, eerie; it was as if I had entered another dimension. It was dark, twigs littered the floor, the trees surrounding were huge, bigger than anything I had ever seen. I heard the crunch of twigs in the clearing in front so I took off again running as fast as I could without a single thought to myself, I could feel my feet object as they splintered under the twigs, how I wish I had put my daps on but you don't think in the moment. You can't, your first thought is to go.

I heard a scream and pushed myself forward, I could see a clearing in the trees to what looked like a meadow? There's a meadow in the woods? As I ran through the trees to the meadow, I noticed Clara lying on the floor but that wasn't what worried me; it was the large ebony wolf towering over her. Was it sniffing her?

I bolted forward without a care; my sister was in danger.

"No! Clara!" The wolf watched me as if I was a little bunny – absolutely no threat at all, although I suppose to it, I was. With all the strength I could muster I ran into its side, only knocking it slightly; which I think was more from shock than anything but it was enough to give me room with Clara so I could check she was okay.

I turned my attention to Clara; she was breathing thankfully; not a scratch on her. What was she doing in the woods? Why did she come out this far? Why wasn't she hurt?

I turned around to find myself face to face with the wolf, its big brown eyes staring at me; it slowly approached me and started sniffing me. Why wasn't I scared? Surely, I should be terrified! This thing was at least twice my size there was no way I'd survive a fight against it, did it know this? Was it waiting to pounce? It stalked even closer, making me close my eyes as I prepared for it to pounce; I was sure I was going to die there. As long as Clara lived, I didn't care.

After a short while I opened my eyes, only to find that the wolf was gone; leaving me all the more confused but I had to take this moment to grab Clara and run. I tried to pick her up but she was too heavy for me; I tried to wake her but she just wasn't waking.

It started getting dark but she still hadn't woken, I just sat there cradling her head; I knew Emily was safe, she was with Josh, she adored Josh and to be fair he adored her, sometimes I was jealous of their bond, I wish I had someone that doted on me like Josh did Emily.

It felt like we had been sat there for days rather than hours, darkness had fully taken the place of what was once a beautiful sun-filled meadow; I couldn't see anything at all, the moon was nowhere to be seen in the ebony sky above. It was like something out of a horror movie as I sat there waiting – at that point I wasn't sure what I was waiting for; the wolf to return and surely kill us or for Clara to wake so we could go home, I couldn't remember the last time I'd felt this drained or defeated.

My thoughts were interrupted by the sound of twigs snapping in the distance dragging me back to reality, I grabbed the closest stick to me just in case it was the wolf from earlier. I looked around praying to see something in the darkness, that was when I saw it; a light which could only be that of a torch.

"Over here! Please, can you help? Hello!" I shouted in hope that whoever this was would hear us and come help, the torch started shining in our direction so I waved my arms as wide as I could.

The light got bigger and bigger until finally I could see a vague figure behind it; they crouched down putting the torch down in front of us so it wasn't shining completely on us.

"What are you girls doing out here on your own? Do you know how dangerous these woods are to Hu—children?" He had a warmth to his voice, it was husky as if from running but he seemed to have a gentle aura, for some reason he felt… safe. With the vague light coming from the torch facing away you could see genuine concern showing across his face as he examined both me and Clara; I'm guessing for injuries; I mean we were in the woods at night – no one ever goes into these woods in the day, never mind at night.

"What happened?" His question seemed to wake me up from whatever daze I was in. Looking at him, not knowing what to do, I moved back a bit, lying Clara's head gently on the grass below.

"Oh… there was a… a… a wolf. It went and then I couldn't carry her. I'm not strong enough." I stuttered with a lot of my words; all we wanted was a day at the lake yet here we were in the middle of a meadow after a wolf almost ate us. I hung my head low, feeling ashamed that I couldn't protect Clara today or even carry her home because she was too heavy; the girls have always been on the larger side growing up. It wouldn't surprise me if they're taller than me in a few years if I'm honest.

"It's okay, calm down, you're safe now. I won't let anything happen to you. I promise." He rubbed my arm as he spoke leaving behind a warmth I'd not experienced before, he said his words with such certainty that I couldn't help but believe him. He started to pick up Clara and carry her in a way I've only seen men on the telly carry their partners after they get married. I wish I was being carried; my feet were sore and bloody because I didn't have any shoes on but at least we were going home, where we would be safe.

"Why don't you carry the torch and I'll carry your sister; that okay with you?"

I chuckled as I said, "Yeah, I think I can manage that." We walked through the woods easily; it was as if he'd walked it a hundred times before. I don't think he even needed the torch if I'm honest, he didn't notice when I shined it at my feet or at the trees to keep an eye on the area around us; that wolf could come back or there could be other animals. This is the whole reason we don't come in here because we aren't sure what kind of things live here.

We finally got back to the lake, all of our stuff was gone; my guess was that Josh had taken it with him to my house which I was both grateful and ungrateful for – it meant I had to walk through the streets in just my bikini and no shoes.

I took over and showed the man the way to my house – as we got closer to home there were more and more streetlights so I was able to study him properly; he only looked young maybe seventeen? He was quite muscly with shoulder length hair, he was wearing a blue t-shirt, I noticed a wolf tattoo on his bicep. I was studying his tattoo when he cleared his throat, he had obviously noticed I'd been staring at him for some time.

"So, what's your name or am I going to have to keep knowing you as blondie?" He chuckled as he said blondie, it made my heart sore. Why was I feeling like this?

"Oh, it's Shannon, Shannon Rye."

"Well, Shannon Rye, it's nice to meet you. I'm Thomas Cannon."

I opened my mouth to respond but as I did my front door flew open and my dad rushed out. It was a surprise to see him I hadn't for nearly a month but my guess is Josh's mom rang him to tell him off. He grabbed Clara out of Thomas' arms. "Alph—"

Thomas cut him off by holding his hand out. "Thomas Cannon, nice to meet you. I found your daughters in the woods whilst I was out for a stroll, please make sure they don't find their way there again. Who knows what could happen."

My dad looked between the three of us both confused and concerned; I gave him a small smile hopefully making him feel somewhat at ease that we were okay.

Thomas rubbed my arm gently, the warmth enveloping me. This is weird, right? Why is his touch so warm? He's like a human radiator, honestly.

"I really hope we meet again soon, Shannon, just not in the woods, okay?" He had such a gentle smile I couldn't help but smile back.

"I hope so too," was all I could think to respond as I watched him walk away, I started questioning everything from today; Why did Clara go in the woods? Why didn't the wolf kill us? Where did Thomas come from? Why could I not stop thinking of him?

One thing I did know was that everything was changing from today; I was going to be a different, better version of myself and no one was going to stop me.

Chapter Two
Six Years Later

Senior Year

It was my senior year of high school. In many ways, yes, I had changed, I no longer looked like a boy with really long hair I had actual curves; which as a teenage girl was amazing. I finally taught myself how to do hair and make-up, since the day at the lake me and Josh had been fairly inseparable. My dad actually looked after us, he was home more often than he wasn't which was honestly a massive weight off my shoulders. We were the closest we'd ever been but I still felt like he was hiding something; I tried asking about Thomas multiple times, if he knew him or even where he came from but he always brushed it off. He preferred to act as if none of it happened which is crazy because it did, I saw the wolf every night in my dreams his chocolate brown eyes melting into my heart, I wasn't even scared of him I felt drawn to him if anything and I wasn't sure why.

My alarm clock started beeping dragging me from the same thoughts I had every day; the man and the wolf. I started getting ready and headed off to school; my dad waving me out the door on my first day. Just as I was leaving my dad's new girlfriend pulled up outside the house, I don't know why but she didn't seem to like me; she waited every day until I was gone before going in and, on the weekend, she didn't even acknowledge me. Obviously, I couldn't say anything to my dad because he loved her and honestly? He deserved happiness more than anyone.

Josh was waiting in his car as cheerful as always. I jumped

in and he drove us to school; I thought the first day of senior year would be exciting but it was fairly boring, in fact the first few months were boring they consisted of nothing but coursework! At least Prom was coming up; me, Meygan and Josh had decided to go together if we didn't have dates – even coordinating our outfits!

Today was a Saturday, me and Meygan decided to go to the next town over to do some prom dress shopping, even if we just browsed, it's nice to get away for a few hours, she was trying on a few fitted dresses but I wanted something big and puffy; something that made me feel like a princess. This shop had nothing like that but we found Meygan's dress! I couldn't imagine anything more perfect for her if I'm honest but I was so happy for her – next was my dress!

"Fancy grabbing a bite to eat before we head back over?" I asked, my stomach grumbling in appreciation.

Meygan giggled. "Ha-ha, yeah, I hear Kenny's make the best burgers."

"Kenny's it is," I mumbled in agreement as I walked towards the restaurant, Meygan followed behind cheerfully.

Chapter Three
The Alpha and the Beta

Thomas

Six years. It had been six years to the date since I'd seen her in the forest, she defended her sister against my wolf despite the danger that it involved. She was human, not a wolf like I imagined; just a small innocent human. She deserved a normal life. I would stay away from her for as long as I could; take a chosen mate rather than make her mine. The way her touch ignited a fire inside of me I would give anything to feel that again; anything. She was only eleven though; eleven, man. I hadn't been with anyone since the day I saw her, I had been holding out for my mate anyway which was hard but once I had actually met her it wasn't hard at all; I wanted nothing more than for her to be my one and only forever. I could never force our world on her, I promised her father that I would let her make her own choice.

There was a knock at the door before my Beta Stefan walked in.

"Alpha, there's been talk of rogues hiding out in the town, we're wondering what action you'd like us to take." Stefan spoke curiously; I only took over as Alpha last year when an army of Rogues attacked another pack whilst my father, our Alpha, was visiting. Unfortunately, we lost him. We also lost both his Beta and his Gamma during the attack. Shortly after my mother, our Luna, died of a broken heart. Our remaining Gamma killed herself; she said she wasn't able to live without her mate, it was understandable, they say that your mate is the final piece of your soul, they make you stronger, happier, they are quite literally the other half of you so when they pass you lose half of your soul, half of you, your only reason to be happy, how can one live without all of that? I'm not sure but it only heightened my respect for my father's beta's mate Kath; she struggles but she's still here thankfully because she's honestly one of the only reasons me and Stefan were doing our jobs so well.

I couldn't even begin to imagine my mate dying, no, I hadn't claimed her and I didn't know if I would but I did know that I loved her more than anything. I'd watched her from the shadows every day since our meeting in the woods, I couldn't go a day without seeing her, who would want to? She was absolutely breath-taking.

"We should go into town and have a look around today, see how their presence is affecting the town then step in if necessary; we need to know how many there are and what their plans are, before we consider making a move." I stood up from my desk following my Beta out the door. I've known Stefan since we were pups, he's my sanity, my rational side, my best friend – I couldn't have done any of this without him. Before being Beta, he was quite reckless, he slept around with any wolf that looked at him; to put it bluntly. But he met his mate last year – maybe two weeks before my father died and she calmed him, brought out the good guy that I grew up with. If it wasn't for her, I don't think I'd have been able to make him my Beta – he was too reckless – it would have been a risk to our pack. It's because of this Jade is the only one who gets away with bossing me about around here because ultimately, she usually does know better. Not that I'd admit that to her anyway.

We travelled to the town in silence. Luckily it was only a

short drive – it was quicker in wolf form because we could cut through the forest – but it was nice to drive too, it gave me even more time to think about things but as usual my mind was wrapped up in the same thing it was every single day; her. I constantly wonder what she'd think to know we were fated together, that she was created by the moon goddess for me. No one else.

Chapter Four
An Old Acquaintance

Shannon

We left the restaurant after what really was the best burger I'd ever eaten in my entire life, we walked back to the car laughing about little things. Meygan was telling me about some big prank she was planning to get her brother with; they were always pranking each other. Just last year he shaved her eyebrows off; the kids at school called her Winnie the pooh for *weeks*. It was hilarious and Meygan really was a good sport, never once getting upset.

As we rounded the corner, I slammed into what felt like a soft wall sending me straight back, dropping to the floor landing pretty badly on my bottom. I sat there in shock for a moment before looking up to see this giant of a man stood there staring at me; great that's all I needed to ruin a perfect day.

He seemed familiar I couldn't quite place where I'd seen him from; probably a magazine with how attractive he was. He had a navy suit on with a baby blue shirt, he had hints of a beard probably shaven off yesterday or something but he had this gorgeous mane of mousy brown hair thrown up in what looked like a messy man bun.

In my moment of admiring him I hadn't even noticed Meygan shouting at him and his friend to watch where they were going, he captivated me like nothing I'd experienced before. He bent down and offered me his hand to help me get up I smiled appreciatively as I took it – I hadn't realised how close we were until I was gazing deep into his big brown eyes, that sense of familiarity taking over, I mumbled, "I know you," under my breath before I could even think to stop myself.

He stood upright when I said this, he must have recognised me too, right? Or was I just having some crazy teenage fantasy?

"You could have seriously hurt her you know!" I was suddenly distracted by Meygan poking and shouting at this god of a man. I rested my hand on Meygan's arm to pull her back a bit.

"Hey, feisty, chill; it was my fault for not looking where I was going. I'm so sorry, sir, and... thank you. For helping me up." I was distracted towards the end... I was nervous, why was I nervous? I looked up at him to see he was smiling, although smirking was probably the better word; he probably got a kick out of teenage girls getting nervous around him.

The air grew colder as the wind picked up; the sign of a storm on its way usually. I looked back up at the man only to see his eyes had changed, they were black, or at least I'm sure they were; I blinked and like that they were back to normal. I was hallucinating, great. I don't think I hit my head though so why would I hallucinate? He said something under his breath but I couldn't hear it, the wind was too loud and the rain had started.

"Well, it was a pleasure to meet you but we must be going," his friend spoke up, I hadn't even noticed him fully with everything going on. He was a bit shorter but definitely looked like they followed the same workout routine. His eyes were still fixed on me as his friend dragged him away, it looked like he was fighting it but then the rain started so me and Meygan ran as fast as we could back to the car soaking wet. We just laughed at each other and started driving home. We knew we would have to get home as fast as we could with the storm approaching.

I finally got through my front door only to be tackled by Emily – I swear she'd be bigger than me by this time next year! She was so tall. Clara was already taller than me; I honestly never thought I was short but there was no doubt, especially when your two younger sisters are taller than you.

"Shannonnnnn, could you straighten my hair pleaseeee? Clara won't do it! She said she has better things t—why are you wet?" She stood up and brushed herself off as if I was a dog that'd just gotten fur over her. She'd developed a little bit of an aversion to mess as of late, Dad said it was a part of puberty but I couldn't care, I loved her no matter what.

"There's a storm coming, me and Meygan got caught in it on our way back. Let me shower and change then I'll be right with you, okay?" I pulled myself up off the floor only to drag myself up the stairs to the bathroom, getting in the shower was just what I needed to help warm myself up after that bloody rain. I climbed out of the shower; wrapping myself up in my robe as I headed towards my bedroom when all of a sudden, the lights went out, just my luck a power cut of all things!

"It's all right, I'll get some candles!" my dad shouted from downstairs. I heard some whispers before heading up to my bedroom but couldn't understand them; probably just Emily and Clara gossiping about something. There was still some light coming through my window thankfully; it made it easier for me to get dressed before I finally headed downstairs. The living room was covered in candles; it was actually really cosy. Suddenly the room was lit up by a bolt of lightning striking the ground on the field over the road; followed by the aggressive grumble of thunder overhead making us all jump. I looked over at my dad and I swear his eyes were fogged over; they looked white but it was hard to see them properly because of the candle light.

"Dad?" I asked softly receiving no response. I repeated; a bit sturdier this time but again no response, so this time I shouted which caught both his and Emily's attention; it was as if they shared a silent conversation before even acknowledging me. Why were they acting weird? It was probably the storm, right? I mean storms make everyone crazy.

"Yes, hunny, is everything okay?" He looked so confused, studying me with concern as if I was the one being weird. What was going on with him?

"You just—are you okay?" I asked him with genuine concern, looking at Emily to see if I was on my own with this. She looked at me as if I was the issue as well, yep, I was the issue. I shook my head concluding it was obviously just something to do with the candle light making his eyes look funny; I mean why else would they be foggy? Once again thunder rumbled overhead but this time it was followed by another sound. One that shocked me more than it should have. "Was? Was that a wolf?" I said quietly, jumping up to go look out the window and hopefully confirm my crazy thought. My dad was behind me, instantly nudging me away from the window, obviously not wanting me to look… but why?

"Of… of course not. They wouldn't come this close to the town, hunny. Listen, I have to go to work. Will you and the girls be, okay?" My dad seemed so nervous, almost upset. What was going on? Why was he being like this? What did Emily know that I didn't?

He rushed out the door before I even had a chance to answer, it was nearly nine p.m. he never went out that late any more. Something was wrong, I could feel it. Should I follow him? No, he would only get angry. I'd ask him tomorrow.

I blew the candles out before heading to bed; Emily and Clara went to bed near enough straight away as well which was nice, they are usually up until stupid o'clock.

I fell asleep as soon as my head hit the pillow.

***

I was woken from my dream by a loud smash downstairs; at first, I wasn't sure, I thought it was likely part of my dream but then I heard another smash, I tried looking out my window but it was too dark to see anything, not to mention the awkward angle the window was at.

I climbed down my ladder as quietly as I could manage, tiptoeing to Emily's bedroom first to make sure she was awake, I gasped when I saw her bed hadn't been slept in; I poked my head around the corner to see if I could see anything but there was nothing, only darkness. I tiptoed to Clara's room thinking Emily had gone in there like she does sometimes but the room was empty as well; where were they? Why weren't they sleeping? I was snapped out of my thoughts by the sound of footsteps on the stairs, I ran to my dad's bedroom locking his bedroom door behind me. I grabbed the house phone off the nightstand but when I brought it up to my ear the line was dead. Typical, the storm had knocked the phone lines down as well. Why did this happen to me? My dad was at work, my sisters were missing and I couldn't even call for help; I was completely on my own.

There was banging at the door, someone was trying to open the door, I screamed as I jumped back; falling over my dad's shoes, I hit my head against his wardrobe. For goddess sake!

There were muffled voices behind the door, I didn't

recognise them as I looked around the room for a weapon when I realised; the window! I'd just climb out of the window! I got to the window just as the door caved in. Without a second thought I climbed onto the windowsill, opening the window as quickly and as wide as possible.

"Get her quickly! GRAB HER!" a man shouted after me, I didn't look back before I jumped out of the window landing on the tool shed.

I landed on the roof with a massive thud; man, the metal against my legs seriously hurt, I whimpered as I got up.

This was the last thing I wanted to be doing right now but those men were trying to grab me, I rolled off the roof, landing on the path below. All I could do was run as I heard the men trying to open my front door. My body protested every move I made because of the pain radiating from every inch of my being.

The wind and the rain pushed me back, fighting with me as I tried to run; it was as if it wanted me to go the other way but I couldn't! The men would be out the door by now chasing after me, hopefully the wind slowed them down too. I heard loud footsteps behind me, I made the mistake of turning around, slowing down ever so slightly only to see a large shadow where I once stood.

All of a sudden, I was knocked from the path with brute force – it was a moment before I even registered that I was falling, I laid on the road in agony, too scared to move when I saw a large wolf stood on the path where I was just running. Why was a wolf this close to town? I'd never seen a wolf outside of those woods; it's as if they knew or there was some sort of boundary in place. My head was pounding from where I hit the floor, the pain in my back was crippling, not knowing what to hold first I clutched my side where the wolf hit me – I think it may have broken something but who cared? I'd be dead any minute I was sure of it. All I could hear was howling, the wolf that knocked me over just stood there looking at me; was it smiling? Can wolves smile? There was something sinister about this wolf, it terrified me; not like the wolf in the forest, this one was dangerous, unpredictable, its eyes were black – I maintained eye contact with it nervously, too scared to look away, not knowing what it was planning.

It stalked towards me slowly until it was stood over me with its paw pushing down on my stomach sending waves of pain through my body. All I could manage was a broken scream before everything went dark. I welcomed darkness thinking that this was it; death was welcoming me, taking the pain away, I couldn't wait to be at peace.

My eye lids were heavy as I tried my hardest to open them, as I gained consciousness, I was enveloped in the worst pain I'd ever felt; my entire body was throbbing, protesting every movement I tried to make to ease my pain. I finally managed to pry my eyes open into a squint; seeing nothing but darkness in front of me I instinctively tried to grab whatever was covering my face only to realise my wrists were restricted. A clattering as I moved them made me realise it was chains; I was chained up. Why was I in chains? Where was I? Why didn't I die?

I cried through the pain I could feel coursing through my arms where I tried so hard to get to my head; it was quiet wherever I was, the only sounds were coming from me, as I tried with what little energy I had to break free. Feeling defeated I gave up trying to get out; just sitting there in darkness I slowly slipped back into unconsciousness. What a day this turned out to be.

Chapter Five
Time Waits for No One

Beep Beep Beep

I was woken up by this irritating beeping sound around me, I was startled when opening my eyes to see this incredibly bright light, it was almost as if the room was glowing; once my eyes had adjusted, I realised that I was in a hospital room. It was a lovely room; very clean looking. The walls were a bright white with ocean blue coloured curtains, the bed I lay on was unusually comfortable with a warm blanket, there didn't seem to be anyone else here so this could be my chance to make a run for it. Get out of here quickly before anyone noticed, I sat up and tried to swing my feet off the bed before realising I couldn't move them. Why couldn't I move my legs? What was going on? My questions were interrupted when the heavy door at the edge of the room suddenly burst open; a tall man walked in followed quickly by a little nurse. I sat there confused, looking at the two people that had rudely came into the room. I wasn't sure how to feel right now, I had no idea where I was, who these people were or even how I'm still alive after everything that happened last night.

"Uh, Alpha, please. Don't. Alpha!" They both stopped in their tracks when they saw me. What was going on? Who were these people? Where was I?

Alpha? What's an Alpha? Or was that his name? Wait – it was that guy! The wall I ran into with Meygan! What's he doing here?

He practically sprinted towards my bed grabbing me and

placing his lips hungrily on mine; kissing me hard. There was a warmth radiating from his lips taking over my body, I never wanted it to leave. I sat there for a moment in shock but as soon as I realised what was going on I tried to push him away. He was too strong though, his grip not giving way, I started hitting him thinking it would loosen him at most but his grip only tightened; I started screaming beneath his lips which startled him enough for me to push him away and punch him in the face. I regretted it though because it hurt; I immediately tried to hide my whimper over my probable broken hand.

"What the hell do you think you're doing?" I screamed at him feeling my anger rise, pushing through to the surface. "Who the hell do you think you are? I don't even know you!"

He stood there looking at me in horror as if I should already have the answers, he stared into my eyes, as if searching for something – but what? I didn't know.

"I, err, I, um—" he stumbled his words before the nurse walked over to him pushing him out of the door forcefully.

"You need to leave now!" She managed to get him out of the room before locking the door and calmly making her way over to me, I was visibly shaking by this point whilst the beeping was only getting faster; I didn't know where I was, who these people were or even what happened and yet this random man thought it was okay to put his lips on me!

"Okay, sweetie, you need to breathe, I know you probably have lots of questions but first I need you to calm down, okay?" The nurse had a soft voice, it was quite soothing, I repeated the breathing gestures she was making in the hope that it would help me calm down. It was helping to be fair; my anger subsiding, the shaking had almost stopped when I noticed the beeping had slowed down, back to what it was before the kiss. The nurse looked a lot more relaxed too, which was comforting; it made me feel safe.

"I'm Hilary, the pack nurse, our doctor will be here soon. She was called away on an emergency unfortunately, now let's hear some of those questions." She had such a lovely smile I couldn't help but trust her.

"Wh-what's a pack?"

"All in good time, hunny, for now let's just get you healed and healthy again before we dive into the deep stuff."

"Wh-who was th-that man?"

"Oh, that was Thomas Cannon, he's…" She paused here, as if she was trying to think of an excuse or an explanation for him – wait where did I know that name from? It sounded so familiar! Why couldn't I place it? Ugh, my head hurt. "He's sort of the man in charge around here, he was so happy to see that you were alive, Miss Rye. I don't think I've ever seen him look so relieved."

"H-how did I get here?"

"One of our guards brought you here, they found you on the side of the road while Thomas fought off a ro—a wolf close by."

"My sisters, are they okay?" I was suddenly filled with panic as I remembered that they weren't home when those men broke in.

"Your sisters are fine, my lovely, they're with your dad, we have already contacted him to say that you're awake so I can't imagine he'll be long."

The nurse didn't get a chance to finish her sentence before my dad and sisters practically threw the door off its hinges; Emily nearly knocking me over as she jumped onto the bed wrapping me in a rib crushing hug. I winced as I felt my body rejecting her affection due to the amount of pain I was already in. Thankfully she jumped straight up and got off me.

"Oh, my goddess! I'm so sorry I forgot." Her eyes searched me for some sign of forgiveness or even just for the first time noticing my visible injuries; I gave her a small smile before moving my attention to my dad who was making his way towards me with his arms outstretched for a hug. I welcomed his hug and realised for the first time I had been holding in my tears, I finally let them fall; eventually breaking down into a sob. Everything that happened in the last twenty-four hours finally hitting me. After what felt like hours of crying, I finally felt all dried up, letting go of my dad, I could see how wet his face was from crying with me. He moved to the chair beside me and I couldn't help but laugh – he was a large man, in all honesty we always joked he was part gorilla because between his hair and his size it was the only thing that made sense but seeing him in this tiny hospital chair was incredibly amusing; I couldn't help but chuckle. The girls were laughing too which drew my attention back to them, remembering that they were gone. I didn't know where they were or who they were with. Heck I didn't even know if they were safe! I could feel my anger building which they must have noticed too because they were fidgeting where they stood.

"Where were you both?" I couldn't contain my anger as I practically spat the words at them – as much as I was glad, that they weren't there because of the men that broke in I still should have been told where they were! I could have headed straight out of my bedroom window rather than checking they were okay; all of this may have been avoidable! They exchanged looks between each other before Clara finally spoke.

"We… we decided to go into Dad's works, we couldn't sleep because of the storm. You were already asleep or we would have told you – we've been going every day since Emily got her w—

erm, new phone for her birthday. We want to start working with him when we turn sixteen so we've been starting our training, I've been going longer obviously but we didn't want to worry you. If we had known we never would have gone, I swear!" You could see how upset they were and honestly, I couldn't stay mad at them, I loved them too much. They returned their stare to the floor before they started to walk towards the door.

"Wait, girls—"

"We have to go but we'll come visit you soon, okay?" Emily gave me a faint smile as she walked out of the door, the guilt they were feeling was painfully obvious. I turned to face my dad, noticing he was also looking down at the floor, guilt spread across his face.

"Dad, it's not the fact that they weren't home, it's the fact I wasn't told."

"I know, hunny, but you have to remember you are not their parent, I know at one point you didn't have a choice and I will be forever grateful for everything you did when your mother left but for now you need to lead your own life and stop worrying for your sisters. They really can take care of themselves." My dad was right, I couldn't deny that but I was in charge; I should have been told, right? Am I wrong?

I couldn't help but ponder over what had happened and what could have happened if they were there, but my depressing thoughts were interrupted by my dad squeezing my hand attentively followed by a low growl ripping through the room. I looked towards the door where I was sure it came from only to see the stupid man from earlier. What was his name? Thomas? I was sure that was what the nurse called him, did he seriously just growl? Or was I losing my mind? Everything seemed weird lately.

"Did you just growl?" I asked the question so abruptly that he just stared at me; yep, I was losing it. I looked away from him, I needed to say something but I couldn't do it whilst looking at him; his gorgeous chocolate brown eyes enticing me more and more the longer I looked at him. I drew my attention back to my hands as I spoke. "You need to leave; I don't want you here!"

My dad gasped before letting go of my hand, sharing glances between me and Thomas, I decided to steal a quick glance at Thomas and it broke my heart to see how sad he looked – I'm not sure why but all I wanted to do was wrap my arms around him and make his sadness go away. I didn't even know this bloke, why was he affecting me so much?

"Hunny, Thomas has sat by your side every day for the past two weeks, he saved your life. He even fought off the wolf so his men could get you to safety."

I didn't know what to say. Why would a complete stranger risk his life for me? Plain old me! I wasn't anything special but clearly, he was; the nurse said he was the boss here. My dad only looked at him with admiration yet he didn't look old enough to be my dad's boss or even the nurses! He had to be in his twenties, late twenties at most. I noticed he was walking towards me slowly before sitting on the edge of my bed and taking my hand; there it was again, the warmth radiating from his touch trailing up my arm and through my body. I realised for the first time since I woke, I couldn't feel any pain, only warmth; it was amazing. I wanted nothing less than to feel like this forever.

"Please, I know I was forceful earlier and I honestly had no right. It was just… seeing you awake for the first time in two weeks I thought I was going to explode from joy. We weren't sure if you would make it through the night with—"

"Two weeks! What do you mean two weeks? The men, the

wolf—it… it was last night! I only met you yesterday and you thought you had some sort of claim over me? Are you fucking crazy?" The *audacity* of this bloke making out he had some sort of right to miss me and kiss me after I bumped into him yesterday. Two weeks? I was sure it was only yesterday? How could I have been asleep for two weeks? No, I couldn't have? Could I?

"Shannon, hunny, you've been in a coma since the day Thomas' men brought you here. To give your—"

I cut him off when I remembered being blindfolded and chained somewhere cold, if they were saving me why would I have been chained up and blindfolded.

"If you were saving me, why was I chained and blindfolded? Why was I left for hours on end somewhere cold until I passed out from the pain?" I could hear my voice breaking as I recalled the events after my waking; trying so hard to break free, being left with only my thoughts; that I was going to die, my sisters were likely dead and no one was going to find my body. Ever. I looked up as I felt warmth against my face; Thomas was moving a stray hair out of my face and placing it behind my ear.

"That was my fault. I told them to bring you back here but they assumed it was as a prisoner, as soon as I dealt with the wolves and got back here, I brought you straight to the hospital, I swear; I still have yet to deal with them for their treatment of you. The only time I have left your bedside is to shower yesterday."

He seemed sincere and gentle; I couldn't help but believe what he was saying. He clearly felt he had some sort of loyalty towards me, whatever that might be.

"Please let me introduce myself formally, my name is Thomas Cannon." He had a boldness that couldn't be denied and seeing the smile on his pink plump lips I couldn't help but smile back.

"Shannon Rye."

"I know who you are, Shannon, I've known you since I helped you that day in the woods six years ago. I've thought of nothing and no one else since."

I gasped, honestly it felt like that one sentence was the missing piece to a puzzle I didn't know I was doing. It was him; the man who was the only thing in my dreams other than that wolf. The one who saved me in the night, he was older now and when I say I liked him like this I mean it. I sat up leaning towards him and pressing my hand against his face checking if he was real; if all of this was real. The warmth was enveloping me – I think he felt it too because he leaned into my touch bringing one of his hands up to hold mine against him, why did I feel this way? Why was I drawn to him? Did he feel the same? No, he couldn't. He looked like he was sculpted by a God and well me – I'm just me. Our thoughts were interrupted when the door flew open and in skipped a short lady.

"Well, helloooo there. I'm so very glad you're awake!" She had such a happy energetic aura I couldn't help but smile and pull my hand back as she skipped towards the bed.

"I figured you'd be hungry after sleeping for two weeks – now, I didn't know what you would like so I brought you a bit of everything, dear."

She nudged Thomas off the bed so that she could bring the bed table over and put the tray down, as soon as I could smell the food my stomach growled in appreciation. She let out a giggle before skipping out of the room; I didn't even get a chance to thank her. Looking at my tray there were all different kinds of things; sandwiches, meatloaf, lasagne, mashed potatoes, vegetables – even jelly and ice cream! I dug in not knowing what to eat first. I tried the mash and honestly – I did *not* know mashed potatoes could taste this good, I let out a moan not even realising as I shovelled a few forkfuls into my mouth. I sampled everything – my favourite being the ice cream; no surprise there though. By the end I was stuffed.

"I'm going to take this to the pack kitchen and give you three some privacy, I'm sure there is a lot you need to discuss." Nurse Hilary rubbed my arm kindly before picking up the tray and heading out of the door; my dad took my hand, smiling kindly at me. You could see the relief in his face that I was okay. Suddenly a growl ripped through the room once again making my dad let go of my hand and turn our attention towards Thomas who was sat on a chair at the bottom of the bed.

"Did you just growl?" There's no way I'm going crazy, he definitely just growled, but why? Seems like a weird thing to do for a man; especially one as important as him.

"I, erm, just, uh, yeah." He stumbled his words along painfully; obviously not knowing how to explain himself, why was my dad not reacting? Did he know something that I didn't?

"What the hell is going on?" I shouted out my last thoughts, not even meaning to but I was so confused, secrets were being kept and I needed to know what.

"You're both hiding something and I want to know what. *Now*."

My dad sighed, obviously he expected me to just ignore all the weird shit going on but I couldn't. He was lying to me, Thomas was—even the girls were lying about something and I had a right to know.

"Hunny, you're right, but when we tell you it will change your life forever. Are you sure you want that? You could go home and lead a completely innocent life; I could even send you to live with your aunts if you like. You could get away from it all."

Another growl radiated from Thomas but this one was louder, angrier; I jumped and turned my attention towards him only to see that his chocolate brown eyes were gone – in their place? Endless black pits.

"Mate. Goes. Nowhere." He was definitely angry he spat these words at my dad through gritted teeth, why did he call me mate? What's a mate? What the hell was going on?

Chapter Six
The Longest Two Weeks of My Life

Thomas

**Two Weeks Ago*

Me and Stefan walked around the town slowly; making sure to check all of the little stores as well but we found absolutely nothing, there was no doubt that we had rogues setting up base in here. You could smell them everywhere, almost as if they wanted us to know they were here. As for finding an actual rogue; we couldn't – not a single one, so I had no idea what they were doing here, their plans, nothing. The fact that no one had gotten hurt was a big plus, although they could just be passing through rather than settling, it was too close to my pack's border for them to risk settling without challenging us.

Our border ended at the lake so we still considered the town under our protection. We even had some wolves living in the town which is how we found out about the rogues; our head warrior David Rye lived on the edge of the town so he was close enough to both to be there quickly where ever we needed him. His daughter Shannon, wow. I hadn't seen her for a few weeks because of all this rogue business, but I hadn't spoken to her at all in the six years it has been since I met her and her sister in the woods. Atticus met her first though, seeing as I was in wolf form, he followed the sweet scent of cherries and lavender – it was intoxicating I can remember how crazy it drove him as I was a mere passenger watching.

He chased the scent, not even caring about who he left behind, which was when we ran into Clara and Emily, Emily managed to run away but Clara ran further into the woods until she tripped and fell in the meadow, hitting her head pretty hard as she slipped into unconsciousness. Atticus nudged her trying to get her to wake – this was when we saw her coming out of the forest in only a bikini, it was an incredible sight; as soon as we made eye contact, I knew I was in love with her. I couldn't help it.

My thoughts were stopped as I turned a corner walking pretty hard into someone, it hit me all at once; her smell, her looks, the electricity that stirred beneath the minimal contact we had just made, all I could do was stand there in shock, in awe of her beauty and that damn intoxicating smell.

It took everything I had in me to stop myself picking her up and taking her home with me, I momentarily focused my attention to the girl that was with her, shouting at us before I offered Shannon my hand, hoping to help her up off the floor, longing for at least one moment of intimacy between us. Although she was my mate and every fibre of my being wanted me to mark her, take her, mate her and make her my Luna, I couldn't; being a Luna when you're a human is a huge risk. It would make her a target because she couldn't protect herself.

"We will protect her," Atticus shouted hungrily in my mind but I ignored him, as much as we could, it was still a lot and she had to make that decision herself; I promised her father that I would allow her to choose six years before when I realised who she was. I am a man of my word and I always will be, it is how my father raised me.

As I helped her up there was a moment where we just stared into each other's eyes; I couldn't help but notice how beautiful they were, it was like looking at the sky on a sunny day. I could feel the sparks invading my body, doing nothing but exciting my raging libido.

"I know you." Her whisper shocked me so much I almost jumped back; did she remember me from that night six years before? I mean I'd changed a lot but I didn't think she'd recognise me or did she know that I'd been secretly stalking her nearly every day for six long years? Watching her grow into the most beautiful woman that I'd ever seen. Her voice was sweet, heavenly – like I was listening to an angel. Goddess, I love every fibre of her, I really do.

It was becoming hard to keep Atticus at bay, he wanted control; he wanted to mate with her and mark her right there, right then. He managed to get through for a second muttering, "*Mate,*" quietly before I was able to take back control, I don't think she would have heard him being human and all that. The sky grew dark, thunderous almost. I hadn't realised, only she had my gaze, my light amongst the progressing storm. That is, until, I watched in dismay as she ran in the opposite direction seeking shelter after the heavens had decided to open up, drenching those who were left exposed. I hadn't noticed Stefan trying to pull me away, trying to get me away from the developing storm; he may be strong but thankfully, I'm stronger. This was the only real interaction I'd had with Shannon in six long years, I couldn't let it end. Not right then, I needed to talk to her, tell her how I feel, that I wanted her, that I needed her. I ran after her in desperation; the wind and the rain pushed me back, as if it knew I shouldn't go after her, I could hardly see between the weather and the tears building in my eyes. I've lost her, her intoxicating scent a mere memory as the rain washed it away.

I ran towards the forest, shifting at the border without a care about ruining my new suit; it always felt exhilarating letting Atticus out but he was just as sad as I was that we'd lost our first chance to speak to her. Of course, he blamed me and blocked me out so that I couldn't talk to him, he just kept running through the woods, hopefully towards the pack house because I had stuff to do.

I mind linked Stefan, "Sorry I ran out, bro, it hurt, I'll meet you back at the pack house, I don't think this storm is going to let up."

"No worries, bro, I get it, she will want you though, I have no doubt just by the way she looked at you today."

As we grew closer to the packs border there was the distinct smell of blood, both old and new invading the air. A whole host of reasons ran through my mind but only one made sense; rogues. Atticus eased his pace, raising his heckles and bared his canines ready for a fight as he approached the pack borders cautiously. The storm rendered our senses useless, our usual perfect vision was replaced by a harsh and stinging sensation as the rain crashed down from the heavens, our usually heightened hearing engulfed by the sound of thunder shaking the sky above. Lightning struck the dirt around the forest, momentarily illuminating the forest around me whilst it shattered the trees in its path. It was almost terrifying. We couldn't hear any movement around us, if the thunder and lightning wasn't bad enough, the howling of the wind left no room for silence in the midst of this earth shattering storm. As we crossed the border the scent of fresh blood grew stronger, Atticus focused as hard as he could to find the source. When he did it took all of our power to stifle a mournful howl at the sight of our deceased pack member, not just any pack member though. It was Jeremy, one of our trainee guards, he only turned sixteen two months ago. He didn't stand a chance, unable to shift, no weapons, his throat was ripped clean out. Something needed to change to prevent this happening again but I couldn't focus on that right now, I had to save my pack.

"Rogues are on the attack, elderly and children get to safety. Warriors get to the border as fast as possible, elites you will protect those at the pack. I want everyone to hurry I don't know how many there are."

"Yes, alpha."

I needed my people safe and these rogues dealt with, why had they killed but not attacked? What were they planning? I was knocked out of my thoughts by a wolf ramming into me, latching onto me with his claws deeply embedded into my side, Atticus tried his hardest to grab him with his teeth but he couldn't, the wolf was digging its claws into us when we were dragged to the floor by another that had jumped onto our back. I could hear the sounds of my pack screaming, linking for help from anyone who was available, it was unbearable, the fear, the pain – as long as my pack survived, I would be okay. I wasn't sure what to do in this moment, I was cornered and on my own – a realisation came to me, this was their plan all along. To take my pack. Suddenly, the rain eased off as lightning struck the ground around us, lighting the forest as I watched Stefan's wolf land on one of the rogues, tearing it away from me. Atticus sank his teeth into one of the remaining wolves before moving onto the rest that seemed to emerge from the shadows surrounding us. This didn't stop us as we tore our way through the crowd around us, it wasn't long before the rest of our warriors turned up and I could feel the relief throughout the pack, we killed around sixty wolves before finally managing to capture one – we had to find out their motive. It was about one a.m. now and my men had been torturing the rogue for an hour when we found out they had a contingency plan in place:

Shannon. *"Mate."* They were going after her if they failed to take the pack. In the hopes to force my hand.

"Stefan, Luke, Gabriel and Jason with me NOW." I couldn't help it we needed to get there and fast, We arrived at Shannon's street, all was quiet, the first thing I noticed was her scent. It wasn't as heavenly as it was earlier today, it was tarnished, tarnished by the smell of fresh blood and rogues. That's when my eyes fell upon her, there in the middle of the road, halfway up the street. Motionless, my heart stopped as I tried to comprehend what was happening. Was she breathing? I watched as the rogue towered menacingly over her, pressing his paw into her stomach, almost crushing her. I wasted no time before I tore down the road, ready to tear this rogue limb from limb for so much as touching my mate. I ripped into the wolf without a second thought, dragging him away from my mate so that she could be rushed to safety.

"Someone get the human out of here now!" Luke shouted through our mind link. I looked behind for a second to see Jason shift, picking her up and carry her towards the pack. I seriously wanted to rip his throat out for having her against his naked body but he was doing his job, he was saving her, unfortunately there was no other way to do it; the rogue tried sinking his canines into my throat forcing my attention straight back to him.

Atticus let out an angry growl before diving on top of the rogue and ripping his throat right out, the wolf coughed and spluttered momentarily before ultimately hitting the floor. The world around me went quiet as I focused on the rogue in front of me, how pitiful he looked as he held his throat, merely delaying his inevitable death. It was nothing less than he deserved for hurting my mate the way that he has, if anything, he's gotten off lightly because if Shannon died… I would make him suffer. I watched as his body stopped jerking, his hands fell loose and his eye bore holes into the ebony sky before I turned around slowly, realisation hitting me as I watched my friends fight the other rogues. Atticus charged and tackled one of the wolves that had cornered Stefan. The sun was starting to rise by the time we had killed the last rogue between here and my pack. We found somewhere desolate, dug a hole and burnt the bodies; nothing special, just a petrol fire. We wouldn't have had burnt at all but the last thing I needed was folks sniffing around and having to explain all of this to local law enforcement. All I could think about right now was Shannon. *"Mate,"* Atticus corrected me again. *"Oh, will you piss off, she has a name."* I blocked Atticus out before heading back to the pack house in the blood-stained clothes we'd found in the woods; we were exhausted.

I asked Jason where he had taken Shannon and his reply angered me.

"The dungeon where we take all prisoners."

"YOU TOOK MY MATE TO THE DUNGEON?" I couldn't control my anger as I pinned him to the wall by his throat, he took the love of my life who was bleeding on the side of the road to a dungeon! What normal person does that? Mate or not; a victim should not be treated that way, I dropped him and ran straight to the dungeon pushing anyone and everyone out of the way.

I finally got there, bursting through the door, there was something that I had never wanted to see, her arms and feet were chained, her eyes had what looked like a tea towel tied around them. I approached her slowly taking the heavy chains off her wrists and ankles, you could see bruises forming where she'd tried to break free, these were werewolves' chains, what idiot would put them on a human? Removing the blindfold, her eyes were swollen and red from where she'd obviously been crying. It was nearly three p.m. – had she really been left in this state for at least twelve hours whilst I was clearing rogue bodies? I felt nothing but shame, she deserved so much better. Better than me. I scooped her up and carried her bridal style; running as fast as I could to the pack hospital.

"Doctor Bane, I need you! Doctor Bane!" We had the best pack doctor in the country. We had a few packs that asked occasionally to use her because she was better than theirs but that was only in rare emergencies; I put Shannon in the Alpha's room which is reserved only for those of great importance.

"Get in here NOW." I mind linked her, practically shouting, because I wasn't waiting a moment longer; she rushed in with nurse Hilary at her side.

"What happened?" she asked pushing me away from the bed and hooking Shannon up to all these different machines; seeing her this way, bleeding profusely, it was terrifying.

"I-I don't know. I found her, rogues they got to her, please you have to save her." I started crying as I begged Doctor Bane to save her, I never thought I'd lose Shannon like this; I thought if anything she'd just live her own life as a human, not die. No, she—she couldn't die! The doctor was running around before more junior doctors and nurses came into the room wheeling Shannon out.

"No! Where are you taking her?" I screamed trying to chase after them, nurse Hilary was at my side trying to comfort her. "YOU CAN'T TAKE HER."

I couldn't help but shout as I watched them wheel her in her bed down the hall eventually turning a corner and out of site, I could feel my tears falling. *"How weak you must look."* Atticus always knew how to make me feel shittier. Some wolf. I fell to the ground, clutching my chest as I felt it growing heavier between sobs when I felt a warm touch on my shoulder.

"Alpha, in order to save her we need to know what's wrong. They're going to be running multiple tests to see what needs doing okay? Doctor Bane is the best doctor in the country not to mention one of the best healers so please go to the family room and wait." I nodded, walking behind me before Stefan showed up embracing me in a hug; I crumbled. I know Alphas were meant to be strong but we had feelings too I couldn't lose her, not then. Not ever.

Doctor Bane walked into the family room sitting down in the chair opposite me; I couldn't read the look on her face. She looked a mix of exhaustion and sadness, she had been gone with Shannon for three hours so I wasn't surprised – she was a healer and could heal almost anything but it always took some of her energy along with it.

"I've healed what I could, Thomas, but you should know she broke nine of her ribs; fractured both of her legs and had quite a severe concussion. She also cracked a part of her spine and although healed, it will take some work for her to get better. You will need to offer as much as your healing as you can too, you only need to hold her hand – the bond will do the rest. I'm surprised she's alive if I'm completely honest. With her kind of injuries a typical human would have died; we've had to put her into a coma for now to give her body a chance to heal on its own. We have to pray to the moon goddess that she wakes up."

I sat there wide eyed, no idea what to say; there was a chance that she wouldn't wake up? A chance that I'd never see those sky blue eyes again, hear her angelic voice or watch her carry my children. I could feel my emotions building up again I wasn't sure which was more overpowering, the sadness or the anger. My fists were balled and my vision blurring through the tears. I was caught off guard by Stefan putting his arms around me making it awkward – I mean I appreciated the gesture but he's not a touchy feely guy so I'm not sure he knew what he was doing.

"You can see her now, Alpha, in fact I would recommend staying with her as much as you can; as her mate you will be able to help her heal faster with your presence. I can take you there now if you like?" She was sympathetic towards me, she must have seen this kind of thing a hundred times over. I nodded my head and got up off the chair slowly; it felt like I had this massive elephant weighing me down, I had to force every move down the corridor which normally wasn't very far but right now it felt like a million miles between me and her.

Doctor Bane kept looking over her shoulder – I'm sure she was checking to see whether I had collapsed or not through the weight I was feeling. We finally got to the door of the Alpha suite… the last place I ever wanted to be again after all this was over; the first thing I noticed was the patient monitor that she was attached to showing us that her heart beat was stable, and all her other observations were normal. The next was the oxygen pieces that were in her nose attached to a machine; there was also an IV going through a vein in her hand, my guess is that it was providing the nutrients easier for her that she needed. I don't know; I really don't. Her beautiful light blonde hair was stained red with blood from where she hit her head, her face pale; like all the life had been sucked from her but she was still the most beautiful creature in existence. She looked so peaceful.

I stood in the doorway staring at her. I couldn't just rush to her side; I had no right. Sure, I was her mate but that didn't mean anything to her, she was human, I'm not sure if she could even feel the bond like I could; how crazy one touch from her could drive me. I didn't deserve her: I mean, after all, I'm the reason she's in this state, the rogues wanted to get to me. To kill me and when they couldn't they must have gone after her; how they knew who she was or where she was I don't know but one thing I did know was that if she survived I would protect her until the day I died, never leaving her side.

"You can come in, Alpha." Doctor Bane pulled me from my thoughts, motioning for me to move towards the bed but I didn't want to; how could I when I was the reason she was there?

"Alpha, she needs your strength if she's going to make a full recovery, now come on."

Doctor Bane grabbed my hand forcefully pulling me over to Shannon's bedside; I moved a stray hair out of her closed eyes, tracing my hand down her cheeks before stroking my thumb over her lips lightly, taking in every inch of her beauty, committing it to memory. I bent over slowly, placing my lips to her forehead; a silent promise from me that I would forever protect her no matter what her choice was. I could never love anyone the way I loved this beautiful woman, I loved her more than life itself.

The days went by slowly; it felt like an eternity. The only time I left her side was to use the toilet and even that was in the same room. Her dad visited daily, so did her sisters. They all blamed themselves for what happened because they weren't home but it wasn't their fault just like it wasn't mine; I didn't choose this life, I didn't choose to have a mate – it… it was forced on me. All I could do was wait; wait until the moment she woke up and I could tell her everything, then pray that she would choose me so we could build a life together.

***

"Alpha… we're going to be easing her medication tonight in the hopes that she will wake up; it will take about twenty-four hours for it to fully leave her system but she may still wake before then. You should go home and shower; you may actually scare her to death if she sees you like that."

I couldn't help but feel excited at the prospect of seeing her open her eyes again, she had a lot more colour in her cheeks now – she definitely looked healthier. They took her for some more scans and x-rays which showed that she was healing faster than they expected which was the best news; the likelihood is it's where I'd been sharing my strength but who knows? She was the strongest woman I had ever met; that I know without her being awake.

I practically skipped out of the room as I headed back to the pack house to shower and change as quickly as I could; I only chucked on some jogging bottoms and a t-shirt. Leaving my hair loose, I headed down to the kitchen to grab something to eat. I also grabbed something for David who was with Shannon at the time; he stayed as often as he could but he had the other two girls to take care of as well – I can't imagine how much all this was hurting him.

Finally back at her side, I planned to stay there now until she woke; I wanted to be the first thing she saw when she opened her eyes – I wanted the first thing she heard to be my declaration of love. Nothing else would do.

When they eventually took out her drip, I started getting excited; this was it, this was the moment I had been waiting for. I squeezed her hand in the hopes it would stir something in her, that she would feel the electricity between us like I did and rush into my arms; I mean I know this is unrealistic but a man can hope.

I jumped up and out of my chair as soon as I woke up; I

looked at her for any sign of consciousness but nothing it was nearly eleven a.m. Fifteen hours ago they stopped her drip; it shouldn't have been much longer, should it? I know Doctor Bane said up to twenty-four hours but this was taking the piss a bit now. *"I want mate,"* It was the only thing Atticus had said to me since we started staying here; I know he longed for her but I did too!

I got up to use the toilet before running out the door in search of Doctor Bane; I needed answers! After walking down the hallway checking all the rooms I finally found her assistant in what looked like the staff room. The nurses that were all sat eating their lunch jumped straight up off their seats to bow their heads as I walked past.

"Where is Doctor Bane?" I asked my question through gritted teeth; it felt like I'd searched the whole damn hospital looking for that woman but she'd vanished into thin air!

The assistant walked towards me; Hilary, I think her name was? I'm not entirely sure but I'm going to call her Hilary anyway, she placed her hand on my arm and steered me towards the door, stepping out into the hallway before she finally spoke.

"Doctor Bane was urgently requested at the Blood Moon pack, Luna Alice needed an emergency caesarean or she would have died; they tried to contact you but you were asleep. They enlisted the help of a witch to transport her there in seconds; I've not heard anything since."

"Why isn't Shannon awake yet?"

"Now that, my lovely, even Doctor Bane couldn't answer; it's all down to Shannon now. Come on, I haven't checked her obs yet."

I stormed ahead of Hilary feeling a mix of frustration and sadness over the fact that Shannon wasn't awake yet; forcing the door open I saw something I didn't expect… It was Shannon! She was awake and sat up!

Hilary looked at me straight away; she must have known what was coming because all I heard was her shouting after me as I ran forward, my only focus on Shannon.

I lost control of Atticus; he forced himself forward kissing her hungrily, tightening his grip with every passionate moment. I tried taking back control but he was too strong; he'd wanted this as much as I did, maybe even more! She started hitting me which felt like nothing; she was weak and he… well, he was a wolf. As soon as I heard her scream, I lost control; forcing Atticus back and blocking him out as he whimpered in the back of my mind, she pushed me back before punching me in the face. It didn't hurt but seeing her cradle her fist the way she was did; all I've done so far is hurt her.

She sat there shouting at me but, if I'm being honest, I wasn't listening, I already hated myself enough for what I'd put her through to listen to her hatred as well; even if it was no less than I deserved.

Hilary grabbed me; pushing me out of the door before locking it so that I couldn't get back in. I paced the hallway for goddess knows how long before I heard the door unlock again, but before I had a chance to go in, I saw her sisters and father racing down the hallway towards her door; they deserved some time to themselves so I decided to wait on a chair close by until I could go in myself and apologise to her.

It felt like an eternity before the door opened; Emily and Clara emerging with tears down their face. I couldn't help but walk over to them, it wasn't nice seeing them upset – they didn't deserve it.

"Hey, girls, are you okay? Please don't cry." I crouched in a bid to make myself look less intimidating, they gave me a small smile but didn't return my gaze.

"Y-yes, Alpha." Their voices were stern like they were trained to be; we taught our warriors to show no fear but it doesn't work when your eyes are swollen and red from crying. I used some tissue that was in my pocket to wipe their tears away.

"Please call me Thomas; take the rest of the week off. Enjoy yourselves, Shannon will be fine. You can even stay at the pack house if you would prefer to be closer."

"B-but," the girls tried to argue but I couldn't let them, I knew the guilt they were carrying because I carried it too. They didn't deserve it though, all they were doing was following orders; they shouldn't have to feel all this weight.

"No buts. I insist. I will mind link my Omega Katherine to prepare some rooms for you on my floor and treat you girls like queens for the week." The girls finally made eye contact, smiling from ear to ear before running off down the hall – no doubt straight to the pack house. I mind linked Katherine explaining the situation and asked her to look after them for me, she was great, Katherine; I knew that they would be in safe hands. Now it was time for me to get up, suck up my pride and go apologise to the only woman I could ever love.

I walked in as quiet as I could so that I wouldn't startle her like I did earlier, I wanted her to like me – love me like I did her but at this rate it wasn't going to happen. I noticed her dad was holding her hand. I couldn't help but feel envious; another man holding her hand! That should be me! Not him! Yes, he was her dad but she was MINE. A growl ripped through my throat before I could stop it, I hoped she wouldn't notice but she did. A look of confusion spread over her face as her dad instinctively let go of her hand, I didn't know what to do so I just stood there quietly afraid of what I might say or even do.

"Did you just growl?" she asked me quietly, almost as if she didn't realise; I just stared at her, admiring her beauty, watching as her anger built before returning her vision to her hands. I shouldn't be here, should I? She'll never forgive me! She'll hate me forever, moving on with her life as I wither away and wait for the moment she realises she loves me.

"You need to leave; I don't want you here!" she shouted at me with such hatred; it felt like a million knives had been sent straight through my heart, I couldn't move, I couldn't think, oh goddess this hurt so bad. Why? I could hear Atticus howling in pain at the back of my head; why can't I move? I should leave; give her space. That's what I'll do. That's when the unexpected happened: her dad defended me. Me. After warning me to let her make her own decision in regards to our mate predicament; he was defending me. I was shocked.

"Hunny, Thomas has sat by your side every day for the past two weeks, he saved your life. He fought off the wolf so his men could get you to safety."

Her dad nodded at me which I took as a sign that I could approach; I slowly made my way towards her, giving her every chance to tell me to back off and leave but she didn't. She just watched me. That was progress, right?

I sat on the edge of the bed taking one of her hands in mine, feeling the electricity radiating through our touch. It was intoxicating, between her scent and the feeling when I touched her, it really was hard to fight Atticus for control. I took advantage of this moment by apologising; I needed her to know I wasn't a bad guy and that I really was in love with her.

"Please, I know I was forceful earlier and I honestly had no right. It was just seeing you awake for the first time in two weeks

I thought I was going to explode from joy. We weren't sure if you would make it through the night with—" Oops. Bad move. Bad move. I could see her anger building before she had even starting shouting at me; I didn't know what to do! Why did I keep getting this wrong? I even looked at her dad for help but he looked just as frightened as me.

"Two weeks! What do you mean two weeks? The men, the wolf – it… it was last night! I only met you yesterday and you thought you had some sort of claim over me? Are you fucking crazy?"

Her dad did try to defend me once again but this woman was on a mission – is it weird I was turned on? FUUUCK. This was honestly the scariest woman I'd ever met which is saying something because my mother was terrifying.

"If you were saving me, why was I chained and blindfolded? Why was I left for hours on end somewhere cold until I passed out from the pain?"

Ouch. That hurt; I mean it's a completely justified question but thinking back to her being in that dungeon, alone – dying. It hurt more than I think she knows but that was my fault again – in Luke's defence he didn't know she was my mate, just that she was a human caught in the cross line and Jason, well, he never should have put any kind of victim down there. I took a breath in before I spoke, I didn't want her to know how upset I was over all of this.

"That was my fault I told them to bring you back here but they assumed it was as a prisoner. As soon as I dealt with the wolves and got back here, I brought you straight to the hospital, I swear; I still have yet to deal with them for their treatment of you. The only time I left your bedside was to shower yesterday."

When she didn't start shouting at me again, I decided it was a good time to carry on… hopefully not angering her more.

"Please let me introduce myself formally, my name is Thomas Cannon."

"Shannon Rye." Oh wow, her voice was like a song. There was no anger behind it; she had also visibly calmed down too, resting her hands in her lap. This was it. This was my chance!

"I know who you are, Shannon, I've known you since I helped you that day in the woods six years ago. I've thought of nothing and no one else since." Her gasp only confirmed that she realised I wasn't a threat to her; that I did care. I watched her frown as if working out an equation before she gave a faint smile holding her hand up to my cheek; I leaned in to her touch, closing my eyes to savour every spark invading my body through her touch. The feeling ended all too quick when bloody Jade bounded through the door with some food for her; shoving me off the bed, forcing me to sit in a chair at the end. Stefan obviously wasn't discreet about Shannon finally being awake; he'd checked every hour to see how she was, they cared almost as much as I did, which shows just how fitted they were to be my Betas.

I watched Shannon attentively as she ate, noticing the odd moan escaping her lips, likely because of how long it had been since she'd eaten or maybe because of how good our cooks are – either way I didn't like it. I should be the one making her moan; when she finished Hilary took her tray and left us so we could have some privacy. Her presence was only preventing the inevitable; it was then that I noticed her dad had taken her hand again, evoking yet another growl to rip through my throat.

"Did you just growl?"

Ah fuck; why couldn't I control myself? She definitely heard that one, I couldn't think of what to say and really stumbled along my words before admitting that I did growl. I had no explanation lined up either. I was just winging it at this point, trying to prevent the bombshell that we had to drop on her, knowing it could be our final few moments together.

"I… erm, just… uh, yeah."

"What the hell is going on? I want to know *now*." Ah, for goddess' sake there's that anger again and here I am like a deer in headlights not knowing what to do or say.

David sighed before clearing his throat; we both knew this was coming but neither of us actually wanted it to.

"Hunny, you're right but when we tell you it will change your life forever. Are you sure you want that? You could go home and lead a completely innocent life; I could even send you to live with your aunts if you like. You could get away from it all."

Send her to live with her aunt? That was never part of the deal! I couldn't hold Atticus back as he completely took control; seething with anger. Practically spitting at David. Letting out an angry growl as he surfaced.

"Mate. Goes. Nowhere."

Chapter Seven
Finally Some Answers

"Thomas, control your wolf." My father was calm when he spoke to Thomas, that is, until he came to the word wolf; what did he mean? I saw no wolf? Why would Thomas have a wolf? Like a pet wolf? What was the alternative? I watched Thomas with interest as he started to relax; his ebony eyes slowly disappearing, replaced with those gorgeous familiar brown ones.

"We agreed Shannon would choose her own path; not us."

Choose my own path? What did they mean? I still had absolutely no clue what was going on here; I looked between the two men in front of me waiting for one of them to at least continue the explanation now that Thomas was calm, when they didn't, I pushed on.

"Well, are you going to tell me? Why would he have a wolf? What does that even mean?"

This time it was Thomas who spoke; he climbed up off his chair and sat on the edge of the bed, taking my hand as he sat down.

"Angel, your dad and I – we're werewolves."

I couldn't control my laughter when he said that they were werewolves, werewolves weren't real; they were a myth, a legend, something you only ever heard of in a book or online. Why couldn't they just be honest with me? I bet they cooked all this up whilst I was in a coma, in a bid to get rid of me and send me to my aunt's like my dad said.

"Werewolves, ha! So, what's really going on?"

"Hunny, Thomas is telling the truth. We are all werewolves; the girls, me, Thomas – even nurse Hilary. Thomas is our Alpha which means he's the head wolf in our pack so to speak."

He paused for a moment giving me a chance to process this; I mean I could sort of believe Thomas was a wolf – the way his eyes kept changing colour, his anger – people actually calling him Alpha. Not to mention he was one giant of a man; I studied him some more, enjoying the warmth radiating from his touch. Maybe this was what my dad meant, maybe this was why his touch was so warm and calming for me, but one thing didn't add up; if my dad and sisters were werewolves, why wasn't I?

"The men that came after you the night of the storm, they were what we call rogue werewolves; ones that don't belong to a pack. The-they went after you to get to me; they tried to kill me and storm our pack but when that didn't work they went after the one thing that they knew would destroy me: you."

Thomas squeezed my hand softly when he spoke; you could see that he cared but why me? We'd only met twice; once when I was eleven and the other day in town, what made me so special?

"Why me?" I needed to know more; my head was spinning with so many questions, I wasn't sure whether to believe them or not. They had no reason to lie but at the same time I just couldn't imagine werewolves being real.

"Because, Shannon, angel, you're my mate. You were created by the moon goddess to be with me; to be my Luna for as long as we both live, to rule side by side as one. Since I met you that day in the woods—"

"When you found us and carried Clara home?"

"Actually no; I met you earlier that day in my wolf form. I followed your scent through the woods and found the girls playing; they were covered in your scent from where you were their main carer at the time; we didn't know this though and assumed Clara was my mate which is why we chased her. It was only when you found us in the meadow that we realised you were our mate, not Clara."

I didn't know what to say; I just sat there wide-eyed in shock as I processed this information, he… he was the wolf. The huge black one that had invaded my dreams every single night since; he was quite literally the man and wolf of my dreams. This was a lot to process but it all made sense; it's how Thomas knew where to find us that night, he wasn't randomly walking through the woods, he had already been there so knew exactly where we were. That was why he helped us; that was why he wanted to know my name – this mate thing, was I really designed by the moon goddess for him? He wanted me to be his forever; rule by his side forever. Thinking about that night I remember my dad did almost call him Alpha but why? Surely if he was a werewolf, I would be one too? Especially if the girls were. I turned my head towards my dad who had been watching me attentively; obviously worried about how I would process all of this.

"If you and the girls are werewolves then why aren't I?"

You could see a mixture of feelings spread across my dad's face; the most prominent was sadness.

"Hunny… I'm not your biological father."

Both Thomas and I gasped at this new piece of information… my guess being that Thomas wasn't aware of this big secret either. I honestly didn't know what to say. It felt like my world was over; everything I thought I knew was wrong, werewolves existed, my dad wasn't my dad. What next?

"But… but why? How? Who?" I couldn't help it – there was so much I didn't know; my whole life… it was a lie.

"I met your mother when you were two years old… she was

the most beautiful woman I had ever met, she wasn't my true mate but honestly I couldn't imagine loving any one more than I loved her, it… it seemed impossible. We went on about five dates before she introduced me to you; you were the smallest, cutest little girl I had ever laid my eyes on and it was then I knew that I was going to be your dad regardless of genes."

You could hear his voice breaking, tears filling his eyes as memories of the past flooded into his mind. I didn't know any of this.

"We had the girls a few years after, I thought… I thought she was happy but she wasn't. She found it difficult at home; she struggled tremendously with depression after Emily, some days I would find her crying on the toilet – other days she would just not get out of bed. I tried everything I could to help her but I… I couldn't. I came home from training one day to find her hurting herself in the bathroom; after that I tried my best to keep anything sharp out of the house, I even brought her to see Doctor Bane here at the pack but because she was human and it wasn't a physical injury, she couldn't do anything. I even suggested a human doctor but your mum wouldn't see one, I'm not sure why. One day I came home to find that she had left; gone. It was you that told me. She was gone when you woke up and bless your little heart you had kept the girls entertained all day; even made them sandwiches so that they wouldn't go hungry. We were so lucky to have you; I'm just sorry I didn't see it at the time. I'm sorry that instead of helping you through the loss of your mum I blamed you. I hated you and practically gave you a dog's life. No, in fact, I treated the dogs better some days. You didn't deserve that; you deserved to be treated like the amazing woman you always have been, and honestly knowing that you're mated to an Alpha – although yes initially I thought it was insane; a human as our future Luna – but the more I realised how much you had done for not only the girls but for me without a grumble; watching you grow into one of the most amazing young women I have ever met – I-I honestly couldn't think of anyone I would rather serve under. I may not be your biological father but I love you more than he ever possibly could."

Hearing my father speak so openly about everything that had happened pulled at my heart strings; I didn't know any of this, the way he felt, Mum's struggles before her departure. I genuinely thought it was my fault that she left but it wasn't and I guess it wasn't her fault either; she was a woman struggling so bad that she needed a way out, she needed to find a way to help herself. I could feel my tears fall down my face as my dad wrapped me in a comforting hug; even if he wasn't my biological dad he was my dad nonetheless and I didn't plan on changing that. I was brought out of my thoughts by my dad sobbing; this was new. I'd never seen my dad cry – he was always this big, strong man that liked to show no sign of weakness; my guess is that's what his werewolf side made him appear as. I hugged him tighter and we sat there until his sobbing subsided enough for him to sit back in his chair; it was getting dark now, I noticed as I looked at the only window in the room. The feeling was coming back in my legs thankfully so I started moving them a bit.

"Is… is she dead?" I couldn't help but ask my dad the only question that kept popping up in my mind; did she kill herself? Did she die? What happened to her?

"No, hunny, well not that I was made aware of anyway. Our previous Alpha – Thomas' father – he sent scouts to find her, we even asked for help from neighbouring packs but we never found anything, it was as if she had disappeared. I gave up looking the night Thomas' brought you back from the lake; I swore then that from that moment onward I would devote my life to my three girls."

He was searching for her that entire time but found nothing? No wonder he struggled so much when it came to looking after us; we were the reminder of what he lost.

Our silence was broken by nurse Hilary re-entering the room.

"Now, gentlemen, it's getting late; Miss Rye will need to rest before Doctor Bane returns in the morning. Please say your goodbyes."

My dad was the first to say goodbye, wrapping me in a tight hug before walking out the door; he did look back and give me a small wave before leaving but I think he was just as exhausted as I was after today's revelations. His eyes were red and puffy from crying; highlighting the obvious dark bags underneath them – I can't believe I didn't notice them; I don't think I'd ever seen him with bags under his eyes; he was obviously more exhausted than I realised.

Thomas walked over to the bed taking my hand gently in his, kissing my knuckles before returning his gaze to me.

"I'm only a phone call away; Hilary will call me for you. Please if you need anything let me know, my angel."

He placed a soft kiss on my forehead and made his way towards the door only to stop before leaving; he turned towards me with a small smile.

"Shannon, whether you choose to go to your aunt's or stay here and rule by my side, I need you to know; from the moment I set my eyes on you, I have loved you more than life itself. You're the only thing I want now and forever but despite all of that I only want you to be happy; if that means you go to your aunt's then so be it but please. Give me a chance. I want to prove to you that you are the only thing in existence that will ever matter to me."

I sat there in awe at him, I couldn't believe what he was saying; he loved me, he truly loved me more than anything in this world but I wasn't sure what to feel at that moment. I needed to sleep; I gave him a small smile as he closed the door behind him. Maybe I could give him a chance; maybe I could be with him; rule by his side and be part of his werewolf family. I laid my head on my pillow only to be consumed by my exhaustion; falling asleep as soon as I closed my eyes.

Chapter Eight
A Father's Perspective

David

Telling Shannon she wasn't my biological daughter was one of the hardest things I've had to do; even at my lowest I've never seen her as anything other than my beautiful daughter, it broke my heart to see the devastation spread across her face, the realisation that she'd been lied to for as long as she could remember. As much as it was a lie it never felt like one; I love her just as much as I do Clara and Emily, without her my girls wouldn't have survived and quite frankly nor would I. I arrived home to find the house empty almost forgetting that Clara had texted saying they were staying at the pack house; Thomas told me the night Shannon was taken in that I was always welcome but I didn't feel like I deserved it.

I walked up to my bedroom, sitting on my bed, I picked up the only photo frame in the house; it held a picture of me and my sweet Emilia on our first date. I'd made her laugh whilst taking the picture and it captured her personality perfectly; before we had our darling Emily she was so full of life, always laughing, making jokes, going out – there wasn't a day in the week her and the girls would be at home unless they were ill. That's why when she had Emily we noticed the change so much – she hardly ever went out, she wouldn't change or shower for days and we would go weeks on end without hearing her laugh.

Sixteen Years Ago

"All right, John, I'll see you later!" I waved goodbye to John as I finished my twelve hour shift on patrol, he's the head warrior; he chooses who patrols, what hours we work, he is also the one who had to train the new warriors.

Rumour has it he's looking for an apprentice to take over as head warrior in a few years; only the strongest of warriors go for that position because it requires only the best, one mishap could cause who knows what chaos. John's been head warrior for nearly thirty years – he was actually the youngest to ever be promoted (he was twenty at the time) and by golly has he created a reputation in that time; we've never had a rogue attack, never had a human cross our barriers or even a wolf taken for that matter. These are many of the reasons I won't be signing up for the position! I want a quiet life with a chosen mate, living in the nearby town; building a family together. I mean sure I could still meet my actual mate but at twenty-four my chances are slim; most wolves meet their mates shortly after their first shift at eighteen – me? I still haven't.

I started walking back to my parents' cottage which was only a five minute walk from the pack house when I thought I could head into town for some pancakes; Dad was the cook in our house so as much as I knew my mom could make them, I didn't fancy getting food poisoning.

I decided to shift, letting my wolf Chase take us there; I got naked, placing my clothes on the floor beforehand, so that Chase could carry them in his mouth. It wasn't long before we were at the border of the trees, shifting so I could dress and leave – crossing over into the town I saw Kenny's open as usual; they did the best pancakes ever. I came here for breakfast a few weeks ago with some of the warrior lads and it was as if I'd just tasted pancakes for the first time, they were that heavenly.

Walking into the restaurant I noticed that they had a new waitress; she was captivating, I had never seen someone so beautiful before. The way her golden blonde hair was wrapped up into a high ponytail with a few strands hanging down by the side of her face, she had the most intoxicating crystal blue eyes surrounded by full, black lashes and her lips. Wow. They were red and plump; just asking to be kissed, she bit her lip as she looked up at me, enticing me to come forward, Goddess, she was beautiful.

"Well, hey there, handsome, table for one?" I could only nod my head to answer her question, too captivated by her beauty to say anything. She smiled as she turned around, taking me to one of the smaller booths closer to the kitchen, her uniform fitted her curves perfectly; it was made for her, it really was. I sat down at the booth as she handed me a menu.

"Why don't you take a look at the menu whilst I get you a drink? What can I get ya?"

"I... uh... erm, coke. Yes. Coke, please."

"Smooth." Chase laughed at me in the back of my head before I pushed him backwards, I'm such an idiot. I watched her walk away serving other customers, laughing with other waitresses as they passed – man I wished I could make her laugh like that.

Finally she returned with a can of coke and a smile for me; it was the best thing I'd ever seen.

"Do you know what you're having then, handsome?"

"Oh... I... erm, I'll have two stacks of pancakes, please."

She chuckled as I stuttered trying to tell her my order, she obviously found my nervousness amusing which was just great.

The first woman I'm attracted to in years and I'm a nervous wreck just talking to her.

She skipped away before returning a bit later with my pancakes; it's safe to say it didn't take long before both plates were empty and I sat there satisfyingly full. Getting up from my table, I left the money there with an unusually large tip for me.

I walked outside instantly getting hit by a cold breeze; it was refreshing I didn't realise that I was warm until it hit me, I start heading towards the forest when I hear someone shouting behind me.

"Erm, sir! Excuse me, excuse me, ouch – sorry. SIRR!"

I turned around only to see the waitress from Kenny's running towards me, pushing through the crowds of people. I stood there confused, wondering why she would have left her shift just to chase after me, finally she caught up with me; she bent over huffing and puffing from the running – I couldn't help but smile at her, she seemed so adorable.

"You… forgot your wallet, phew." She stood up straight, wiping a bead of sweat off her forehead, whilst slapping my wallet in my hand with her other hand.

"Dude, you're fast, did you know that?"

"Go out with me?" She looked at me wide-eyed for a moment before a smile spread across her face.

"YESSSS!"

I stumbled back a bit; I'd be lying if I said I didn't think that this drop dead gorgeous woman was going to reject me because I did. I'm sure my heart skipped a beat when she said yes, her eyes shining with joy, her wide smile. I was already in love and we hadn't even had our first date yet.

Fast Forward Three Years

"You can do this, hunny! Push! PUSH!"

I watched as the love of my life pushed our second daughter into the world; technically she was our first daughter by blood but I had no doubt in my mind that she was our second daughter. Hearing her cry was like music to my ears, I watched as Doctor Bane placed our crying infant on her mother's chest only for her to settle down almost instantly looking up at her mother. Doctor Bane called me over to cut the cord and honestly it was the best thing ever. My eyes swelled with tears of joy looking at the love between my two girls on the bed. Emilia's eyes met with mine and I couldn't help but swell with pride, her beautiful golden locks fell carefree over her shoulders. She was tired, but to look at her you wouldn't know. Her eyes sparkled with love and excitement, a big smile across her face as she spoke.

"I'd like to name her Clara after your mother." Well that was all I needed. I fell to my knees in sobs of both pure joy and sadness; my mother passed away last year. It was hard, the only thing that got me through it was Emilia and Shannon otherwise I don't think I'd have survived the grief; she adored Shannon, was forever spoiling her, giving her anything and everything. She would have loved Clara too, this meant the world to me, my family was complete. I felt whole.

Nearly Six Years Later

"Emilia, hunny, are you okay?"

I woke up to my beautiful Emily jumping on our bed, I looked at the clock: five a.m. I let out a sigh before rolling over to face my love, who was just laid there staring into space; this meant a bad day for her usually.

"My love, why don't you go back to sleep? I can sort the children out this morning."

I received no response from her as I climbed out of bed. Picking Emily up as I walked out of the room, we headed downstairs and put the telly on. Cwtched up on the settee watching a film, I fell asleep again; woken by Shannon running into the room wrapping her arms around my neck.

"Good morning, Daddyyy!" she squealed in excitement. I'd been training so hard lately ready to take over as head warrior I hadn't seen much of my little girls, which broke my heart more than I care to admit.

"Good morning, my princess!" I wrapped my arms around her giving her the tightest hug I could without crushing her.

"No, Daddy, I'm going to be a doctor!"

"Well, you will always be daddy's little princess, doctor or not!" I twirled her around the room before setting her down on her feet and making all three girls' breakfast.

It wasn't long before we were walking to school to drop Shannon and Clara off.

"Now you two have the best day ever! I will see you here at pickup okay?"

I gave them both a kiss before watching them skip through the front door hand in hand; they were so cute.

"Right then, my little Emmy bobemmy, let's take you to nursery, shall we?"

I dropped Emily to nursery and headed home to check on Emilia, she worried me when she got into this state. I walked through the door heading straight upstairs; she hadn't moved. She had stayed in the exact same position for five hours and goddess knows how long before Emily came in. I tried to talk to her but it was as if she was an empty vessel; her spirit was no longer there. Her once gorgeous golden hair was now a greasy, knotted mess that hung off the bed like a dead weight, her once exciting crystal blue eyes were now dull and lifeless, her lips were cracked and looked so sore; I honestly don't remember the last time she had a shower, she had an awful smell coming from her but I couldn't tell her that. I loved her no matter what she looked like; I closed the door before heading downstairs and tidying up the mess that was made during breakfast.

It wasn't long before I had all my girls home, laughing, eating dinner and watching a film before bed. It was bliss.

This was my routine for the rest of the weekend but Sunday it was as if a switch had been flipped! Emilia was up, showered and cooking breakfast like normal, laughing with the kids as they ate; it was these moments I longed for, it was these moments that made it easier.

I headed to work three a.m. Monday morning as per my usual shift, feeling confident that Emilia would have a fantastic day getting the girls to school before getting some time to herself. I'd even finish a little early to meet her at the school and walk home with them. Yes, that sounded great.

The day went by pretty quickly; I was looking forward to my early finish and walking home with my girls. I finished at two thirty p.m. heading straight for the school. I was a few minutes early so I just stood there waiting looking around for signs of Emilia but I didn't see her. Panic started to set in but I calmed myself down; she was probably just late, three fifteen came and most of the kids had left but none of my girls had come out. I approached the school office slowly with concern; the lady at the front desk came out to greet me.

"Hi, I'm, erm, looking for my daughters; Shannon, Clara and Emily Rye. They're usually brought round to the front so they can come out together."

I could feel the panic rising as the woman looked at me confused.

"I'm sorry sir but the girls wasn't in tod—"

She didn't get chance to finish her sentence before I was already heading home, running as fast as my feet could carry me. Within minutes I was home and bounding through the front door, relief flooding through me as I saw all three girls sitting in the living room colouring, crusts scattered around them from what looked like toast and sandwiches.

The girls ran over to me in excitement almost tackling me to the ground in their desperate hug, it was the best hug I think I'd ever had after I thought something had happened. Almost instantly, Emily and Clara went back to their colouring; I held onto Shannon.

"Shannon, hunny, where's Mommy?"

"I'm not sure, Daddy, Emily woke me up because she couldn't find you; I couldn't find Mommy either, we haven't seen her all day."

Haven't seen her all day? Where was Emilia? It broke my heart to think how scared they must have felt waking up unable to find us, how awful would that make me? Leaving my three beautiful daughters at home alone all day, even if I didn't know Emilia had left I should have checked on them.

"Wh-who looked after you, Shannon?" Even though I asked I already knew the answer and it broke my heart.

"I did, silly, I made a bit of a mess though. I'm sorry, Daddy, can you forgive me?"

"Oh, honey, don't you ever apologise again, you're my big brave girl, okay?"

I squeezed Shannon tightly, kissing her on the forehead

before I headed up to our bedroom only to find nothing. Emilia wasn't there; she'd taken her clothes, her shoes, everything without leaving so much as a note. I checked the entire house; the only thing left of her was the picture frame that sat on her bedside table with our first picture together in it. I sat on the bed cradling the small frame, sobs eventually breaking through as it felt like my heart had been ripped out of my chest slowly and painfully.

What do I do?

Shannon

I tossed and turned all night getting hardly any sleep. I honestly felt like crying when I saw the sunlight creeping through the curtains; I was trying to make sense over everything I found out last night. My whole life is basically one big lie!

Not only is my dad not my dad but he's also the head warrior to a pack of werewolves that up until yesterday I genuinely believed didn't exist! What's next? Vampires? Witches? Heck may as well go the whole hog and say the tooth fairy!

It does make sense though I guess; the wolves coming to town, even meeting Thomas' wolf in the meadow. He didn't feel like a threat, he didn't hurt Clara and he didn't hurt me. He just left us there in the middle of the woods. Wait but why would he leave me there if I was his... What did he call it again? Mate.

Why didn't he come back straight away and take us home where we'd be safe, why leave us in the middle of the woods? I wonder if that's why he's so warm to me; this mate bond as he called it, maybe that's why his touch warms my body, why I'm mesmerised every time I look at him, why all I want to do is kiss him. I don't know any more! My dad and Thomas both said I had to decide though; whether I was going to accept Thomas and be his Luna or… leave.

I mean I love my aunt to bits but the idea of moving to England to be with her made me feel uncomfortable, she was my mom's sister, so my guess is she's human. She's actually the only member of my mom's family we've ever met; Mom said that she wasn't close to them any more, they turned their back on her when she met my dad, she never said why though just that they didn't agree with it.

I sat up in the bed, throwing my legs off the side of the bed, I headed to the bathroom so I could have a wash and freshen up a bit; there were towels and stuff in there including a little bag with what looked like my stuff in – Dad must have brought it here when I was brought in. It felt so good to wash and change into some clean clothes rather than being stuck in the hospital gown that they had changed me into; I walked out of the bathroom to find nurse Hilary changing the sheets on my bed, a smile spread across her face when she saw me.

"Good morning, my lovely! How did you sleep?" Her happiness was definitely contagious; I could feel my own smile spreading from cheek to cheek.

"Oh, erm, okay actually."

"Good to hear it! The breakfast cart will be around soon, okay?"

She started to walk towards the door with my dirty sheets when I spoke; not even realising I was asking until it was too late.

"So, you're a werewolf too, I take it?"

She turned around to face me, she looked pretty relaxed, obviously not bothered by my question at all.

"I am, hunny. Well, we all are." She paused for a moment, I'm assuming not knowing where to go from there, she turned around again going back towards the door only saying one thing.

"Doctor Bane will be in soon; she's excited to meet you."

The morning went by pretty quickly; I didn't get any visitors, at the very least I thought Thomas would be in. I still needed answers!

There was a knock at the door before an older lady walked in – she had long grey hair, thin black glasses and the most incredible violet-coloured eyes. Wait, why were her eyes that colour? Maybe it was a wolf thing?

"Are you a wolf too?" She looked at me as if I'd just interrupted an important thought that she had now lost, was this Doctor Bane?

"Now, now. If you ask everyone who enters the room that question, we'll be here all day. It's nice to see you, Miss Rye, I am Doctor Bane."

She walked over to my bed checking the different machines, making notes on her clipboard alongside the occasional look in my direction. When she was done, she walked over to my bed, sitting in the chair my father sat in last night.

"How are you feeling?"

"How am I feeling? Well, I've just found out werewolves exist, my dad is not my dad; oh, and apparently I'm mated to an Alpha wolf which makes me an immediate target seeing as I nearly died two weeks ago."

She let out a small chuckle whilst moving her hand caringly towards mine.

"That's a lot for you to process so young, isn't it? Well, I suppose it's a lot for any person to process at any age."

"Doctor Bane?"

"Yes, my dear?"

"May I ask you something?" I'm not sure why but I had a

feeling that she would be able to give me an honest opinion on my predicament. I had absolutely no idea what to do or even who to ask so there was a big possibility that she may be my only hope right then.

"Of course, you can; it's whether I can think of an answer we ought to worry about."

We shared a giggle whilst I thought of how to word what I was going to ask her; I mean I wasn't entirely sure of any of it myself like.

"I have to choose between living my life as a human, possibly moving to my aunt's or… accepting Thomas' word about whatever a mate is, be his Luna, and live with werewolves forever. What would you do?"

I could see her thinking about what I had said, possibly wording her answer as carefully as possible.

"Miss—"

"Shannon." I had to correct her; I hate it when people address me formally – it feels awkward. She gave me a small smile before she continued.

"Shannon, tell me; what do you feel when you look at Thomas?"

Why was she answering my question with a question; a silly one at that, I didn't feel anything, or at least I didn't think I did – did I? I mean he's handsome sure, he's also kind and considerate – annoyingly forceful but just one look at him and I feel content, safe. Sure, yesterday I was angry but looking back it was more the situation surrounding it rather than him. Then I remembered how all I wanted to do was make him happy after I saw the look on his face when I tried to send him away; it hurt to see him so sad if I'm honest.

"I-I feel like I want to make him happy."

"And when he touches you, what do you feel?"

I thought back to the kiss yesterday how warm it felt, how right it felt, how I mustered all my energy to fight it because it was wrong… but it wasn't. I mean the kiss was amazing but that shouldn't have been how my first kiss went. *Yes, that's right! I'm nearly eighteen and I've never kissed a boy.* When he held my hand though, all the pain went away; I could feel the warmth spreading through my body making everything feel better, leaving nothing but the feeling of his touch soaring through my body, exciting my core.

"He's warm, very warm; it's nice, is it a werewolf thing? Yesterday it made all the pain I was feeling disappear; leaving only his touch." She smiled as I spoke, listening attentively, waiting for me to finish before she spoke.

"You see Miss—Shannon, although humans can't feel the pull like us wolves do, they do feel some sort of pull from the mate bond, which to me it sounds like you are feeling. The warmth you feel will feel like electricity to Thomas, igniting every single part of his being, making him want you more and more. They say a mate is one half of your soul, they make you strong, they make you happy but most of all they complete you – without your mate you will forever feel like you are missing a piece of yourself. Some wolves don't get a mate and have to take a chosen mate – like your father did your mother but we will forever search for our mates; it's what we are raised to do, both a blessing and a curse. I can't tell you what to do in regard to your choice, but I hope with all of this added information you can make the right choice. Not for Thomas, not for your dad. For you."

I sat there for a second in shock, processing everything Doctor Bane just told me; was I really that important to Thomas?

Was I the other half of his soul? Were we really destined to be together? I watched as Doctor Bane stood up from the chair, heading towards the door.

"Shannon… the reason I think you healed so well – I mean being a human you should have died from your injuries, but you didn't. You're strong. You have a fire in you that I don't think even you have realised yet; Thomas may have shared his strength with you to get you through, but I believe you could have done it on your own. I expect you will do great things. You, regardless of which life you choose. You can go home tomorrow, okay?"

"Thank you, Doctor Bane, erm, could you please tell everyone I don't want any visitors today please? I-I have a lot to think about."

"Of course, and please call me Geraldine… Luna." She gave me a small smile before she headed out the door leaving me with just my thoughts.

At least I could go home tomorrow, but I mean, what do I do? Do I go home, finish school, and build a life without Thomas? No. I-I don't think I could. It would likely drive him crazy being so close to me but not being able to have me; if what Doctor – Geraldine said was true, I'm surprised he's been able to go six years without me.

I could go to my aunt's? At least then he could move on and be with someone who could feel it back; be a proper Luna for him and the pack without needing to ask questions every ten minutes.

Why is this so hard?

Chapter Nine
A Visit to Crimson Rock

Thomas

"Shannon, whether you choose to go to your aunt's or stay here and rule by my side, I need you to know; from the moment I set my eyes on you, I have loved you more than life itself. You're the only thing I want now and forever but despite all of that I only want you to be happy; if that means you go to your aunt's then so be it but please. Give me a chance. I want to prove to you that you are the only thing in existence that will ever matter to me."

I couldn't leave without telling her how I feel, I wanted to put everything out there before she made her decision – I couldn't help but feel hopeful seeing her smile the way she did, her beautiful eyes twinkling like stars as she looked at me. Wow, she really was mesmerising, she stirred something in me that I have never felt before; it was a mix of fear and excitement.

"She will choose us, I know it; we were destined to be together."

Atticus spoke with such confidence that I couldn't help but listen, I could feel how happy he was at the prospect of Shannon accepting us; it was rubbing off on me and soon I was grinning ear to ear.

"Well, you look happy, things go well with Shannon?"

Stefan was waiting for me downstairs, he patted my back as we walked out the door – he said he had something he needed to tell me so we were going for a run, Atticus needed to stretch his legs and so did Stefan's wolf Cyrus. We hadn't shifted since the night of the rogue attack. I'd been here and Jade's been poorly according to him, but she seemed fine when she brought Shannon food. I don't know, she can be a mystery at times – he probably just wanted an excuse to stay in the bedroom with her.

"I think I may have gotten through to her, Stef. I really do."

"That's amazing, bro, shall we head to the lake for a change?"

"That actually sounds great!"

I hadn't been to the lake properly in years; a refreshing swim and some bro time was exactly what I needed. We stripped off at the tree border folding our clothes neatly so that our wolves could carry them, then we shifted; thankfully, long gone are the days that it was painful to shift. In the beginning it was agony; your bones would have to break in order to move into a different position, the pain was horrendous, it got easier over time though – our bodies adjust to the movements and the breaking. I remember my first shift took about three and a half hours, I felt every single break, every single movement, I remember begging my father not to make me do it again; to kill me instead. Once transformed though it was amazing – I was faster, my senses were a thousand times better than they were before, I was stronger and I loved every second of it. Now it only takes about ten seconds at most to shift, it needs to be quick just in case of an attack or a fight; we need to be able to shift before we can get hurt, we can't do that if we are still shifting three hours later, my father made it law that shifting became part of the training so that we were the fastest and we could bear the pain otherwise we'd likely struggle longer. Although I'd prefer this over being one of the first werewolves. Legend has it the first werewolf was cursed by a gypsy witch, he had stolen a precious necklace of hers. When she found out she cursed him; every single full moon he would change into this uncontrollable monstrous beast, he had no control during this shift, he was basically a killing machine and anyone who lived through one of his attacks would become like him. Eventually they were able to find ways to lock themselves away and not hurt anyone but when he met someone and they had children or any of his creations had children, they didn't shift at every full moon; they were able to shift when they wanted to at the age of eighteen and have more control over themselves, they were known as shape-shifting wolves – this is where we eventually developed from. The original werewolves are thought to have been completely destroyed by the witches and vampires because of the risk they posed to our world, but who knows whether it was true or not?

It's a weird feeling when Atticus has control; it's like I'm a passenger in a car, sure I can see what he's doing and feel most of what he's feeling but I can't fully control him. I have to just hope for the best. Sometimes I can overpower him and take control but it's hard, it takes a lot of energy; after all, our wolves are the strongest part of us. They are where we get our power from; without them we're just… human.

It was quiet through the woods; no birds, no deer, no rabbits, nothing. The only sound surrounding us was our wolves' paws hitting the ground, breaking the odd twig that had fallen on our path. We shifted at the edge of the forest; putting our clothes back on before stepping into the clearing. We noticed that there wasn't anyone here – I mean it wasn't entirely unusual because people knew that there were wolves in the forest but there was still usually one or two people here, hanging around or playing in the water. Stefan was the first to dive in – still fully clothed might I add, sending a big splash into the air as he did so. I couldn't help but laugh at him before following him in myself; we swam around for a bit, splashing each other, telling jokes and just overall having fun.

We got out of the water finally, our clothes dripping wet, we sat there in awe as we watched the moon at its peak, I prefer coming out at night; it meant I could be a bit more… myself. It sounds silly I know but after dark I never really see anyone so I'm not expected to be the big Alpha that everyone looks up to. I can… Well, I can be me. The guy who wants to have fun with his friends, take the woman he loves out on a proper date, go to the cinema, but I can't. I have to think solely about the pack and what I can do to help or improve it. It's my life, it's always been expected of me and it will be expected of my children too.

"Hey, Tom." Stefan nudged at my arm moving my focus back to him.

"Oh sorry – hey."

"What were you thinking about?"

"Oh… the pack."

"Dude, I swear that's all you ever think about."

"It's all I'm supposed to think about, Stef, it's the way I was trained to think."

"You need to take time for yourself too, mate, you're an amazing Alpha, everyone adores you. You are allowed to have a life as well as the pack." I thought about what he said, did the pack really not have to be my life? Could I do more than just be an Alpha? I pushed that thought to the back of my head; this wasn't what we came here for.

"What did you want to talk about?"

"Oh yeah, it's Jade… she's pregnant! I'm gonna be a dad!" You could see the grin spread across his face illuminated by the moonlight.

"That's amazing, dude! Congratulations!" I hit his arm before pulling him into a big hug. I couldn't believe it he was going to be a dad. He'll be a great dad and Jade will be an amazing mam, this is the best day I've had in a while by far! We joked about baby names and how I hoped the baby didn't inherit his fat nose… that thing was huge, but ultimately, I was chuffed for him honestly. I couldn't help but think about Shannon carrying my pups and how good a mother she would be; I suppose she had already had enough practice with her two sisters all those years ago. I wondered if she would want kids with me? That all depended on whether she chose to stay with me, leave her life, her innocence and be my mate; my Luna, my everything.

Me and Stefan decided to shift so that we could go home, tomorrow was going to be a busy day; I had to drive over to Crimson Rock lake to see how Luna Alice and Alpha Kye were doing after their pup's birth. I really didn't want to, I wanted to spend the day with Shannon, find out how she felt about… Well, everything but it's tradition between the packs to visit the Luna and Alpha after they have their first heir. The funny part was that they had triplets – girl, boy, girl. So even though the son was born second he would take his rightful place as Alpha because as per tradition a girl could not. These were the first werewolf triplets born to a pure Alpha bloodline in centuries though so it was a very big deal. That's why Doctor Bane had to do an emergency caesarean when things weren't going as smoothly as they liked, we couldn't risk losing Alice or the babies.

I slept well last night, the best I have in ages – I think it's because I know that Shannon's awake, I decided to visit Shannon before going down for breakfast. I thought she'd be asleep because it was so early but when I got there she was in the shower so I turned around in defeat, getting a bite to eat before starting my two hour journey to the Crimson Rock pack.

Alpha Kye was waiting for me when I reached the Crimson Rock pack house – they had a smaller pack to ours maybe three to four hundred werewolves in total, it was nice. They had cosy little cottages scattered around and then a house that was a little larger than a mansion situated in between them all; I got out of the car only to be pulled into a friendly hug by Kye, he was only a year or two older than me so we got along better than we did the other alphas who were still stuck in the old ways, refusing to consider change.

"Thomas, it's so good to see you! Where is your Luna?" He looked around me and into the car; he obviously expected me to bring Shannon considering she was at the pack.

"She's still recovering, a lot to process for a human, I guess." I looked around realising that there were no other cars here, where were the other Alphas?

"Uh, Kye, where is everyone?"

"You are the only one coming actually."

"Wait, why?"

"Because you are the only person I know that will keep our secret."

"What secret?"

"You have to see it for yourself." Kye turned around, gesturing for me to follow him. I was in shock over the fact that he managed to get the Alphas not to come never mind that he had a secret, was it to do with Alice? The pups? I followed him, growing more intrigued by the minute to know what their secret was.

Chapter Ten
The Big Secret

I followed Kye through his pack house admiring the paintings that hung on the walls as we climbed the stairs. I smiled politely towards anyone that acknowledged me (as a visiting Alpha should). When we came up to the third floor which only Alphas had access to, I noticed that he had added a key code lock which definitely wasn't there when I visited last summer.

As we walked through the door, I noticed three warriors stood close by; obviously watching the door to make sure that only an Alpha came upstairs, this was all completely new. Kye wasn't this high security last year – in fact he was a lot more relaxed than I am with my pack; whatever was going on was big.

"Kye, what's going on? Why are there guards stationed up here?"

"Thomas, I will not speak about it out here. We will go to my room and discuss it there." Kye looked almost angry when he spoke – his eyes darting to each guard, almost questioning whether they were listening to us. Why were we going to his room though? Surely something this important should be discussed in his office? I stayed quiet as we walked down the hallway, he obviously didn't want to risk anyone finding out so I knew better than to challenge him. We passed his office, heading towards a door at the end which I'm assuming was his and Alice's bedroom, he opened the door to invite me inside; I was surprised at how bright it was. They had floor to ceiling windows on the one side of the room with some French doors placed in the middle leading out onto the balcony. There were plants everywhere, like a greenhouse, they looked nice against their bare white walls and black four poster bed.

"Thomas, hii!" Alice squealed in excitement before wrapping me up in a warm hug, I haven't seen them since last summer when I came to sign a new alliance as Alpha. Unfortunately when you take over as Alpha all former alliances have to be re-signed or negotiated because they're no longer valid but it's how things have to be done now after some issues in the past.

"Alice, it's so great to see you, it feels like forever. How are you feeling?" She let me go when a low growl ripped through the air, obviously coming from Kye and I can't say I blame him but I've known Alice for years – even longer than I've known him so of course we're going to be excited. I'd definitely react the same way though, wolves are possessive by nature, we can't help it.

"I'm okay considering." She looked almost nervous, if it was getting Alice nervous it must be big. She was never afraid of anything after everything she went through.

"Thomas, if you will, come and meet my son, Theodore – or Teddy as Alice keeps bloody calling him." You could see the pride in his face as he looked at his son, the next heir to his pack but there was something else that spread over his face. Concern. I walked towards the crib and looked down at the little heir; I couldn't help but coo over him. He had these big chubby cheeks, a kind of golden-brown eyes that were honestly like something I had never seen, they were almost glowing. I put my hands towards his cheeks slowly when all of a sudden, his eyes turned black, I watched as his hair grew longer, paws replaced his tiny hands, his arms and legs changed position in the way we did when we shift. I watched as this baby transformed into an ebony wolf cub, his fur shining gold where the light hit. I stumbled back in amazement, completely astonished by what had just happened.

"Kye. What? How?"

I turned back to Kye and Alice who were just looking at me, waiting for me to react to their sudden revelation.

"We—we don't know. We've looked as far as we could without arousing suspicion but we can't find anything. Thomas – he was born a wolf, then he shifted into his human form. We can't explain it, it's never happened before. Can you understand now why we're being so secretive? If we told anyone we'd be placing a target on the pack, on him."

I stood there for a moment, not knowing how to process this information – it was both terrifying and amazing, he could shift at will – no pain, no struggle. I couldn't help but envy him, what I'd have given to not have to go through the pain when shifting. Alice walked over to me, grabbing my hand, she slowly pulled me over to another crib.

"Thomas, that's not all… Annabelle, we think that she's a healer."

"Well, I mean that's impossible, healers don't get their powers until they get their wolves at thirteen." I looked down at the infant in front of me to be met with the most fluorescent violet eyes I had ever seen, even brighter than Doctor Bane's.

"Thomas, watch." I watched in horror as Alice stabbed her hand with a knife on her bedside dresser before placing her finger in little Annabelle's grip, I watched as the cut on her hand healed before my eyes, Annabelle's eyes glowing the entire time. I gasped when I saw it was healed in less than a minute.

"But—" I stopped mid-thought I had no idea what I wanted to say, I'd never seen anything like what these little ones were displaying – especially as infants.

"She would have to have her wolf already, right? I mean to have her powers? Has she shifted like little Teddy has?" I felt like I was babbling but I had no idea what to say, what to ask, what to even do, I couldn't take my eyes away from little Annabelle. "What about your third?" I walked over to the third crib to find a smaller baby; she had the lightest blue eyes I had ever seen. They almost blended in with the whites of her eyes, she looked up at me smiling; from wind I'm guessing but it was adorable none the less.

"As far as we're aware, Adira is completely ordinary."

"Kye, Alice… this… this is amazing. I mean not for you, you will definitely have your work cut out for you especially with Teddy."

"Yes but, Thomas, we can't risk it getting out; as far as we're aware, he's the first werewolf to be able to do this, same as Annabelle. I've never heard of infants having powers before."

You could see the fear in Kye's eyes as he spoke, fear of the unknown, fear of something happening to his children, if anybody found out about them who knows what could happen!

"Kye, why are you trusting me?"

"Because out of everyone in the world, I know that you will do nothing to put my children or my pack in danger. I know that even though you're the youngest Alpha, you're the one we all look up to, you are the only one that thinks of the greater good over themselves. We need to ask something big of you. It involves your mate too, I guess, which is why I hoped you would have brought her." He looked so serious when he spoke, whatever it was I knew that I would do it; if he needed warriors for protection they were his; if he needed supplies, done. Alice was like a sister to me and has been since we rescued her from rogues six years ago, we recognised her alpha aura straight away. It turned out her pack had been massacred by werewolf hunters back in Ireland. We were only there on vacation when we found her, she was just skin and bone. We saved her and brought her back here to live with us, it was at the next Alpha meeting Kye nearly mated and marked her right in the middle of the meeting room – they accepted each other straight away and it was like her happy ending.

"Anything, you both know that."

"Thomas – we want you and Shannon to raise our children if anything were to happen to us."

I couldn't help but gasp, what an honour. They want us to look after the three most important things in the world to them if they are not able to. I couldn't help but smile at how highly they held me in their mind – I didn't even have to think about it. I knew the answer and I didn't think Shannon would object.

"We would be honoured but I'm sure there's no need."

"Thomas, our witch – Aisling, she had a premonition. We won't watch them grow up, we know that and we've come to terms with it but you and Shannon, you will play a key part in their lives. Aisling is able to put a sort of mask over the babies to hide their eyes but it's not strong enough to cover Teddy's shifting, she will be coming up soon to put their masks on but we need her to do another spell as well. It's an attachment spell – it ties the pups to us, then when we die it transfers the tie to you and Shannon. Upon our death the pups will be teleported straight to you for protection; it's a simple spell which is just cast by grouping the blood."

Wow, that was a lot to process, they were asking, knowing we'd accept because their witch had seen it, they knew they wouldn't live long enough to watch their pups grow yet they were okay with it. Why weren't they trying to change it? The future can always be changed, they didn't have to die, we didn't have to have the pups, they should be with their mom and dad not me or Shannon.

"What can we do to change it?"

"Thomas, we can't."

"Bullshit!" I could feel the anger rising in me, they were just giving up! They weren't willing to fight for their life, I'd lose my friends and the pups would lose their parents all because they didn't want to try!

"Thomas, calm down, if we don't die the pups won't reach their full potential, they won't change the world – we've had this discussion! What do you think all of this is for? The security, the codes, the warriors! We are trying to live as long as we can! I don't want to die, I don't want our babies to grow up without us but it's for the greater good! We don't have a choice!" Alice cried as she shouted at me, I had never seen her like this, she looked as if she was at war with herself; why was I such an idiot? Of course they didn't want to die, of course they had thought of absolutely everything they could but their deaths were inevitable in whatever sick future we had coming.

"I-I'm sorry, I didn't mean—"

"I know, but, Thomas, we need to know that you will take care of our pups no matter what. We can't save ourselves, we can't even save our pack. But we can save our pups. We will conduct the spell today and Aisling will explain the rest."

Kye's eyes fogged over before a mist appeared in the room which quickly transformed into a young woman; she had long ebony hair, the darkest eyes I had ever seen and rose-coloured lips. There was no doubt she was beautiful and despite her heavy gothic makeup she wasn't menacing at all, she walked towards me and held her hand out – I shook it as she introduced herself explaining everything in regards to how the spell would work.

"So, I've already gathered the ingredients for the potion; I've already visited Doctor Bane, who gave me a vial of Shannon's blood to add to it. Once it's mixed you must all drink it, even the pups and Shannon. I can put it in a container for you to take with you, Thomas – as long as Shannon drinks it in the next forty-eight hours the spell will take hold. It will not take hold until Shannon has drunk hers; once she has, you will all feel it, it's like a surge of energy through your body – one similar to that of marking. It bonds you in a similar way as that of the mate bond."

We all nodded, understanding the steps. We had individual knives to cut making sure to put our hands over her cauldron at the same time, the blood was the final ingredient – the adults had to be added first to link us and then the pups were added second – linking them to us. Aisling muttered in cursive whilst we did this but I couldn't hear her over the pups crying because of their cuts. We finally got them settled – Annabelle healed her siblings without even touching them, it was as if they didn't need touch for Annabelle to heal them, I guess they were already bonded by being triplets, the only reason we knew it was her was because her eyes were glowing. It was mesmerising.

When the pups were settled, Aisling poured the potion into cups for the adults, then into bottles of Alice's milk for the pups. We clicked our glasses before we drank it like a shot, sending it all down at once. It was awful, it had a metallic taste from all the different blood, mixed with something that tasted like socks and the after taste was similar to morning breath. We each held a baby and fed them, they protested at first but gave in in the end thankfully – I'm not sure what would have happened if they kept refusing.

"Here, Thomas, you must get your mate to drink this in the next forty-eight hours or we will have to repeat the process." Aisling handed me a bottle of the potion; I was surprised to see how red it was considering all of the other stuff that was in there – it kind of looked like cherryade.

"I will, it's getting dark now, I must head back to my pack. Hopefully I can see Shannon tonight." I shook hands with Aisling, gave Alice a hug and gave each of the pups a small kiss on the forehead before walking downstairs with Kye.

"Listen, Kye, I have to tell Stefan what's going on. He's my Beta and I trust him."

"I understand, but only him and Shannon, with a secret like this we don't know who we can trust. I will forever be in your debt, Thomas."

"There's no need." We shared a hug before I got in my car, starting my two hour journey back to my pack, it was relatively quicker than earlier – I'm guessing because of how distracted I was by today's revelations.

I tried to go and see Shannon but Nurse Hilary said that she wasn't allowing visitors. I was really looking forward to seeing her – hopefully I can tomorrow, we have much to discuss. For now, though I can go and get some rest, I have a feeling I'm not going to get much going forward.

Chapter Eleven
A Life Changing Decision

Shannon

Thankfully, I only saw Hilary after Doctor Bane left yesterday; she had to check me over and bring me some dinner, she did say that Thomas came by but once she told him that I didn't want visitors he left with no trouble. It was pretty late when she told me though so I wonder where he was all day? I mean surely if I was his mate he would have been here first thing rather than out gallivanting all day, it made me question whether he was even being honest with me about his feelings, about being his mate, even about wanting me as his Luna. I mean what even is a Luna? I know it means moon but what does it mean for werewolves? He said I would *"rule by his side"* but what does that even mean? Is it like a queen? How can a human rule over werewolves? It doesn't make any sense whatsoever.

My thoughts were interrupted by a knock at the door, followed by Hilary walking in with some breakfast – it smelled so good that my stomach grumbled in appreciation. I smiled as she approached the bed, giving me my tray as she pulled my table over.

"Shannon, Alpha Thomas is here. Is he okay to come in?" I nodded eagerly, the idea of seeing Thomas again gave me butterflies in the pit of my stomach – or was that the hunger? I had no idea. He walked in casually; dressed rather formal in a black suit with a baby pink shirt and black tie, his hair looked different today, it was a sort of golden brown colour pulled back tightly into a neat bun. His eyes sparkled as our eyes met; a grin spreading across his face from ear to ear – how was it possible for someone to be this good looking?

"Good morning, my angel."

Thomas walked over to the bed, placing a kiss on my forehead before sitting down in the chair beside me, I noticed him carrying a small bottle of what looked like cherryade – it was still quite early, who drank pop at this time?

"G-good morning, Thomas."

I couldn't help but stutter as I spoke, still in shock over how gorgeous this man was, I decided to move my focus to my scrambled eggs that were sat neatly next to my toast, I shovelled a lot more into my mouth than I intended to – almost choking in the process but it was definitely the distraction I needed.

"Shannon, I was wondering if you had made your decision at all yet?"

I moved my focus back to Thomas only to see he wasn't even looking at me; he was focusing on the drink in his hand, moving it between his palms. I swallowed what was left in my mouth so that I could speak, I already had an idea of what I wanted to say but I still had questions that I needed answering.

"I wanted to know if you could answer some questions for me first, I have so many and they are the only thing stopping me from making a decision right now."

This caught Thomas' attention enough for him to move his gaze back to me, he looked worried more than anything – I guess the unknown was really getting to him.

"Anything."

"That night, six years ago, when your wolf left us in the meadow – why did it take you so long to come back and help us?"

This question had plagued my mind a lot since everything was revealed – it didn't make sense, why would he leave us there in the middle of the meadow? Did he know Clara was a wolf and think she would protect us? But she was unconscious how could she?

"I well… I came back to the pack, shifting before Atticus could take me back to the meadow and mark you. You were only eleven, and human. I thought we had it wrong, I thought the moon goddess had it wrong. I went straight to my father's office and told him everything. I didn't even consider what danger I had put you in just leaving you there – if the guards had found you I'm not even sure what would have happened. I just assumed you'd carry Clara home, I only went back to the meadow because Atticus kept howling at me to."

"Who's Atticus?"

"Oh, Atticus is my wolf, our wolves, although they are a part of us, they are another being entirely with their own thoughts and feelings." He giggled a bit at the end, obviously remembering how new I am to all of this. He cleared his throat before carrying on. "When I came back to the meadow and I saw you were still there I felt awful… I swore that I'd be there for you whenever you needed me from that day forward. But I broke that promise two weeks ago. I wasn't there when the rogues broke into your house and nearly killed you in the street, I can never forgive myself for that." I watched as the pain spread across his face, the idea of me being hurt by *rogues* was obviously distressing him but I wasn't hurt and he was there when it mattered, he saved me. I moved the table away from the bed so I could climb down from it, kneeling down on the cold floor with my hands on his looking him straight in the eyes.

"But, Thomas, you were there – sure you weren't there when they broke in but you were there when it mattered. You saved my life if you hadn't showed up that wolf would have killed me and although at the time I'd have welcomed death I'm glad you saved me."

With the smallest ounce of courage, I had I raised myself up from the floor, maintaining eye contact with Thomas as I placed my lips against his, a warmth spreading through my body, starting a fire in my core. He sat there in shock for a moment before returning the kiss, he wrapped his arms around my waist – lifting me up so that he could deepen the kiss. The longer we kissed, the more passionate it was getting so I pulled away, placing myself on my bed – a safe distance away so that we could both cool down.

"So, uh, what are rogues?"

I found it hard to speak, I was still trying to catch my breath from our kiss. It was amazing; exactly what I always pictured kisses like, it was as if electricity was coursing through my body, creating a burning desire in places I didn't know I could feel things.

"Rogues are werewolves without a pack; in my opinion they are the most dangerous of our kind because they're unpredictable. There are some rogues that leave their pack for whatever reason; a mate rejection, a loss, some even leave because they want to live more like a human – not that they will ever fully be able to do that but they try. Then there are the rogues that are banished from their packs for their crimes; it is usually only for certain crimes because anything severe enough would warrant execution in some packs but those who are banished will never be able to join another pack. To take in a rogue you must contact their previous pack Alpha, like a reference, and if they were banished, they would never be accepted. They are forced to hunt and live like a normal wolf would for their own survival. This means that their beast-like tendencies will eventually take hold – forcing them to act more animal than man, in most their wolf will fully take over leaving them unpredictable and dangerous."

"Wow, what crime would require banishment?"

"That's a good question; I suppose it would be something like causing harm to someone in the pack on purpose, repeated offences or even just being caught trying to cause harm. I've never had to banish anyone myself but around sixteen years ago my father had to banish a warrior's son because he was feeding pack secrets to werewolf hunters at the promise of sanctuary once they took my father out. His parents followed him in the end, asking my father to allow them to leave. Which he did, with the promise that if needed they could return as long as their loyalty stayed to him but, unfortunately, we found their bodies not far from the border killed by other rogues it looked like. We had a funeral for them before we burnt their bodies."

I sat there in shock; I honestly couldn't believe what I was hearing – not only were there werewolves but there were werewolf hunters and then different kind of wolves at that! Oh, and each wolf had its own different name, personality, body – everything! Why was there so much to learn?

"Wow, that's a lot to process. Where do I fit into all of this? What does a Luna do?"

"You, my angel, are the love of my life, the woman sculpted by the moon goddess herself to be a Luna. It's like a queen, shall we say? You will help me do anything and everything that we feel is in the pack's best interest, you want a new cottage for Dorothy down the road then you've got it – you think we need to get down on our knees at twelve p.m. every day and say hail Shannon, you got it." I couldn't help but chuckle at the hail Shannon, the idea of a whole pack getting down on their knees and shouting was very amusing. "Ultimately there isn't a set list of things that you have to do, we will work as a team to make sure the pack runs smoothly, to make sure our members are safe, happy and comfortable always."

"How many members are there?"

"We are actually one of the largest in the country, our records showed nine hundred and sixty-nine members at the beginning of the year – not including pregnant wolves or new-borns at the time though – so it could be a few more now. There is only one pack bigger than ours and that's Alpha Edmund's pack Crescent Water – he has about sixteen hundred now, he recently combined with another pack when their leaders were killed by hunters." A look of concern spread across his face at the mention of the hunters, although I guess I'm not surprised. They must be powerful if they can kill all of one pack's leaders.

"What is this pack called? I mean if that one has a name, yours does too, right?"

He lifted his head as he chuckled at my question; why did I feel like an absolute idiot? Asking all of these questions that were obviously quite silly to him but I knew nothing! A few days ago, as far as I was aware werewolves weren't real and everyone was human, not just me, this was all so new to me – I felt like a child.

"*Our* pack is called Forest Lake." He put emphasis on the our obviously trying to make me realise that it was our pack not just his or theirs, it was ours, I belonged here, didn't I?

"What happens if I accept that I'm your mate, your Luna? Where do we go from here?"

"Well, first I'd need you to drink from this—" he gestured to the bottle in his hand – so it wasn't for him? It was for me? Why did he think I was going to drink some random flask he'd brought me without any details? "And then we will host a dinner tomorrow night; inviting all the pack members to introduce you as their new Luna. For you to become a Luna though, we will need to mate, and I will need to mark you before the next full moon which is when we will have your Luna ceremony."

I sat there with my mouth open not knowing how to process half of what he just said – does he mean mating as in sex? What the hell does marking mean? Will it hurt? Why does none of this sound pleasant for me?

"What—what is marking?" I was already terrified about knowing the answer, it doesn't sound like it's pleasant but maybe it would be something cute like matching tattoos? Or was that just wishful thinking?

"So marking is when me and Atticus sort of mould together in order for both the human and wolf side to be present, we will extend our canines and sink them right into your marking spot by here—" he moved my top to the side, gently caressing the lower part of my neck with his fingertips; sending a chill through my body. "It's painful at first I've heard, might be even more so with you being human but once the pain has gone and we've sealed it with a lick it's supposed to be one of the biggest pleasures you will ever feel; especially if done while mating."

"And mating. That's sex, right?" He nodded, looking as embarrassed as I felt about this small fact, I didn't want to stay on this subject for long so I switched my attention to the flask.

"What is in there?"

"So, this is something I came to speak to you about last night – it's a potion made by the witch at Crimson Rock."

"No, wait – witches are real too?" I couldn't help but

interrupt him, how frigging cool is that? All the stuff I've read and seen on telly about witches is all true! They're just intertwined with werewolf affairs.

"Yes, my love – this potion binds not only us together but the Alpha and Luna of Crimson Rock pack, if they were to die it would teleport their children to our exact location as soon as it happened."

"Wait but why? Is this normal procedure for leaders with children?"

"It is not… but they are not ordinary children and I honestly wouldn't ask if it wasn't completely necessary but their witch had a premonition and the only way that their children will reach their full potential is if their parents die and we take over their training."

"But why me – what can I offer them?"

"You can offer them a warm, loving family, a gentle touch – I've seen the way you care about your sisters and I'm telling you right now I have no doubt you were destined for it. Plus, I'll be right by your side the entire time."

"What is different about them?" My curiosity was getting the better of me.

"You kind of have to see it to believe it, angel, I promise I will take you to visit them soon, okay? Do you trust me?" I thought for a moment realising that yes, I did trust him; I trusted him more than anyone, so I held my hand out for the flask. Before putting it in my hand he stared at me; looking for any signs of doubt in my eyes but I had none – for the first time I was sure of something. I knew that whatever these babies were they obviously needed protecting otherwise they wouldn't have just done this for no reason. I took the lid off, ignoring the copper smell coming from the bottle. I drank it as fast as I could, ignoring the foul taste that came with it. We sat there quietly for a moment, Thomas watching me like a hawk when all of a sudden, I felt a strong wave of energy surge through me; I can't even describe it – in that moment I felt strong, I felt powerful I felt like I could do anything. I could feel it getting stronger and stronger; I risked a glance at Thomas and all I could see was fear in his eyes, it looked as if his whole body was glowing, it was getting brighter by the minute. I looked down at my hands and gasped as I saw them glowing just like Thomas; getting brighter and brighter as time progressed, the energy getting overwhelming. I mustered a scream before I fell back in the bed; darkness taking over as I slipped into unconsciousness again.

Chapter Twelve
New Adjustments

I woke up feeling quite groggy, it felt like I had had way too much to drink the night before. My head was throbbing, the light was burning my eyes as I opened them – even my mouth tasted horrible; like I hadn't brushed my teeth in a month. It was an awful feeling, I tried to lift my head but it felt too heavy so I just pulled my hand up to cradle it softly, I heard shuffling from beside the bed but I couldn't look that way; I just moaned in acknowledgement.

"Shannon, angel, are you okay?" It was Thomas, he stood over me examining every inch of my face obviously relieved that I was alive but also looking for the source of my pain. "I-I'll get Doctor Bane, okay?" He ran out of the room as quick as he could; I could hear him shouting down the corridor which meant that he had left the door open – for some reason if the door wasn't open you honestly wouldn't hear a thing, can you soundproof rooms? If so, I think that's what was going on. I heard footsteps coming closer before eventually I saw Doctor Bane towering over me.

"Hi, Shannon, how are you feeling?"

"It feels like a hangover." You could hear the annoyance in my voice as she shined her little torch in my eyes, checking for a reaction, I assumed, before checking all my other observations.

"Hmm, everything seems to be working okay, everything is normal – Thomas, what did you give her?"

"It was a potion. You already know which, otherwise, you wouldn't have given Aisling the final ingredient."

He furrowed his brows at her, it was if they were having a silent conversation – what did they know that I didn't?

"I told Aisling she needed to fully recover before taking that potion! You're lucky you didn't kill her!" You could see the anger building inside Doctor Bane, it was the first time I'd seen her anything but calm. She was scary, even Thomas looked at the floor rather than her as she shouted at him.

"What ingredient?" I couldn't help my curiosity; I knew it was a potion but I didn't know what was in it, why would Doctor Bane have ingredients that a witch could need? That seemed weird. I finally managed to drag myself up as Doctor Bane gasped, her anger building further – I swear you could almost see the smoke coming out of her ears! She turned towards Thomas who backed away slightly as he caught a glimpse of her face.

"*You didn't even tell her what she was bloody drinking?*" Oh wow. He's in trouble and it's my fault; I wanted to jump up and defend him but I didn't have the energy to.

"No, I knew it was a potion binding us, I-I just didn't know what was in it and in Thomas' defence I didn't think to ask once I knew it was for the protection of his friends' babies." This was all I could think to do to try and calm her down, take her anger away from Thomas – I should have asked what was in it but I wasn't too worried I knew he wouldn't do anything to hurt me, he just obviously wasn't told as much as he thought.

"Angel, the ingredient Doctor Bane gave the witch was a vial of your blood; Luna Alice and Alpha Kye thought that I was bringing you with me to visit but when they saw that I hadn't brought you they made other arrangements. The potion required the blood of the four adults to be added first, binding us together, then we had to add the three babies' blood – all whilst Aisling the witch stirred and spoke the spell. We were all meant to drink at the same time but because you weren't there, we decided that you would drink it last to complete the spell. Did you feel it once you drank it? The power coursing through your veins, the strength of the three werewolves coming together as one – it… it was incredible."

That was what I felt before I passed out; the energy, the strength, it was our energies all being merged, bonded like he said. I was in shock; when he mentioned the blood being added to the potion, I couldn't help but gasp, I had literally drunk six other people's blood without even thinking to question him because I was sure I could trust him, I felt sick thinking about it but what could I do now? It was done, it's probably for the best I didn't know because I definitely wouldn't have drank it. I know that for a fact. Doctor Bane walked over to me, putting her palm to my head.

"I'm going to get you some pain killers and something to eat. Hopefully, it is just like a hangover from where everything came to you at once; overwhelming your already fragile body." She had a small smile now but shot Thomas a dirty look as she left the room which made me giggle, the giggle drew his attention back to me. I watched as a smile spread across his face whilst looking at me, sending butterflies straight to my core. It's starting to get annoying feeling like this.

"Thomas, I want to be your Luna, I really do. I just. I don't want to mess it up; it's a lot of changes, a lot of pressure and if I'm honest I'm not sure how much more I can take."

"Angel, we don't have to rush into anything! We will do it all at your pace, I promise, just please give me – give the pack – a chance and I know you will love it."

"Why do you keep calling me angel? How can you say it's at my pace when I just drank a potion that nearly killed me, bonding me to you, two people I've never met and three special babies that you can't tell me about because *I have to see it for myself*? Since meeting you I've nearly died twice, found out that my entire life was a lie, I'm destined to be stuck with a man I don't know, live in a way that I never believed existed. Like how is any of this benefitting me, huh? Maybe I should just go and live with my aunt in England, just to live a less confusing life."

I'm actually not sure why I tried to create an argument; the more I thought about it the more I did genuinely believe I belong here, I was attracted to Thomas in a way that I'd never felt before, I felt stronger around him, even happier. It's only when I looked at him, I realised just how plain and miserable my life was before all of this, before him. Maybe it was a defence mechanism, seeing whether he would argue back, lose interest, maybe even kick me out. I'm not sure, I just know with everything going on I was just trying to figure out what was safe. I looked up and saw sadness as our eyes met, why did I keep hurting him this way? Why couldn't I just give in?

"I call you angel because every time I hear your voice, every time I look at you – it's… it's as if I'm looking at an angel, hearing an angel's song; even when you're angry all I can see is beauty radiating from you. It's all I've seen since Atticus first met you in those woods, it's the exact reason I haven't looked at nor been with another woman ever. In my eyes no woman or wolf is comparable to you, I am sorry I forced the potion on you so soon – if I'm honest I'm still a little freaked out over it myself and if there was any other way to do it, I would have but unfortunately there wasn't. I can't promise you the simple life you had before, Shannon, because I can't give you that in any way, shape or form but what I can promise is to love you until the day I die, worship you like the angel I see you as and give you the life that you deserve. I know things have been forced and hasty so far but I promise we will go at your pace – if we have to wait until next month for your Luna ceremony then so be it. All I want is your happiness, forever and always."

I looked at him in disbelief, everything he was saying was so raw and true, you could see that he only spoke from the heart as he sat there, his eyes pleading with me to give him a chance and, in all honesty, I was listening. My heart was practically singing as I finally made my decision, I was going to stay with Thomas and see where things went, my head was trying to argue, see everything practically, but for once I thought I'd listen to my heart.

"Okay, Thomas, I will be your Luna. I will stay."

He nearly hit the roof with how high he jumped off his chair, making his way towards the bed, he put his hand on my chin tilting my head so that I was looking directly into his eyes as his lips were forced upon mine; sending jolts of electricity through my body, lighting a fire in my core, his tongue forced its way into my mouth exploring it excitedly when we were interrupted by a knock at the door. Thomas growled angrily at whoever was at the door, obviously displeased by our interruption, he walked back to his chair like a little boy sulking over a lost toy. Doctor Bane walked in sharing glances between me and Thomas, knowing what we were up to, she let out a small giggle as she approached the bed.

"Well, Shannon dear, you're free to go, seeing as you're not dead and quite obviously feeling better I see no reason to keep you here. But I do suggest you get plenty of rest the next few days, okay?"

I nodded eagerly, excited to be getting out of this hospital room at last. The excitement was short lived though when I realised, I had no idea where I went from here, did I go back to my dad's? Did I have to stay at the pack? Where? I watched Doctor Bane leave the room quietly, taking any leftover equipment with her because it was no longer needed.

"Thomas, where do I go from here?"

He looked confused as I spoke, did he really not know what I meant?

"I mean, do I still go back to my dad's? Or stay with you?"

"You can stay here at the pack house – on the Alpha floor; you can stay in my room with me. Or, um, if you aren't comfortable with sharing my bed… I… I guess I could ask one of the Omegas to sort out a room close to mine to—uh, give you your own space?"

You could see how sad he was at the prospect of me having my own room but I'm not sure how comfortable I'd be sharing his bed; although I guess I didn't have much of a choice really seeing as I was his Luna, his forever and always.

"Erm, I guess sharing with you is fine. That's what a Luna would normally do, right? Just, erm, no trying for that mating ceremony that you have mentioned."

He let out a chuckle and you could see the excitement in his eyes, seeing him so happy made me realise I made the right choice, I mean what's a few uncomfortable nights before I accept how infatuated with him I am?

"Wait, what about my clothes and stuff?"

"I've already mind linked an Omega to go get it all from your father's house."

"What's an Omega and a mind link?"

"So, werewolves have ranks within the pack – we have the Alpha and the Luna at the top, then it's the Betas, then the Gammas, then it's the Deltas which are basically a backup for the

Gamma, then we have Elites which we actually only introduced a few years ago here – these are our strongest warriors who protect the weaker wolves during battle, then there are our warriors, then there are the Omegas. The Omegas basically help keep the pack going by cooking, cleaning, childcare – that kind of thing. Then mind linking is something only wolves can do, we can basically talk to each other through our minds."

This was a lot of information to process at once, so many levels of werewolves and they can all talk to each other with what – a form of telepathy? It was crazy how different things were here and it was making my head hurt trying to think about it, there was a whole new world just down the street from where I was brought up. I started packing my things into the duffle bag that was left in the bathroom; silently thanking myself for getting washed and dressed earlier, even if I had passed out at least I was clean. Not that it would stop me washing the scent of hospital off my body as soon as we got to Thomas' room.

"I'm ready."

I looked at him only to see a large toothy grin spread from cheek to cheek, I took his hand and he navigated us through the hospital before finally leaving and stopping outside. The air was crisp and refreshing; all I could smell was nature, there was no air pollution or anything – it was relaxing. We walked through the grounds hand in hand, smiling at the people we passed who nodded at Thomas politely; my guess is this was their way of showing respect to their alpha. We passed maybe twenty cottages before we were in front of a building that looked like a hotel. I was surprised to see a large drive in front of the hotel leading to a road that carried on into the forest; I've never known a road to be here although I've never been stupid enough to go near the forest. Thomas squeezed my hand attentively, I looked up to see him smiling down at me, it was lovely to see him so happy. I couldn't help but feel excited myself for what was to come.

"Welcome home, my angel."

We walked through the door to be greeted by a grand entrance; in the middle was a huge staircase going off in both directions towards the top, giant arch windows stood at the top of the staircase letting in light which bounced off a large – what looked like crystal – chandelier. The entire entrance floor was just marbled tile with a lovely red runner starting at the door and going all the way up the stairs. The whole room was just pure white, making it very bright in here; I couldn't help but wonder if it was the white that made it seem so large. We scaled the stairs together with my hand resting upon the intricately carved banister; admiring its beauty as I walked, it was a dark oak kind of wood which contrasted beautifully with how light it was in here. I noticed the red runner carried on through the hallways as well.

"That there is the Gammas' side of this floor." Thomas gestured to the right side as we headed towards another grand staircase. "And that is the Deltas', they share the floor because it was easier that way when introducing the leaders to the one pack house."

We climbed the other staircase before coming to another floor; this one had large wooden doors off to the right and then another set to the left. Thomas gestured to the right side before he spoke. "That is our Betas, Stefan and Jade's side of this floor, it is where they will grow old and their pups will grow up – that is until the new Beta takes over. The other side we use for visiting leaders."

We walked up yet another beautiful staircase to find only one set of double wooden doors.

“This, my sweet angel, is our floor; we have this entire floor to ourselves, each floor is fitted with its own kitchen, lounge and bedrooms but ours are bigger obviously.” We walked through the big double doors and I was shocked to see how big the entrance was, there was a small dip with one or two steps leading down to a very open plan living area. A gorgeous corner sofa sat in the middle facing what had to be the biggest television I’d seen in my entire life, behind that was a pool table and an archway leading into a small kitchen. It was big enough for a six chair dining table but it was small in comparison to the living area, there was everything you’d have in a normal kitchen plus more, there were blenders for any occasion, two coffee machines – it was quite overwhelming.

“Uh, Thomas – where is your bedroom?”

“Our bedroom is right up here.” He took me down a small corridor where to my surprise there were even more rooms. We were right at the end when he finally opened a door; the first thing that caught my eye was the large French doors with arch windows either side, leading to what I assumed was a balcony. I couldn’t believe how beautiful the room was; it had a big white sleigh bed to the right with some gorgeous geometric bedding made neatly on it, there was silver carpet down with a large shaggy ochre coloured rug in the middle of the room. It was dark now and honestly that looked like the comfiest bed ever; I couldn’t wait to get in.

“Are you hungry? I could make us some food?” Thomas placed my bag on the bed and walked towards the door. “Why don’t you shower and meet me in the living area, okay?” I nodded as he closed the door, heading back towards the kitchen to start making our food.

I walked towards the door next to the bed hoping it was the

bathroom only to find a very large walk-in closet, the right side full of tailor-made suits all lined up neatly along the wall, with drawers underneath full of other clothes I'm guessing. On the left I noticed some of my stuff with what looked like some added new stuff. I walked towards what I assumed was my side to look through some of the drawers, there were lots of bottoms in them, some I hadn't seen before. Most of it had tags on – the only exceptions were my actual clothes from home. I pulled out a lovely pair of Teddy bear pyjamas from the bottom drawer. I tried the door on the other side of the bed. Finally, the bathroom! There were already towels on the unit so I locked the door and fumbled with the shower before there was finally hot water coming out of the shower head. I stepped inside; immediately relaxed by the hot water trickling down my body, I washed my hair and my body with the toiletries that were on the side, I'm pretty sure they were Thomas' but at this point I didn't care. I dried myself off before changing into the new pyjamas and heading towards the living area; I was surprised to hear the sound of laughter as I approached the opening to the living area. I looked over to the settee feeling slightly nervous at the thought of entertaining people when a familiar face smiled towards me; it was the lady who brought me the selection of food when I woke up from my coma, the thought brought a smile to my face helping me relax. Thomas rushed over to my side steering me towards the settee.

"Shannon, this is my Beta, Stefan, and his lovely mate, Jade."

I smiled at both visitors only to be tackled by Jade for a hug.

"I'm so glad you decided to stay! We're going to be the best of friends; I just know it!'

Chapter Thirteen
A New Environment

When I say that this was the comfiest bed, I had ever slept in I mean it; it was like sleeping on air and the way the blanket enveloped us both comfortably was heavenly, it was the best sleep of my entire life. I opened my eyes looking around the room as sunlight peeked through the gaps in the curtains, my eyes rested on the man sleeping next to me; he looked so peaceful, his hair a tangled mess caught up around his head, his lips pursed as if having a nightmare, I cupped my hand to his cheek noticing that it relaxed almost instantly – was this because of the mate bond? Could he feel my touch even in his sleep? I hadn't even noticed that he had his arms wrapped tightly around me until he pulled me closer to him, my body now pressed against him and it felt right. It sounds silly but we fitted perfectly together there on his bed. He buried his face deep into my neck; inhaling deeply as he did. I could feel sparks erupting, heading straight for my core – why did he make me feel like this?

"Good morning, my angel," Thomas whispered in a husky voice, he pulled away slightly so he could look at me better. "I've dreamt about waking up next to you for six years and it's better than I ever thought it could be, how did you sleep?"

"Amazing actually, you have the comfiest bed ever."

"We do, my angel, what's mine is yours, remember? For now, and forever."

"Oh, uh, yeah. How did you sleep?"

"Better than I've ever slept, having you in my arms was like a dream come true. Let's stay here forever."

"When did you put your arms around me?" I tried getting up but Thomas' grip only tightened around me.

"They've been there all night, you seemed to be having a nightmare not long after going to sleep so I tried to calm you down by cwtching you and it worked… I just sort of fell asleep, comforted by your scent."

"My scent?"

"Yeah, a werewolf's mate has an intoxicating scent that only their mate can smell, it helps calm them, it's one of the things that draw them to each other in the beginning."

"Oh, well, what does it smell like?"

"So, it's different for everyone – your scent is sweet – it's a mix of cherries and fresh lavender. It's the best smell in the world."

I laid there for a moment thinking about how different things were going to be from now on, I wouldn't be living with my family, wouldn't be able to hang out with Josh or Meygan like I used to. What would I say in school? Wait – SCHOOL!

"Thomas, how will I get to school from now on?" He groaned as he moved, taking his arms away from my waist, he sat up on the bed facing me as he spoke.

"Shannon, you honestly don't think you can carry on with school, do you?"

"Erm, excuse me?"

"Shannon, you are to be my – our – Luna. I need you here and I need you safe. You can't protect yourself so I need you on pack grounds."

I couldn't help the shock that had no doubt spread across my face; why couldn't I finish school? Surely, I wasn't at much risk, it was school. I'd already missed so much I didn't want to miss any more, and prom was coming up! I was so excited to be going, I couldn't miss out. I couldn't.

"Thomas, you, you can't expect me to give up school. I've already given up so much to stay here and… and be your Luna! I want to see my friends and it's not like they can come here, is it?"

"Shannon, all I want is for you to be safe – just over two weeks ago you were attacked because of me… I… I don't know what I would do if I couldn't protect you again."

You could see how upset he was, thinking back to the night that I was hurt. I could see that this was a battle that I wasn't going to win so I decided to get up and have a wash before getting dressed.

"Thomas, do you think you could introduce me to the pack today then? It would be nice to meet everyone and start my Luna duties, if I'm going to be stuck here, I may as well have something to do."

I could see that I had hurt him by saying stuck here but it was how I felt right then unfortunately. I was sure that would change eventually but I just wanted some sort of normality for a change. I'd been comatose for two weeks only to wake up and watch my life change drastically.

"Of course! I can't wait to introduce you to everyone!" He jumped off the bed, and walked over slowly, holding his hand out. We walked hand in hand through the hallway to where we put our shoes last night and out the door, down the stairs all the way until we reached the entrance way. Instead of going out the door we turned left entering a very large what looked like a ballroom with tables everywhere. A buffet table at the very end was surrounded by different pack members.

"This is where meals are served for pack members that wish

to eat here; obviously as you know everyone has their own eating facilities but we do like to have stuff like this set up ready for anyone who wants it. Breakfast is served between seven and ten thirty, lunch is served between twelve and two thirty, dinner is then served from four until around eight – it was from five but we brought it forward for some pups so that they would get to socialise with other pack members. Then any leftovers go through that door there where there are seven large fridges; one for each day so that it doesn't get muddled up and it makes waste more manageable."

He pointed out a door on the other side of the room, showing where the food goes. He was really organised with everything around the pack: it surprised me. At home my dad couldn't organise a sock drawer never mind a whole pack.

"People are free to help themselves to leftovers, the doors are always unlocked because of it, I'd hate for anyone to go hungry. Hey, look, there's Jade and Stefan!" Thomas waved over at the two people sat in the far corner before making his way over there, leaving me by the door. I'm not very confident and yeah, we'd had fun last night but I still didn't know them, saying that – I didn't really know Thomas either, why was all of this so bloody frustrating? Feeling defeated I hung my head low and started to walk over towards their table when my stomach grumbled at the sweet smell of sausage coming from the buffet table, realising my hunger, I decided to make a detour and grab an actual plate of food before sitting down with them. I grabbed a plate and waited patiently for my turn to go towards the selection of yummy food. Using the tongs I grabbed some sausages and bacon before moving onto the scrambled egg, I went to grab the spoon for the eggs when all of sudden a tall woman appeared before me, she obviously took very great care in her appearance with the amount of makeup and perfume she was wearing.

"Erm, excuse me, I was about to grab that."

I was quite proud of myself; I hardly ever stood up for myself, I just let everyone walk over me all the time but nope, not this time. Or so I thought. As soon as we made eye contact my confidence diminished. I didn't realise exactly how tall she was beforehand but now I could see she towered over me, obviously a werewolf. I just picked a fight with a bloody werewolf! She just looked at me and laughed.

"Who even are you? I mean, which poor lump got saddled with you? A human!"

I wished I could make myself invisible right then, she was just in hysterics. Was Thomas really that badly off with a human as a mate? How did she even know I was human?

"T-T-Tho—"

"Are you stupid as well? Can you not talk? Oh, hunny, tell your mate I know a real woman when he wants one." She slammed the spoon for the eggs into my chest, it was so hard I coughed at first. I watched as she chuckled menacingly again, obviously finding the fact that I was human very amusing. "Come on then? Who got saddled with this dim-witted human as a mate? No need to hide, we all want to know!"

There were a few chuckles amongst the people around us, they obviously found it amusing too that someone could get a human for a mate; poor Thomas. I knew I should have left, not come here – why did I ever think I could do this? My thoughts were interrupted by Thomas, his voice echoed in this great hall, silencing everyone, forcing their attention only upon him.

"*Silence! Verity – how dare you speak of your future Luna in such a horrible way.*"

The woman – I mean, Verity – stopped for a moment,

looking between me and Thomas only to start laughing again.

"A human? For Luna? That's hilarious, she is not my Luna." She only just managed to say Luna before Thomas had her pinned against the wall by her throat; she pulled at his hand trying to free herself of his grip.

"*She will be your Luna or you will leave. You have no importance; you won't be missed.*"

Thomas dragged her away from the wall and threw her to the floor before turning back to me, snaking his arm around my waist as he smiled at me. I watched Verity crawl away until she could get back up on her feet, running out of the door. Everyone stole a quick glance at me and Thomas before they turned back to whatever they were doing before Verity's performance. I stood on my tiptoes and placed a kiss on Thomas' cheek.

"Thank you."

"For what, my angel?"

"Defending me."

I walked over to Stefan and Jade's table with Thomas, finally with a plate full of food so that I could eat. They were both polite but it was pretty obvious that we were interrupting something; we ate our food quietly before Jade was the first to speak.

"So, Shannon, Thomas told us that he's having a special dinner tonight to introduce you to the pack."

"Well, I said more of a party so it wasn't as formal."

"Same thing, Thomas."

I giggled as I watched them argue about whether it was a party or a dinner; Stefan was sat next to Jade finding the exchange amusing too.

"The whole point in the conversation was to see if she wanted to come dress shopping, Thomas, now shut your mouth and let me speak to her."

Thomas held his hands up in obvious surrender; smirking at how angry he had managed to get Jade.

"I'd actually love that if I'm allowed."

"What do you mean if you're allowed?"

"Well, Thomas won't allow me off pack grounds at the moment because I can't protect myself."

"Oh, won't he now?" Jade was glaring at Thomas, her anger reaching the surface slowly when I watched Thomas put his hands up in defeat again.

"Fine, you can go. But you will have to have guards with both of you so that we know you're safe."

Jade calmed down immediately, excitement taking over; she was practically jumping in her seat. I didn't feel comfortable with the idea of guards but getting away for a few hours would definitely be worth it before I came back to my life of solitude as their unwanted, weak, human Luna.

Chapter Fourteen
Meeting the Pack

The car ride into town was pretty fast; Jade insisted on driving me and her, despite Stefan's objections, so the guards were in a car behind us. I was pretty glad to be honest – it felt awkward as it is knowing you aren't strong enough to protect yourself from an attack never mind being forced to have guards as well. But why did Jade have guards as well? She's a werewolf! Surely, she could protect herself if push came to shove like.

We got out of the car together, walking down the street I noticed we were walking towards the shop me and Meygan went to when we bumped into Thomas. Walking in with Jade was different though, it wasn't as funny as it was with Meygan – it felt like more of a chore, I mean after all I was only here to get away from the grounds for a little while. I'd only been consciously there for what four days? Yet, already I was fed up and bored. How was I meant to spend the rest of my life there with Thomas – never leaving, growing old, popping out the kids that he wants… without a second thought to what I want! I really wish that I was a werewolf so I would feel the pull in the same way he did.

"Shannon, this dress would look amazing on you, especially with how blue your eyes are! Try it on." Jade practically threw the dress at me as she finished speaking, I looked down at the frilly light blue dress – it really was lovely, I guess. I walked towards the fitting room ready to try it on. It had only one strap which went over my left shoulder, it had beautiful darker blue fabric flowers sewed onto the strap fading into the detail along my chest, there were intricate flowers sewn carefully into the light blue fabric, then there was a ribbon placed neatly and perfectly around the waist line of the dress. The skirt part below the belt was light and flowy, it felt lovely on; I couldn't help but admire myself in the mirror as my blonde hair cascaded over it. I think I'll wear this tonight then, honestly couldn't get any better than it I don't think. I opened the curtain surprised to see Jade wasn't there waiting to see it on me.

"Jade?" I walked towards the front of the shop where I left her but she was nowhere to be seen, I noticed her guards over the other side of the room so I approached them. "Erm, excuse me, Caydence, was it?"

"Cayden, Luna."

"Oh, I'm so sorry! I'm really bad with names, I, erm, I was just wondering if you knew where Jade was?"

"She's using the staff bathroom, apparently you can get morning sickness all day and not just in the morning." Cayden rolled his eyes when he finished speaking; I'm not sure whether that was because of me or Jade, I didn't get much chance to think about it before Jade emerged from behind him looking rather tired. Her eyes widened as she looked at me; admiring me from top to bottom.

"Wow, Shannon! You look *amazing*! You have to wear that tonight; Thomas won't be able to control himself!"

I couldn't help but blush as she spoke; I didn't want to think about Thomas losing control but it was nice to know that someone found me attractive if I'm honest.

"Oh, stop it!" I couldn't help but giggle as I spoke, maybe this could be fun after all. "Have you got a dress for yourself?"

"Yeah, none of my dresses fit any more unfortunately. Let's

pay and head to Kenny's, I'm starving!"

We paid for our dresses; or should I say Thomas paid since he gave Jade his credit card. Walking to Kenny's, Jade started to tell me about the guards that we had with us. All four of them were in the Elite squad as she called them. Cayden and Tommy, Jade's guards, both had mates who were warriors but my guards, Jason and Tobias, had Omega mates, I'm not entirely sure Jason liked me because of the looks he kept giving me when he thought I wasn't looking. I suppose I was going to get that a lot though, no one at the pack wanted a human Luna – they got stuck with me in the same way that I got stuck with them. We sat in a booth at the back of Kenny's, I wanted more privacy so that I could actually talk to Jade about a few things without other humans hearing; once we ordered I decided to start the conversation.

"So, Cayden said you were pregnant, is that true?"

"Oh, yeah it is. I guess amongst everything we never officially told you. Why didn't Thomas tell you?"

"Oh, I'm sure with everything going on it slipped his mind. Is that why you had to have guards as well then? I mean being a Beta werewolf I just assumed that you would protect yourself."

"Yeah, pregnant werewolves can't shift – well, I mean, they can but they shouldn't – there's always a risk that the baby wouldn't survive, we've lost a few pups that way sadly. There have also been cases of moms being stuck shifted until delivery which ultimately led to their death. We have better facilities now so I don't think death is likely but there will always be a chance. I think there's only been a few instances of shifting during pregnancy where both survived."

"Oh, wow, that must suck, does your wolf mind?"

"No, ultimately the baby is Callie and Cyrus' too so she will do whatever it takes to protect it as well. It's actually why you'll find our mates harder to control during pregnancy; their wolves are constantly in protection mode. You'll find that out soon though."

"Excuse me?"

"Well, Thomas is twenty-four now, it's actually pretty late for him to find his mate and start mating. The pack needs an heir to ensure its survival."

"I'm not even eighteen yet, I have no intention of giving Thomas an heir anytime soon, I've never even had sex!" I couldn't help but feel my anger towards Jade building at the thought of everyone just assuming that I would get pregnant A.S.A.P. Like who does that? I agreed to see how things go, meet the pack and get to know Thomas. He even said that he would wait until next full moon to complete the Luna ceremony if needs be. I stood up from the table and walked out. Not even thinking about Jade or the two elites that had been made to guard me because I'm just a stupid weak human. I found Tobias waiting outside – we didn't expect them to come in if they didn't want to so him and Jason hung outside, both stood straight as I approached them.

"I wish to go home, please."

"Where's Beta Jade?"

"Inside with her guards seeing as they actually like her, now I can go myself or you can take me. Either way I am finished here and I would like to return to my future Alpha."

The two men opened the door to their car for me before driving off; I noticed Jason's eyes went foggy a few times meaning that he was mind linking, probably telling Jade we had left and Thomas how rude I was to them. But who cares?

"Listen, I understand that you guys don't want a human for a Luna; I'm weak and more than likely an extra job to you but

I'd appreciate it if you got to know me as a person before coming to your conclusions about me as your Luna. I've seen the way you look at me and, no, I won't be telling Thomas but I'd like it if you could give me a chance, we're stuck with each other either way."

I looked at both men; they were both obviously thinking about what I said, digesting the information. Jason just hung his head; obviously annoyed he got caught but what can we do? I really didn't blame them for the way they felt, they had every right to but I just wanted a chance to prove myself, I wanted this to work.

"For what it's worth, Luna; I'm not all that bothered about you being human, you make our Alpha happy and once you mate, he can mark you which will make him stronger. That's enough for me."

"Thank you, Tobias."

The rest of the drive was quiet, when we finally arrived back at the pack house I jumped out of the car before Tobias was able to park. I ran straight up the stairs towards the alpha floor, when I finally got there, I jumped on the bed and broke into a sob. I wasn't even sure what I was crying about; all my emotions built up today, trying on my dress, arguing with Jade, knowing that Jason clearly disliked me. The only thing I regretted was arguing with Jade, she only meant well but as usual I had to ruin it. I could feel sparks trickling down my back as Thomas was by my side stroking me.

"What's wrong, my angel?"

I looked up into his soft, brown eyes and couldn't help but smile. Why was I even fighting my feelings for him? As bonkers as it sounds; I love him, I know I do. In my heart, it beats for him and only him – it's just my head couldn't make sense of it. I'd not known him long enough to fall in love with him personally; but he'd been both the man and wolf of my dreams since I saw them in the woods six years ago. I couldn't imagine being anywhere else now; even my argument about school was forgotten because deep down I knew it. I love him.

"I love you, Thomas, it doesn't make sense but I do. I love you."

A large toothy, grin spread across his face before he picked me up, pulling me onto his lap and kissing me passionately. I kissed him back; granting his tongue access to my mouth again, all I could feel was pleasure flowing through me as we kissed. His member hardening underneath me; I threw my head back moaning as he trailed kisses down my neck, reaching the area where he said he would mark me, he sucked it hard – I moaned in pleasure again, not wanting him to stop when there was someone knocking at the door. Thomas let out a deep growl which made me chuckle.

"Shannon, it's me, Jade. Can we talk?"

Ah shit, Jade, I really need to apologise but for the first time I was enjoying my time with Thomas; I suppose me and Thomas have forever to enjoy each other's company.

"Yes, come in."

Thomas let out another growl, looking at me confused as I spoke; I climbed off his lap and straightened myself up, thankfully he did the same. Jade walked in looking at the floor, carrying a couple of bags, I forgot about the dress and other bits we bought. I felt even more guilty now.

"I'm sorry, I shouldn't have used my Alpha growl, Jade."

Oh, so that's why she was looking at the floor, she was intimidated. Makes sense I guess, he is higher up than her, she looked up, finally giving us both a small smile.

"I uh, I thought we could get ready together... for the, uh, party. I'm sorry for interrupting and if I upset you."

"Wait, why would you have upset her?" You could see Thomas' anger building as he looked at Jade, I had to speak soon before he did something he'd regret.

"No, Thomas, it was me. I... I shouldn't have run off, we were just talking about things in the pack and I got annoyed at something. It was entirely my fault."

"Well, what annoyed you?"

"I told her she would be expected to give you an heir to the pack sooner rather than later."

You could see both anger and fear flash across his face as he rushed over to me apologetically.

"I promise you, Shannon; I am going at your pace. I won't be expecting you to give me or the pack an heir until you're ready, same with marking and the same with mating. This is all at your pace. I swear." You could hear the panic in his voice as he spoke, holding me in a protective embrace as he spoke; I forced myself out of his warm, comforting embrace so that I could look him in the eyes as I spoke.

"I know, Thomas, but like I said I love you. There's just a lot expected of me from the pack and I just panicked a little bit but I'm okay. Let's just take it day by day, together."

Jade cleared her throat from the other side of the room.

"So, I thought we could get ready together. The party is only a few hours away after all."

I had almost forgotten Jade was there; I took my attention away from Thomas to smile at Jade who still looked quite sad.

"That actually sounds really great, why don't I turn some music on and we can get started?"

I was actually feeling pretty excited for the party; I know that everyone hated the idea of a human Luna but we'd all got to make the best of this unfortunately. After fumbling with Thomas' radio for a little while, I finally managed to get it working. Dancing over to Jade I decided to take the bags away from her whilst she shooed Thomas away; a smile finally forming its way across her face.

Jade helped me do my hair; I had a half-up, half-down curly hairstyle, it looked really nice against my baby blue dress. Jade straightened her hair, the way her hair was layered into her face made me slightly jealous, her gorgeous ebony locks framed her face perfectly, a few violet streaks going through it; showing her rebellious and fun side. Her dress was a colour similar to the streaks in her hair; she looked so beautiful. I decided on very light makeup; only mascara, rouge and some blush but Jade went quite heavy on it, it still looked lovely though. The dark makeup only made her emerald green eyes pop out more and even though she was pale it contrasted quite well.

"Jade, you look so beautiful."

"Clean up well for a pregnant wolf, eh?"

"You do! You're practically glowing!"

I couldn't help but giggle as she stood there posing in front of me, I watched as her eyes went foggy – probably mind linking the men.

"They're waiting for us downstairs."

I nodded, suddenly feeling very nervous. It was as if there were a million butterflies in my stomach as I thought about the walk downstairs, meeting the pack, there was no going back from here.

"Jade, what—what if they don't like me?"

"Shannon, they are going to love you and if they don't then fuck them. Like Thomas said they know where the door is. They will love and respect their Luna in the same way the Alpha and Betas already do."

"But I'm just a human, I'm weak."

"You are in no way weak, you heard Doctor Bane say it herself, most humans would have died after everything you have gone through. You are stronger than you believe. You just need to realise it."

I couldn't help but smile at the way Jade spoke about me; we really were going to be the best of friends! She walked over to me; placing her arm in mine and guided me towards the door.

"We'll do this together."

We smiled at each other in unity before heading out the door and down the stairs; Thomas and Stefan stood at the bottom of the stairs, both their jaws hit the floor when they noticed us. I thought that Jade would have taken Stefan's arm when we reached the bottom of the stairs but she just held tightly onto mine as Thomas took my other arm. This was what I needed; I could walk into the party with my head held high. As we walked into the ball room the first thing I noticed was that there weren't as many tables as there was this morning; Thomas must have had some cleared to make it easier to dance. Everyone was dressed so smart; the women in ball gowns and the men in suits, it was so lovely to see. I noticed that everyone had stopped what they were doing to look at us. I kept a smile as we carried on walking; the first person to approach us was an older looking woman – maybe early sixties?

"Angel, I would like to introduce you to my personal Omega, Katherine; Katherine has been with me since I was a pup, sometimes more than my own mother. Katherine, this is my beautiful mate and our Luna, Shannon Rye."

Katherine shook my hand rather excitedly as I smiled at her, it was lovely. I'm not sure what I was so worried about!

"Oh, Shannon, lovely, you have no idea how long I've waited for this day! He's absolutely infatuated with you."

"Ha-ha, I realised that not so long ago." I couldn't help but laugh as she spoke about how all she's heard since the day in the forest is Shannon this, Shannon that. He really has loved me from day one, I looked at Thomas admiring him as if all of this information was completely new to me but it wasn't, it was all I'd heard in fact.

"Katherine, I hate to cut this short but I must introduce Shannon to the other pack members too."

"Oh, of course, I'm so sorry."

I held Katherine's hand in mine as I spoke. "Don't apologise! In fact, I look forward to hearing those stories one day."

We walked around for about forty-five minutes speaking with pack members who so far seemed to like me and were happy to have a human as their Luna, one of the warriors was even mated to a human but they hadn't accepted them yet sadly. I walked over to an empty table because I needed a few minutes to rest; those heels were not made for walking! I had no idea how Jade did it! She hadn't stopped dancing since we got there and her heels were taller than mine. I was watching Jade and Stefan on the dance floor when I suddenly felt a spark flow through my arm; it wasn't a Thomas spark though, it was more of large static shock. I turned around only to find a woman sat there.

"Hi, I'm Luna Alice. I came from the Crimson Rock pack."

"Oh, uh, wow, you're the Luna I drank the potion for, right?"

I saw the fear spread across her face as she leaned into me to whisper, "Yes, but you must not speak about it so openly. No one is supposed to know for everyone's safety."

"Ah yes, I'm sorry, it's just nice to finally meet you. Thomas speaks so highly of you and your husband – Kye, is it?"

Alice sat back in her chair visibly relaxing after my apology and change of subject.

"Yes, Kye. They've known each other years, even longer than I have known Thomas but Thomas likes to think he's known me longer because before me Kye wasn't the greatest person, his father even delayed his Alpha ceremony because of it. He has always been like a big brother to me, I was so excited to hear when he had found you, a bit disappointed when I—"

"—Heard that I was human? I'm getting that a lot." I couldn't help but slump forward in defeat; everyone was so nice in person today but you could see their distaste behind their masks. I wondered if Thomas noticed or whether he was just unaware but it was definitely there. I felt that familiar static shock on my back as Alice placed her hand there.

"I was going to say when I heard you hadn't accepted him straight away; I mean I get it, you feel out of place here, a human among werewolves. I felt the same for a while but you'll get used to it and the pack will get over it, it just takes time."

"Why did you feel out of place? You're a wolf; pure Alpha as Thomas tells me which is very rare apparently."

"He didn't tell you how we met, did he?"

"No, not really."

"Thomas and his family were in Ireland, on holiday I believe, when they came across a group of rogues that had captured me. This was a few weeks before he met you if I remember correctly, they could tell that I was an alpha – I'm not sure how the rogues hadn't realised but anyway. Thomas and his parents asked them kindly to return me pretending I was their daughter – unfortunately I had already been with the rogues a year by that point; beaten and starved, abused. I thought it was never ending until Thomas and his parents slaughtered the rogues; bringing me here with them, if they hadn't, I think I would have died there. Shortly after my return I met Kye at an Alpha meeting, Thomas was furious to find out he was my mate after the reputation he had built out but it all worked out for the best and here we are now; six years later, three beautiful babies and an alliance stronger than ever."

I couldn't help the shock that must have spread across my face at the thought of this beautiful, kind woman being abused by rogues for a whole year; the thought of what could have happened if Thomas hadn't found her.

"How did you end up with the rogues?"

"Sadly, some werewolf hunters found out about my pack, about our weak spots, secret tunnels, whatever they needed to gain access secretly. They snuck in whilst we slept and murdered everyone; my mother, she died protecting me, they thought I was dead too but I just lay there under her corpse until I was sure they were gone, daylight broke and I ran, looking for shelter in nearby packs but I didn't make it to one – the rogues found me before I had the chance."

Women, this woman had been through so much and here was me complaining over having to be with Thomas forever; a guy that adored me and only wanted my happiness for now and forever. We were interrupted by Thomas and a similarly large man I guessed was Kye.

"Kye, this is my beautiful Luna, Shannon; Shannon, this is Kye – I see you and Alice have already met."

I stood up and held my hand out to Kye whilst bowing slightly; I'm not exactly sure what you are meant to do when you meet an Alpha but his chuckling told me this was not it. He pulled me into a tight hug which was followed by the same static shock

I felt with Alice making us both jump back a bit.

"It's the bond, Aisling said we'd feel something when we touch. Like you do with a mate just nowhere near as strong."

We all nodded in agreement; they all knew what it meant except for me but it was the only thing that made sense to me.

Alice and Kye said their goodbyes as they started their journey home; leaving me to carry on meeting and greeting with the pack members. I met Jason's mate who was really lovely, she didn't seem to have a problem with me so who knows what his problem was? The more I mingled and laughed with the other members I realised that as much as, yes, they were werewolves and I was a human, we weren't all that different – the wolves were the only thing separating us really. It was nice though, I really did feel like I belong here; I'd been around wolves my whole life without realising, maybe I *was* destined by the moon goddess to be here. My mother and father brought me up to believe in the moon goddess but in different ways; my mother believed that she was a woman trapped on the moon, separated from her long-lost love. Whereas my father, he believed that she was the one in charge of fate, she knew what was going to happen and when it would. I guess it makes sense that they had different views with Dad being a werewolf but the idea of the moon goddess always stuck with me and I loved it; it made it easier to believe what Thomas said about mates and everything. I understood now why Dad never mentioned the moon goddess after Mum left; he had obviously lost faith in her for a while. I wonder if Lori was his true mate? As if they knew my thoughts I watched as Dad, Emily, Clara and Lori appeared through the door. I was starting to think they wouldn't show up seeing as the party was nearly over but I guess there were warriors still on shift. Thomas had changed the rota so that both the day and night warriors could come, my dad searched the room before his eyes fell on me, a smile spreading across his face, they all walked over. The girls ran towards me, tackling me to the floor in a large embrace; I couldn't help but laugh as I hugged them back, my dad finally caught up and spoke first.

"Now, girls, is that how we treat our future Luna?" He spoke kindly, trying to hide his amusement as he helped me up; pulling me into a hug as he did.

"I've missed you so much, my sweet girl!" He sounded so sad that I couldn't help but squeeze him tighter.

"I've missed you too, Dad!" The biggest smile I'd ever seen spread across his face as I called him dad, he will forever be my dad. There was no doubt about it.

I noticed Lori by the side of him, squirming uncomfortably, I broke the embrace with my dad and held my hand out towards Lori.

"Hi, Lori, it's nice to formally meet you." She just looked at my hand before giving me a similarly dirty look.

"Luna." You could see the disgust across her face as she spoke through gritted teeth ignoring my hand completely.

"So, how is life at the pack house, my sweet? Is Thomas treating you right?"

"He's fine, Dad, he—"

We were interrupted by a familiar voice.

"Mother? What are you doing here by that?" I turned around only to come face to face with Verity; the she-wolf from the other day.

"Lori is your mom?"

"No shit, stupid, why are you talking to her?"

"Talk to my daughter, *our* future Luna, like that again and I will deal with you *myself*."

I hadn't seen my father this angry in ages; you could see it slowly bubbling up to the surface, when to my surprise Jason walked over to us, he'd been quite obviously avoiding me all night so why would he appear now?

"Jason, take your sister home please, she is no longer welcome here."

Jason nodded at my father before quite literally dragging Verity kicking and screaming out the door which grabbed the attention of Thomas who rushed straight over to us.

"What happened? She didn't start on you again, did she?"

"What do you mean again, Thomas? You are supposed to be looking after her!"

"Dad, Thomas, chill; it's nothing I can't handle myself. Now if you will excuse me, it has been a long day and I would like to go to bed."

"I'll come with you, my angel."

I put my hands on Thomas' chest as I spoke. "No, it's fine, you enjoy the party. I can put myself to bed." I gave him a kiss on the cheek before giving my dad and sisters a hug to say goodbye, I then went upstairs to bed, I couldn't wait to get some sleep.

Verity

**An Unknown Enemy*

Jason dragged me out of the pack house towards our small cottage at the edge of the forest; I tried to fight him but being an Elite, he has always been stronger than me.

"Jason, let me go!"

"No! Verity, what did you think you were going to achieve

by pulling a stunt like that back there? If Thomas had seen he would have banished you on the spot after the shit you said this morning to our Luna."

I could hear the anger in his voice; practically spitting his words at me rather than speaking! He wouldn't even look at me; I'd done nothing wrong! She didn't deserve to be our Luna, there were so many other people that deserved it more… mainly me!

"That *human* will never be *my* Luna! She doesn't deserve it, Jase, we need a wolf for our Luna! She'll never be suitable!"

Jason turned around sharply, picking me up by my arms, up against the wall of our house. You could feel his anger radiating from him; it was quite intimidating and I was so tempted to cower before submitting it but I couldn't. I knew what I felt, she would not be my Luna.

"I know, Ver, and I have a plan but you have to trust me, we will get rid of her. One way or another. I promise. Mom is already working on a lead of someone she thinks may be interested in taking Shannon off our hands but we have to wait and see for now."

He loosened his grip, finally placing me back on the ground gently so I could walk.

"If Mom's so keen on getting rid of her, why was she there acting nicely towards her?"

"She's dating Shannon's dad; it would be strange if she wasn't. Mom's been following this lead since she found out about Shannon being Thomas' mate three years ago. We hoped that it would be you with how close you both always were but obviously not, we'll get rid of Shannon and you will be Luna. I promise. We had hoped the rogue attack would have sorted it but she's stronger than we thought, you have to be patient for now."

Chapter Fifteen
A Luna in the Making

Thomas

As people started to leave the party, I noticed a lot of the Omegas had started cleaning up; it was nearly one a.m. No one deserved to stay up this late cleaning when it wasn't necessary. I walked over to them slowly, I hadn't realised how tired I was until now – they looked up at me in confusion as I approached.

"All of you are dismissed; go home and rest, I don't want to hear of anyone in here cleaning before ten a.m. tomorrow morning, you guys deserve it. Tonight was amazing. Thank you."

They gasped as I said thank you – this shocked me more than anything; was I always that rude to them? Did I just not notice?

"Uh, Alpha – what about breakfast? We can't make and serve with it like this."

"The pack can make their own breakfast; besides there is leftover in the fridge. I'm sure they will survive."

I chuckled at the idea of Stefan burning Jade's morning omelette but they would have to make do; everyone deserves a break, especially these. They do so much for everyone and we don't realise.

"Please, go home, guys."

They smiled at me before finally leaving; it was nice to see them so happy as they left the pack house. I shut the doors and headed up to our floor where I knew Shannon would be sleeping soundly. Walking into my bedroom I breathed in her scent; it was intoxicating, honestly it was like a drug to me, I couldn't get enough. I walked into the en-suite having a quick shower before changing into a clean pair of pyjamas and climbing into bed next to my angel. Just as I wrapped my arm around her she rolled over, facing me, she put her leg and arm over me, trapping me in this heated position. I moved my arm down deciding to stroke her leg; I couldn't believe how smooth it was. I wasn't even aware she was wearing shorts until now. Trailing my fingers along her thigh, reaching her shorts I dragged my hand back down and slowly repeated the process whilst thinking about how beautiful she was when a scent filled my nostrils shocking me to my core; it was her arousal. She was… turned on?

"Mate! Mate now," Atticus growled at me both possessively and hungrily. I blocked him, jumping out of the bed, going straight for a cold shower to either calm myself or find a release before I couldn't hold Atticus back; why did she have to have this effect on me? It was driving us both into horny, crazy beasts! I knew it would be worth the wait though, I did.

The sun creeped into the room waking me from my heavenly slumber; I woke up entangled in my beautiful mate, goddess, she was intoxicating, ignoring my raging hard libido I jumped out of bed and headed for yet another cold shower to calm myself. I don't even remember the last time I satisfied myself, nothing felt good enough since I met Shannon – I just wanted to be inside her, hear her screaming my name, feel her release. Mark her, make her mine forever. Growing up, it's the norm to save yourself for your mate; it's what our parents made us believe was best and I'm glad I did. Yes, it's not the norm to be a virgin at nearly twenty-five but I needed to make sure my mate had nothing to worry about when I found her and once I did, it definitely made saving myself a lot easier, even if I thought about it. I have no doubt in my mind Atticus would take control and attack them first.

Once satisfied that I was clean and calm enough I walked into my closet and got dressed before approaching my bed, nudging Shannon awake.

"Shannon, angel, it's time to get up." She stirred slightly before rolling over and hugging my pillow. "Come on, sweetness, today we start your Luna training."

You could see that this woke her up straight away; she got out of bed and headed straight to the bathroom, I couldn't help but moan when I saw her shorts had wedged themselves nicely between her butt cheeks, shaping her perfect ass nicely. Shannon stopped abruptly by the door in confusion; obviously not understanding the reason behind my moan.

"Is everything okay, Tom?"

"Yeah, everything's fine. I'm going to make us some breakfast, okay?" I put my hand over my trousers hoping to hide my raging libido from her; if I was a female wolf, I'm sure I'd be in heat, this was driving me crazy. I walked out into the kitchen, searching for the plates and pans before I could finally make some scrambled eggs on toast for me and Shannon. I wasn't the best at cooking but I could definitely manage this! As I plated our food up, Shannon walked into the kitchen wearing simple black leggings, a black vest and a checked shirt. She looked absolutely stunning as always, I hit the jackpot when it came to mates, human or not she is better than I ever imagined my Luna to be.

"I made scrambled eggs on toast, nothing fancy but enough to get us started."

"Oh, wow, thanks. Why are we not eating downstairs?"

"I gave the Omegas the morning off; they do more around here than anyone really so they deserve a break."

"That's really kind of you, Tom."

We ate breakfast and headed towards my office where I showed Shannon the paperwork for all of our orders; what to do if we need/want something before we started looking at files for our members, each member had a file stating where they live, children, spouse etc… As a Luna Shannon was expected to know each member and at least something about their lives, seeing as it was early days she wasn't expected to know straight away but she seemed eager to learn which was great.

"Tom, there's at least fifteen warriors, five elites and goddess knows how many Omegas here that have young children. Where do all the young ones go when they have to work?"

"I've actually never thought about it; normally the mother would just stay home until they are old enough to go into the school, why do you ask?"

"Well, I mean if we had a day-care built and trained some of the Omega staff to care for the young ones that would free up so many wolves to do their jobs. I mean they could even put them there to keep on top of training; not to mention we could make it into a panic room so that if there was another attack there would be a safe space for everyone that can't fight and we wouldn't have to worry because we'd know that no one could get in there."

"Angel, that's brilliant! I can't believe I haven't thought of it before, such an obvious solution too! I'll set up a meeting with the contractors who are upgrading the gym and see what we can do; you should be there though, it's your first job as Luna."

I couldn't stop smiling at how brilliant my mate was; she was already thinking of things that could make a huge difference to the pack! I honestly couldn't believe we hadn't thought of this sooner though – it seems so obvious now! Looking at her you could see how proud she was and it honestly melted my heart, I love her more than she could ever know.

"Angel, will you go on a date with me tomorrow night please?"

The words escaped my mouth before I had really thought them through but it definitely felt right; how was she ever going to accept me if I couldn't put her first and let her get to know the real me? The man the moon goddess made for her? I needed to show her that I was hers like she was mine. I watched as her smile grew even wider, making my heart skip a beat.

"I'd love to, my Alpha."

The way her smiled turned quite mischievous as she said Alpha, biting her bottom lip and looking at me under her long beautiful lashes sent an exciting shiver through me; I could not wait for this date.

Chapter Sixteen
Our First Date

I left Thomas alone in his office so I could go find Jade; heading straight to the Beta floor but I only found Stefan.

"Hey, uh, Stefan. Have you seen Jade at all?"

"Well, with her being my mate I see her a lot."

He chuckled as he spoke, I couldn't help but flush in embarrassment as he stated the obvious to my stupid question.

"She's gone down to feast on leftovers from the party; you'll find her in the ballroom more than likely."

I shouted, "Thanks," as I ran back down the stairs towards the ballroom; sure enough, there she was surrounded by five or six different plates of food, thoroughly enjoying herself. I approached the table slowly, I jumped out of my skin when she growled at me for trying to take a seat, her eyes completely charcoal by this point, it was only when they focused on my undoubtedly horrified face that she relaxed obviously seeing no threat.

"Oh, my goddess, Shannon, I'm sorry! I thought you were the annoying Omega that keeps trying to get me to leave."

She picked up another sandwich as she spoke; I chuckled and sat down, I'm impressed by how much this woman can eat, there were already three empty plates on the table.

"It's all right, Jade, I'm not taking your food, I actually thought that I would ask you to come shopping tomorrow."

"Yeah, sure. What are we shopping for?"

"Thomas asked me out on our first date! I need the perfect

dress and I know you are the perfect person to help with that!"

She dropped the food in her hand before jumping up and down in excitement.

"Oh, my goddess, Shannon! I already have the perfect dress in mind!"

"I knew you would be the best to ask, now sit down and calm yourself before Stefan kills me for nearly sending you into labour!"

She chuckled as she sat back down, picking up the sandwich that she had started before the excitement.

"You must be made up, Shan; I don't think Thomas has ever asked anyone on a date you know."

"I'm sure that's not true, you've seen how all the women fawn over him here. He's probably been with most of them."

"Thomas isn't like that, Shan; give him a chance. I mean you can't say you've never dated or gone out with anyone, can you?"

"Actually, Jade, I can."

"Wait. So, you've never been with anyone? Not a date, a kiss, nothing?"

"I haven't, no. I wanted to wait until I found someone I loved enough to and well… Until Thomas, I hadn't."

She gasped dramatically before leaning closer to me so that she could whisper.

"You're a virgin?"

The several gasps around the room told me that there was more than just me and Jade in this conversation, I chuckled at the obviousness, looking around to see if anyone made eye contact but it didn't happen; they averted their gaze as soon as I looked towards them, this only made me chuckle more.

"Yes, I'm not ashamed of it either. All I've ever wanted is to spend forever with the person I love; saving myself was part of this."

I said this a bit louder than needed but I wanted everyone to know that I had nothing to hide in terms of my sexuality; I'd never struggled with my drive but since sharing the bed with Thomas I'd been driving myself crazy, having some very vivid, wet dreams so to speak; I found I couldn't keep my hands off him either. I was kind of gutted that he hadn't tried anything yet if I'm honest. I'd been gagging for it for days but after my objections about it I had to at least act like I wasn't all that interested in it. I even upped it a gear that morning by pulling my shorts up; he groaned on the bed quite aggressively and I stopped abruptly in the hope he'd grab me, pull me onto the bed and take me there. When he didn't, I questioned whether it was all okay but he just wanted breakfast. I could feel the disappointment and sexual frustration flashing through my brain once again.

The idea of sex running through my mind I could feel myself getting horny once again, feeling a burning wetness seeping through my underwear, I shifted nervously in my seat, only drawn from my thoughts by Jade clearing her thoughts.

"Uh, um, Shan?"

"Oh, err, yeah?"

"I can smell your arousal from here."

"Wait, what?"

"Werewolves have heightened senses, that includes smell. And, well, you're quite obviously aroused, what were you thinking about?"

I was sure by this point I was looking like a tomato through the embarrassment.

"Uhm, Thomas."

"Well, girl, if you get like that just thinking about him, I'm surprised you're able to share a bed without him mating and marking with you."

"See, that's the thing. I've wanted it so many times but he's just not tried anything."

"Why has he gotta try anything? You get up those stairs and you ride your man."

"You know what? You're right! I'm a strong woman and if I want sex, I'm having it!"

I ran out of the ballroom hearing Jade shout faintly behind me, "You go, girl!" I came to the top of the stairs by the Delta side when I was grabbed and thrown against one of the doors to what I assumed was a supply closet, I went through the door like it was paper, my head was throbbing as I tried to regain my footing. All of a sudden, I was pushed back down to the floor when I heard a voice.

"Oh, look she's back where she belongs – beneath me." I looked up at the person who was now chuckling quite sinisterly above me.

"V-V-V-Verity."

"Oh, you really are a bumbling buffoon, aren't you?"

She bent over and grabbed me by the throat, pinning me against the wall; I clawed at her hands and wrists, trying to break free from her strong grasp, kicking my feet towards her but nothing made her budge. She just chuckled more and more.

"Listen here and listen close; you will not go on this date with Thomas tomorrow or I will make sure that it's the last thing that you *ever* do. You got that? I should be his Luna, not you."

With what little courage I could muster I stood on my tippy toes, grabbing Verity's arms to allow myself to take in some restricted breaths before I could speak.

"I am his mate, so I am his *Luna.*" Unfortunately due to the lack of air the last word came out as more of a cough, which made her laugh more.

"A human will never make a good *Luna. Ever.*"

I could feel myself getting light-headed from the lack of oxygen; if she didn't let me go soon I would either pass out or die, I heard footsteps behind her when I heard a voice I didn't expect to hear.

"Verity, what the fuck are you doing?" Jason's voice was enough to make Verity drop me there and then, she bent over as I coughed, gasping for as much air as I could take, looking straight into my eyes before she spoke.

"Heed my warning, Shannon, if you go on that date tomorrow, I will kill you."

She walked away and soon Jason was at my side, helping me up off the floor and walking me up the stairs towards the Alpha floor.

"I'm so sorry, Luna; I'm not sure what's gotten into her. I heard about the day-care you and Thomas are building, it's a wonderful idea. My mate, Skye, and I, we just found out we're going to have a pup and I know afterwards she would love to train for the day-care; providing that's okay with you and Alpha."

I coughed a bit before finally managing to speak.

"That would be great, Jason, I will tell Thomas. Congratulations on the pup, you will make an amazing dad, I'm sure."

We stopped outside the alpha door when Jason grabbed my hand quickly; I looked at him only to see a look of desperation spread across his face.

"Luna, thank you but I must ask something of you."

"What's that?" I stood there rubbing my neck, trying to alleviate the pain radiating with pain from Verity's hold.

"Please don't tell Alpha about this, I'll get Verity in check I promise. I can't lose her."

I nodded in agreement before heading through the doors straight to my bedroom; thankfully Thomas wasn't home yet so it's not like he would see the bruise at least. I got ready for bed and went to sleep as soon as my head hit the pillow. I don't care what Verity said, I'm going on this date tomorrow, Jason said he'd keep her in check and that was good enough for me.

We were only in town maybe three hours at most; I didn't wake until eleven a.m. and, surprisingly, Thomas just left me in bed today. I'm not sure why I'm so tired – it's probably from Verity nearly killing me last night. I wore a scarf today to hide my bruises, hoping that no one would see them, I trusted Jason to sort Verity out; as much as he was her brother, he was also an elite and knew exactly how serious an attack on the Luna was. Rushing to my floor, me and Jade chucked our shopping bags down before I started getting ready. She curled my hair tightly before brushing it into cascading loose curls, still quite light makeup with a dark red lipstick to go with the beautiful dress that Jade chose. It was a dark red skater girl type dress that fell just above my knees, the back was part open at the back and then rose-patterned lace covering my shoulders, she had also introduced me to these strapless bra things that you basically stick to your chest to keep them up. Once ready we walked downstairs together; it was only ten minutes to six so I didn't expect Thomas to be there waiting; he looked so smart, his hair slicked back into a man bun, a black suit with a white shirt, a rose in his pocket and then a dozen beautiful roses sat in his arms with a heart shaped box in the other. His mouth dropped as he watched me approaching him, his eyes sparkling under the nearly full moon, wow he looked amazing.

"You really are an angel, aren't you?"

"Well, don't you look handsome there, Alpha?" Jade nudged me as she spoke, pushing me closer to him as he gave me the flowers and box.

"These are beautiful, Tom, thank you." I handed them to Jade slowly. "Do you think you could put these in my room for me please?"

"Of course, I can!" She looked so excited as her and Stefan ran up the stairs towards our room; I already knew they were going to be there all night but I didn't care, I love their company, it's weird with just me and Thomas.

"Angel, do you mind if we walk?"

"Not at all."

He offered me his arm as we walked towards the forest, I noticed there was something glowing inside the forest; it was only as we got to the opening, I realised that he had laid out a path of LED candles and rose petals, going further into the forest. I couldn't stop the gasp escaping my lips as I realised how much effort he'd put into just one small part of our date, tears started to fill my eyes as I looked up at him.

"Oh, Shannon, I'm sorry. You hate it, don't you?" You could hear the panic in his voice as he pulled me into him.

"No, Tom, Thomas. I… I love it. Thank you." I stood on my tippy toes so that I could place a kiss onto his cheek before we started following his beautifully lit path. After what felt like a short walk, we reached a clearing. Looking round I realised that we were in the meadow, the same meadow I met Atticus in six years ago, the same one that a young Thomas came and carried Clara from. There was another candlelit path leading to what looked like a small picnic blanket. As we got closer, I noticed that it was definitely a small picnic blanket with a basket, some glasses and even a sheet held up by some poles.

"I thought we could enjoy dinner and a movie in the place that I realised I loved you, the place that I decided I would do anything to make you mine, and protect you forever."

"Oh, Thomas, this. This is beautiful. No one has ever done anything like this for me before." I couldn't help the tears as they fell from my cheeks; they were good tears, happy tears.

"I'm glad, I don't want anyone to ever make you this happy. That's my job, forever."

He pulled me over and we sat on the picnic blanket, it was surprisingly really comfortable. He handed me a glass and popped the cork on the champagne he had brought us, he held his glass towards me before speaking.

"To new beginnings, to our future together."

We said cheers and sipped our champagne happily before Thomas started a movie; after a few glasses of champagne, I was feeling fairly confident in myself, not quite drunk but not hundred per cent sober either.

"Thomas, how many women have you been with?"

He spat out his drink, obviously shocked by my new found confidence.

"I, erm, I…"

"It's okay, you can tell me. I know you must have women throwing themselves at you every day."

He chuckled as he spoke which didn't help my confidence much but I stared at him intently waiting for his answer.

"Shannon, I've not been with… anyone. I-I'm a virgin." He looked at the floor when he spoke; did he really expect me to believe that he was a virgin?

"Bullshit, why lie?"

"It's not a lie, Shannon, I swear."

"Then why? We all get needs! I mean not to mention you've

ignored all of my signals!"

"I was waiting for my—wait, what signals?"

"Don't act dumb! When we're in bed you ignore all of my advances; wrapping myself around you, wearing very short stuff, heck the other day I even pulled my shorts up in the hope that you would pounce."

"You've been doing all that on *purpose*? Angel, when I leave the room or I shower it's so that I don't take you there on the bed without permission! You've been driving me crazy for days! Why wouldn't you fucking say anything?"

I could see his anger and frustration building, ready to burst. I was done arguing, this was already turning me on; he'd wanted me all this time but I was just too naive to notice, I climbed onto his lap, wrapping my arms around his neck, placing my lips to his – this was more than what I wanted; I needed this. I could feel my body burning, throbbing for him, he sat there for a moment before returning my kiss hungrily. I could feel his hardening member below my core; causing a moan to escape my lips as I lifted my head back. He took full advantage, sucking my neck leaving trails of kisses down it as he sucked, he undid the clasp around my neck, pulling the dress up and over my head in one swift move. I used my hands to try and cover my exposed body out of instinct, only to find him grabbing both my wrists and pinning me onto the picnic blanket while he towered over me, a look of admiration spread across his face as he looked me up and down. I couldn't help but moan more at the feel of all this, he bent down and ripped my sticky bra off my left breast allowing it to bounce freely, the feeling made me scream at first; it did hurt being pulled off so quickly but an intense pleasure followed that I've never felt before as he bit down hard, sucking on my already erect nipples. He did the same with my right breast and honestly all I could do was moan, I could feel the wetness between my thighs was only growing the more he touched me; I didn't even realise that he had let my hands go until I felt his hand caressing my left thigh, slowly making its way up to my burning wet core. It was an anticipation I'd never felt before; I wanted him to touch me so bad I was practically begging as he ripped my pants off.

"T-Thomas, please."

He looked at me intently before grasping my core, slipping two fingers inside whilst he circled my clit with his thumb.

"That's *Alpha* to you, little Luna."

His voice was hoarse and hungry; he really did want this just as bad as I did. He picked up the speed before inserting three fingers and I couldn't control myself as I could feel the pressure inside me building.

"Say it, who am I?"

"Alph—*my Alpha*!" I couldn't help but scream as I felt myself release; breathless, coming down from the wonderful feeling that took over me then. I looked up at Thomas whose eyes were now black with lust; he took his trousers and boxers off to reveal his large hard member, I didn't know they were that big! I couldn't help it as my eyes widened looking at the size of his member before realising where it had to go, I gasped not sure if it could fit. He smiled, obviously proud of his size, he made his way down to the blanket before positioning himself at my entrance.

"You're so wet, angel."

I could only moan in agreement, arching my back as he moved his member around my core. Feeling the pressure build, I knew I needed him inside me.

"Alpha, please," I begged, hoping he would end this torment.

"As you wish, *my Luna*. This may hurt in the beginning but

I promise it gets better, okay? If you need to stop, just tell me."

I nodded as I prepared for him to enter me; he entered me slowly, filling me almost instantly and I couldn't help but gasp as my body adjusted to his size. He started thrusting inside me slowly; still not fully in before he gave one big thrust which honestly felt like he'd broken me at first, I screamed as the pain sent shock waves through me, he stayed there waiting for the pain to go away, once it died down, I nodded towards him to carry on and my goddess was he right. I could feel myself building as he hit all the right spots; getting faster and faster chasing his release as mine too built.

"Fuck, angel, fuck."

I wrapped my arms around him before he pulled me up so that I was in his lap, wow this was a whole new kind of sensation, I threw my head back to scream as my pressure was ready to build when I felt it. He sunk his canines into my neck; it felt as if my neck was on fire, I screamed so loud but the harder he bit the better it felt and it was what pushed me over the edge in the end. Screaming "Alpha" as I felt myself pool in his legs, he reached his climax at the same time, sending his seed deep inside me. We both collapsed on the picnic blanket, hot and sweaty, curled up together. I passed out from exhaustion.

Chapter Seventeen
The Full Moon

Thomas

Shannon and I collapsed onto the picnic blanket; hot and sweaty, I could still feel the ecstasy from the moment pumping through my veins, it was the most amazing feeling. Now she was mine. Forever. I watched as she fell asleep cwtched up to me; she was breath-taking, how is it possible to love someone as much as I love her? I licked her neck gently; sealing my mark there, she moaned in her sleep, obviously feeling the connection between us. I wrapped the picnic blanket around us when there was the sound of twigs breaking close by; this sent me into high alert – jumping up and getting ready to shift at the sight of danger, when who should come into the clearing? Verity. What the hell was she doing here? I put my boxers and trousers on quickly before I approached her; all she seemed to do lately was follow me like a lost sheep and the way she spoke to Shannon the other day was disgusting, nobody should have to put up with that, that's why I warned her that if she set one more foot out of line she would be banished.

"Can I help you, Verity?"

"I, erm, Thomas. I thought I could keep you company tonight; I went to your office but some of the warriors saw you come this way so I, err, followed the candlelit path and well, I didn't think Shannon would be here."

"Why would my mate not be here, Verity?"

"She's not your mate, Thomas, she can't be! She's weak; she doesn't deserve you!"

"Verity, you will leave now. If you say one more word about my mate, *your Luna,* I will not hesitate to rip out your throat out right here, right now. Do you understand?"

I couldn't help but let Atticus take over at this point; why does she think she has such a right to speak about Shannon the way she does? It's disgusting, her and her mother only want one thing; *power*. Her mother tried going after my father too before he met and marked my mother; she didn't do anything after my mother came into the picture though she did try to get with any ranking male she could! Even rejected her true mate because he was an Omega; it nearly killed him but he was granted a second chance mate luckily and moved to her pack where she was the Beta. The irony of it. I don't believe Verity has been given a true mate yet; not that she deserved one though. I walked back over to my sleeping mate whilst Verity ran off whimpering; no doubt to her mother. I scooped Shannon up still wrapped in the picnic blanket and walked back to the pack house; mind linking a few Omegas to grab our things for us; thankfully they were happy to but I try not to use them for personal things because it's not their job. Since Shannon has been here, I've noticed how badly we treat them by how kindly she treats them. It's weird.

We arrived back at the room and sure enough there was Jade and Stefan, watching our television and eating our food. They jumped when I closed the door; slamming it slightly, I nodded in acknowledgement as they sat there smirking at us. I was surprised Shannon hadn't woken, when I laid her in bed she just lay there contently. I walked back out to the living area; making sure to close the door quietly.

"So, you guys have been here all night then?"

"Well, we thought you wouldn't mind seeing as we thought you'd be out all night."

"Yeah, well, Verity turned up, didn't she."

"Wait, she what?" Jade's jaw dropped as she spoke; a look of disgust spread across her face.

"Yep! I managed to get rid of her but you know what it is like; she talks about Shannon so horribly and I don't get it, she's done nothing wrong."

"Just banish her already."

"You know I can't, an Alpha has to be fair. I can't just banish her after only one incident and then her saying stupid shit."

"Well, it won't stop me ripping her head off if I catch her hurting her."

"Yeah, even Atticus threatened to rip her throat out."

"Well, good on Atticus." Stefan and Jade got up to leave when they stopped right beside me. "What's that smell?"

"Oh my! You guys mated, didn't you! Did you mark her?"

I couldn't help the wide grin that spread across my face as I nodded, causing Jade to jump up and down in excitement.

"Aw, I'm made up for you, bro. Do you think we could whip up a quick Luna ceremony for the full moon tomorrow?"

"No, I did think about it but we don't know how her body will react to being marked; with her being human and all it could take a lot of energy."

"I guess that's a good point, at least we can still watch the first shift ceremony."

"Can't wait, now get out!" I couldn't help but laugh as I guided my two best friends out of the door, I locked it and then decided to jump into bed with my beautiful angel.

I woke the next morning; wrapped in the most intoxicating smell ever, I couldn't help but nuzzle into my Luna who was still fast asleep next to me, she hadn't moved all night, why? She should be awake by now surely? I checked the time: eleven a.m. She had been asleep for fourteen hours give or take, that's weird.

"Dude, where are you? You were meant be here at nine!" A mind link from Stefan dragged me away from my thoughts; I jumped out of bed and had the quickest wash I think in history, chucked on some jogging bottoms and a t-shirt. Today was the full moon; everyone in the pack had to help prepare for the shifting ceremony, I ran out the door and headed towards our small stadium as quick as I could. We actually only had it built last year so that everyone could watch the new wolves shifting on their eighteenth birthday, you get your wolf at thirteen but your body isn't physically ready to shift until you're eighteen and even then it's quite painful.

I walked into the stadium to see that nearly everything was set up; there were towels and water laid out on a long table at the front of the stadium, changes of clothes stacked either side for after the switch, we even make sure to have warriors are on hand to help carry the teens home that are too exhausted to walk after the switch. Between the pain and the changes your body goes through it is a lot on a young wolf's body so we do recommend that they don't overdo it especially when we know the next two weeks of agony they are about to go through; yes, it's cruel but it's definitely better in the long run, not only for the pack but for them. The quicker the shift the better your chances are during a fight unfortunately. We like our warriors to be the fastest in the country; we even train the Omegas because there are more of them and they deserve a chance at a fair fight if we were attacked. We recently upgraded an Omega after the last rogue attack. The Omega managed to kill three rogues that had tried to enter through the kitchen door; he is now being trained as a warrior.

The day went by pretty quickly, I headed back to my room to check on Shannon for the first time all day; it was nearly nine p.m. and although I asked Jade to check on her for me Stefan said that she wasn't feeling the best so didn't manage to. I walked through the doors only to find nothing, no sign of movement from Shannon and entering the bedroom my heart dropped to see that she was still in the exact same position as this morning, the same one she was in when I brought her home last night. I opened my mind-link focusing on Doctor Bane; hopefully hers was open, I know she was preparing herself for tonight's shifting which she always has to be on hand for just in case. Thankfully it was open.

"Doctor Bane, I need you to come to the alpha room straight away please. There is something up with Shannon."

"I'll be there in five."

Sure enough, she barged through the door five minutes later with a few small pieces of medical equipment and Nurse Hilary by her side.

"What happened, Alpha? How long has she been asleep?"

"Well, we, sort of, mated and I marked her last night. She's been asleep since."

"Why wasn't I called sooner?" I could see the anger bubbling its way to the surface and my revelation, not to mention my ignorance to Shannon's condition. I couldn't help but feel ashamed; she's my mate I should have noticed, not focused on the bloody shifting ceremony, why am I such a bad mate?

"I, I've been out all day, helping prepare for the shifting ceremony. I, I'm sorry."

I looked up to see Doctor Bane walking over to me with a small smile.

"I've checked all of her readings and thankfully she's okay, my guess is her human form is changing slightly to accommodate to her new position as your mate and our Luna. She may even gain a few wolf-like abilities. It isn't uncommon for humans to gain something when bitten by a werewolf, I will come back and check on her tomorrow but, Alpha, I may have to move her to the hospital again if she hasn't woken in a few days, just to keep a closer eye on her. Congratulations, though. I'll see you at midnight."

I nodded at Doctor Bane and Hilary as they left the room; I couldn't help but feel guilty over the fact that once again it was my fault that she may end up in the hospital. I showered and changed before making my way back to the stadium; I made sure to lock the door so that I knew she was safe whilst I wasn't there. The stadium was already filling up which wasn't surprising – it was a requirement that everyone attended with only a few exceptions; young children, pregnant she-wolves and any elderly that weren't up to it. It was a great honour to be there during someone's first shift, and after a few years we decided that we would do it together.

Midnight came around quick, as the moon hit its highest peak our shifters started to strip off. It wasn't long before the screams were heard, it's an awful noise, you can hear the bones cracking at different speeds, some of the shifters were vomiting between screaming and some were just crying. It made me feel sick to my stomach watching them go through it, you want nothing more than to go down there and help them in any way possible, but you can't any more; a few years ago, we had one of the quickest shifts in history and the poor kid mauled his mother by accident during the shift. Thankfully she lived but now has a hideous scar. We made it a requirement then that no one could be close to those that were shifting, we have had no incidents since thankfully. I noticed as a young man at the back shifted into a light grey wolf; his wolf was beautiful, it's not often you get a grey wolf, I think I have only ever seen one or two. No doubt David Rye would be all over it, finding out what is so special about his wolf, a few more wolves transformed swiftly and easily – no doubt relieved that it was over. It was then that I noticed a young girl shifting at the back of the group; her wolf was white with violet eyes, this meant only one thing – a healer. A true healer in the pack once again, these were rare as well; yes, we had Doctor Bane, but she was the first true healer our pack has had in a century. It was weird that this girl's eyes never changed at thirteen but it wasn't uncommon for them to find out late. I searched the crowd to find Doctor Bane only to see her with a huge smile across her face as she stared at our new true healer. Suddenly, the light grey wolf from earlier started acting up, sniffing the air and pawing at the ground, searching the stadium until his eyes fell upon the new true healer. He bounded towards her nearly knocking her over as he reached her, it was quite funny, it definitely explained why he was light grey – a true healer's mate is usually as close to white as you can get because they are a pair essentially. They would do great things in years to come, I could feel it. They switched back to their human form and headed back towards the houses; a few chuckles erupted through the crowd because we all knew what they were going to do, after they left the rest of the wolves followed suit in transforming, some found their mate and some didn't. They would hopefully find them eventually. It's just not everyone finds them straight away unfortunately. I helped tidy up and put things away before I finally went home myself, I cwtched up in bed with Shannon; holding her as tight as I could, praying to the moon goddess that she would wake soon. I need her to wake soon.

Chapter Eighteen
She Is My Luna

Jason

I woke up this morning feeling refreshed but anxious, I couldn't stop thinking about how Verity almost killed the Luna a few weeks ago. I hated her in the beginning – the idea of a human as our Luna sickened me but she had settled in really well, she was even close mates with Skye which meant we saw each other a lot and, in all honesty, I couldn't imagine the pack without her. My thoughts were interrupted by the sweet smell of cinnamon with a hint of pine; indicating Skye had come in. Sure enough I looked towards the door and there she was. My beautiful mate; we'd been together nearly two years now and I couldn't imagine my life without her, she was perfect. Her scent had changed recently because of the pregnancy but it was still the most intoxicating thing I'd ever smelled. My smile grew wide as she approached; climbing on top of me placing a small kiss on my lips.

"Good morning, sweetness. What are you up to today?"

"Well, my prince, today I'm helping Luna Shannon pick out colour schemes for the day-care. She hasn't long mind linked me actually, to say that the structure is ready so she's heading over there; seeing as I'm being trained as the manager, we figured it was appropriate for me to go."

"Ooo, Manager Skye Hopkins. I like it!"

I grabbed her, throwing her gently against the bed, leaning down so that I could kiss her growing bump, she was around eight weeks pregnant and we had our first scan that morning; werewolves are only pregnant for five months usually, six at the most if they go overdue but with the way Skye was showing already, I didn't think going over would be an issue.

"What time are we seeing Doctor Bane again?"

"Ten thirty so you need to hurry up and change. You've got twenty minutes." She laughed as I rushed around getting washed and dressed; I'd been waiting for this day for weeks and here it was, today I could see our baby for the first time, knowing she was carrying my pup only made me love her more – I didn't think it was possible to love someone as much as I loved her but I did. My mother tried to get me to reject Skye but it wasn't happening, I could never, I love her more than anything, I prayed to the moon goddess that Verity would get her very own mate and love him like I do Skye but it's never happened; maybe if it did, she would drop this obsession she has with Thomas. We walked hand in hand to the pack hospital; the biggest smiles across our faces, Doctor Bane was waiting for us already in the maternity wing.

"Jason, Skye! Welcome, and congratulations obviously."

"Thank you, Doctor Bane,"

"If you lie on this bed here, I can get a proper look at your little one, would you be all right with our apprentice healer Kaitlyn sitting in and seeing if she can sense the pup?"

"Not at all, we would be honoured."

Doctor Bane's eyes fogged over, shortly after there was a knock at the door and our apprentice healer Kaitlyn walked in shyly.

"Hi, thank you for letting me do this. You're actually my first patients."

"Well, we're honoured. Aren't we, Jason?"

"Of course."

I smiled brightly as Kaitlyn walked over to the bed and Skye lifted her blouse.

"Thank you, Skye. Kaitlyn, I want you to place your hands on Skye's lower stomach and close your eyes. Focusing on the heartbeat inside, the pup growing in there, okay?"

Kaitlyn nodded, her hands gently placed on Skye's stomach. I watched as her hands slowly started to glow, even Doctor Bane looked shocked at this small revelation but the shock soon turned to pride as she watched Kaitlyn concentrating on my mate's stomach, keeping her breathing shallow as she did. When the glowing stopped, she looked up at us with a wide smile.

"Oh wow, I saw them, I saw your babies."

"Wait, babies? As in plural? There's more than one?"

Skye and Doctor Bane gasped before Doctor Bane started fumbling around with the ultrasound machine, wow no wonder she was showing already, we were having more than one!

"Let's have a look, shall we? Skye, this will be cold a second, okay?"

Skye nodded as Doctor Bane put some kind of gel on her stomach before putting a weird probe over the gel that was connected to a machine, she looked at the screen for a little while before she turned it to us; I looked at the screen but it was all a grey and black blur, I couldn't really tell what was what.

"Okay so see here; here is baby number one's head – and here, well, here is baby number two's head, if I move it around a bit then we can see parts of their body but they're not in the right position to check everything. If I press this though you can hear their heartbeat."

She flicked a switch and the most beautiful sound filled the room; it was like two very fast drums going at different beats, it was amazing, I looked up at Skye with tears in my eyes. This only made her more amazing in my eyes; she was training to be a manager of the day-care, pregnant with twins and yet she still managed to look as beautiful as the day I met her. When I saw the tears falling down her cheeks, I couldn't help but let mine out as well, I was going to have the perfect family I'd always dreamed of.

"Here, I've printed you off a few pictures; why don't you come back next week and we can get a better look at these trouble twins, okay?"

I took the pictures whilst Sky cleaned her stomach and got up, I couldn't help but laugh at the idea of trouble twins; if the way I was as a pup is anything to go by, we would definitely have our hands full. Me and Skye went our separate ways once we left the hospital; she had plans with Luna Shannon and me? I had to pay a visit to my mother and sister. I walked towards the very end of the pack grounds, quite literally the furthest you can go – Alpha Thomas' father moved us here when he was Alpha because my mother wouldn't leave him alone. Mom never really did anything with it, it was still the same bland, depressing cabin that I remember from my childhood. I pushed the door open and it creaked in objection; obviously in need of some good oil in the hinges, I was surprised to see dust and cobwebs everywhere, honestly, I'm surprised Verity could live here considering how high maintenance she is.

"Mom? Ver?"

I heard the pounding of footsteps in the rooms upstairs before Verity was on the stairs and tackling me to the ground in excitement.

"JJ! You haven't come here in forever!"

"To what do we owe this visit then?" I looked up to see my mom walking down the stairs slowly, her lips pursed and brows furrowed in disgust.

"I-I wanted to tell you in person, Skye's pregnant! With twins!" I beamed with pride as I pulled the scan photos out of my pocket; only to be pulled into another hug by Verity.

"That's amazing! I'm going to be an aunty!"

"Tsk, Verity get off him. They will be worthless Omegas like their worthless mother. You should have rejected her the moment you found her like I said."

Verity climbed off me and it was a good job because I could feel my anger rising.

"She is not worthless; you seem to forget Nana and Papa were Omegas."

"Oh, Jason, why do you think I killed them?"

Me and Verity both gasped, she couldn't have. Could she? How evil was this woman?

"No. No. You didn't, don't lie."

"Oh, I did, Jason. It was the night I met your father; I waited until they were asleep and I placed a lit candle under the curtains in the living room. I went for a run after I saw that the curtains had finally caught fire, during my run I ran into a lone rogue, which was when we created you. He couldn't join the pack unfortunately; his crimes were too severe so we just had a love affair outside of pack borders until recently actually. He is now the leader of the rogues after the attack recently, he loves me knowing what I did and he'll love me more once he knows our Luna is dead."

My jaw was dropped, my back against the wall, I couldn't believe what I was hearing; she was a monster.

"You won't kill Shannon – I, I won't let you. I'll tell Thomas."

She walked over to me and had me pinned against the wall

holding my throat. I tried to hurt her but I was still too in shock to make sense of any of it. Even Verity stood back with her mouth dropped; not knowing what to say or do, tears slowly escaping her eyes.

"You will tell Thomas *nothing.* If you so much as try, I will kill that little slut you call a mate and rip out those pups right in front of you, do you want their death on your hands? Once that human is out of the way, Verity will be our Luna and you can live a quiet life wherever you choose. Understand?"

"Y-ye-yes, Mother."

She threw me to the ground with great force, I coughed and spluttered trying to catch my breath as quick as I could; a menacing smile spread across her face as she watched me trying to catch my breath before she eventually left. Verity regained her focus, giving me a glass of water, I gained my composure and was finally able to stand up.

"Ver, we can't let her do this. Shannon's a good person, she's done nothing wrong."

"She took my man, Jason; she deserves what's coming for her. Your babies don't, though; look after them and focus on Skye, we'll take care of the rest. You don't have to have any involvement."

"But, Ver, I'm already involved. I can't tell Thomas but I will stop it. One way or another."

I walked out of the house, my mind swimming with all this new information. Shannon didn't deserve to die, but neither did my mate or my pups. What did I do?

Chapter Nineteen
New Abilities

My dreams were strange; wolves everywhere, following me, listening to me, letting me live with them – the Alpha, a large black one, kept hiding from me, it looked just like Thomas but it wasn't, it didn't make sense. My vision started blurring before finally I was able to open my eyes.

"T-T-Thomas?" I looked around realising that I wasn't in the field any more, I wasn't in my bed either. For the first time I noticed the familiar beeping by my side; ugh, I was in the bloody hospital again. I thought about Thomas, the last thing I remembered was him mating with me and then marking me. I touched my mark, sending tingles through my body as I thought of Thomas again; suddenly he was all that filled my mind. *"Where is he?"* I asked myself looking around the room, I threw my legs off the bed about to get up when another voice filled my mind; making me jump that badly I lost my balance, landing with a thud on my bottom, disconnecting myself from all the machines.

"Shannon? Is that you?" I screamed in impulse; this is it. I've gone crazy, I'm having a mental breakdown, everything the past few weeks was an aspect of my imagination and now I'm hearing voices. Suddenly the door burst open; about ten nurses came rushing in followed by Doctor Bane and another young lady that I'd not seen before, I started crying, overwhelmed by everyone being in the room.

"False alarm! Everyone clear out, only me and Kaitlyn need

to be here." Doctor Bane shouted at all the nurses fussing over me, trying to get me up off the floor and check that I was okay. Just then the door burst open and there he was; my god-like mate, stood in the doorway, eyes focused on me and only me. He pushed through the crowd of nurses, making his way to me, a look of concern and lust spread across his face. He tilted my head up; studying my expression looking for any sign of injury or hesitation before forcing his lips on mine; sending waves of sparks through my body, straight to my core, I wanted him so bad right then.

"Uh-hum; you have company still here; I'd like to see to my patient please, Alpha."

I'm sure Thomas was blushing as he pulled away from me, sitting in the chair beside my bed; I sat on the bed as Doctor Bane approached me.

"Shannon, do you mind lying down so that Kaitlyn here can do a quick assessment of you?"

"Uh, Doctor Bane, I would prefer it if you checked her first; no offence, Kaitlyn."

"Thomas, as much as I'd like to; as Kaitlyn grows stronger, I grow slightly weaker. I'll never completely lose my power but the newest healer will always be stronger."

I nodded at Kaitlyn, giving her a small smile to let her know that it was okay to approach.

"Hi, Kaitlyn, it's nice to meet you. I'm Shannon."

"It's nice to meet you, Luna; I'm Kaitlyn. We found out three nights ago that I'm the next generation true healer, may I touch your stomach please?"

"Of course, please call me Shannon. It sounds like you're just as important as me now."

We both chuckled as I pulled my shirt up; I didn't even

realise I had been changed at this point, she said three nights ago but I didn't know her then or remember Thomas saying we found a new healer, I wondered how long I'd been asleep then? I wasn't even freaked out by this point; I seemed to make a habit of going into comas apparently. I watched Kaitlyn put her hands on my stomach, her hands started glowing as she hummed quietly, this must be what Doctor Bane meant by a "quick assessment".

"T-Thomas, is she meant to glow?"

"Yes, it's normal, my angel."

"Oh okay, how long have I been asleep?"

"Four long nights, Shannon. Did you hear me earlier?"

"What do you mean?"

"Shannon, you mind linked me."

"What? That's impossible! I-I'm not a wolf."

"Shannon, sometimes when humans are marked, they develop certain abilities that wolves have. I actually wouldn't be surprised if you developed more when we have the Luna ceremony next full moon."

I sat there shocked when the voice popped into my mind. *"Can you hear me baby? Focus on me, speak in your mind and only your mind."* His voice made me jump, it was weird hearing him like this; I wasn't sure if I liked it but I did like he said and focused on Thomas. *"I, erm, Thomas? Can you hear me?"* I watched him as a small smile spread across his face, telling me that he had definitely heard me, our thoughts were taken by Doctor Bane walking forward; placing a hand on Kaitlyn's back.

"Kaitlyn, is something wrong? You've been there a while now?"

Kaitlyn pulled her hands away; looking between me and Doctor Bane confused.

"I-I can't read you, Luna, it's as if there's a block. I get nothing from you."

"What does that mean?" I couldn't help but look around at everyone; not knowing what to say when Doctor Bane placed her hands in the same place only for her brows to furrow in confusion too.

"I-I've never known anything like it; we can't read you, Shannon. How do you feel?"

"I feel fine, a bit nauseous but that's probably because I'm starving."

"You can go home if you want, all your observations were fine the entire time you were here, it was just a case of waiting for you to wake up."

"Yeah, I'd like to go home please."

"That's no issue but please rest, give it a few days before you have any erm… extracurricular activities shall we say?"

I couldn't help but laugh as Doctor Bane and Kaitlyn whispered; discussing my condition and what could have caused it, why they couldn't read me, I was surprised I could hear their low whispers if I'm honest but it could be one of those wolf-like abilities Doctor Bane discussed with us.

The next few weeks went by pretty quickly; I have my Luna ceremony tonight during the full moon so me and Jade are picking our dresses up today from town, not to mention Jade wants to pick up a few baby bits so we will be gone most of the day giving Thomas time to get on with setting up for both the Luna and the shifting ceremony.

Me and Jade walked arm in arm down to the cars where Jason, Luke, Ryan and Scott were waiting to escort us; we rode in Jade's car behind the men, we stopped at the pack house only to see Verity running out and giving the boys some water bottles. That was unusually nice of her; although saying that since me and Skye had become really close friends, so had Jason – maybe Verity was changing too? She'd not said anything to or about me since Thomas marked me and it was kind of a relief; I worried a lot that first week after waking up but anytime I saw her she was all smiles. Me and Skye ran into each other at breakfast and had been practically inseparable since. She was going to come today but she had a check-up with Doctor Bane, I tried to get Jason to go but he insisted on coming with us; like he did anytime I left the pack grounds, it made me feel safer though, knowing he was there for me.

I have been working on my mind linking and I can now link: Thomas, Jade, Stefan, Skye and Jason. I'm working on my dad and sisters next but Thomas thinks that once I am marked as Luna tomorrow, I'll be able to link the whole pack. But that sounds like a lot of work if I'm honest. We arrived in town rather quickly; picking up our dresses first before grabbing a drink and heading to the other shops, Jason pulled me away from the others rather hastily.

"Shannon, I need your help."

"Sure, Jase, is everything okay?"

"I want to propose to Skye."

I couldn't help but jump up and down in excitement for them both! Everything was coming together for them; the twins, they were even moving into the pack house after my insistence and now Jason was going to propose! It was like a love story, I couldn't wait for this honestly.

"You have to do it tonight! New moon, new beginnings!"

"That sounds awesome, really. But I need help choosing a ring, do you think you could help?"

"Yesss! Come on!"

I dragged him towards the jewellers on the corner; they sell the most beautiful stuff; I had no doubt they would have something that Skye deserved.

We walked in and the sales lady walked straight over to us; she had such a sweet voice; I couldn't help but smile looking at her small stature.

"Good afternoon, what can I help you with today?"

"We're looking for an engagement ring please."

"Right this way."

She walked us over to a small glass case; I was right, they had the most beautiful things. That's when I saw it; her perfect ring. It was in a tiara shape with a rose gold finish, diamonds surrounding a big oval one on the front. It was stunning.

"That one, Jase, she'd love it. She always says that you're her prince, make her your princess."

A large smile spread across his face as he nodded then ordered one in her size; thankfully they had one in the back otherwise he would have had to wait a week. We waited whilst he had a small message engraved into the ring, on the inside, it read "*forever and always, my love*". We left the shop; Jason hadn't stopped smiling since we bought it. Jade asked where we went but Jason swore me to secrecy so I just told her to wait and see, it was kind of exciting only me and Jason knowing. We picked up more baby stuff than was needed; you'd think Jade was having quadruplets the amount she bought but who cares, it's all fun, even Jason grabbed a few bits, putting them in his trunk. He was so excited for everything to come it was adorable. He's a completely different person to when we first met. We all got in the car excited for the full moon when all of a sudden me and Jade watched the boys' car lose control, going around in circles, heading straight for us.

"JADE, STOP, TURN—DO SOMETHING—THEY'RE

GOING TO—"

I watched in horror as the men's car spiralled into us, sending our car off the road, down the slope into the field below, me and Jade screamed the entire way down; I saw the boys' car come to a halt not far in front of ours. The sound of wolves echoed around us; everything went dark.

Chapter Twenty
An Enemy Turned Friend Is a Friend to the End

Jason

Me and the lads got back in the car; excited for what was to come. Not only do we crown Shannon as our Luna tonight, I get to propose to the love of my life; the woman I physically could not live without, she is my reason for living, her and those pups are my everything. Shannon helped me pick out the absolutely perfect ring; I had no doubt Skye would love it, I picked up the water Verity gave us earlier, we completely forgot about it amongst everything going on. It was quite refreshing with the sliced lemon and cucumber in it, it was unusually kind for her to do something like that but I think she's changing slowly; I've not heard anything more about revenge on Shannon so I'm hoping her and Mother have decided against it, but I knew better than that. My mother doesn't give up, she bides her time; works out her strategies, she was pure evil.

My thoughts were interrupted by coughing behind me; I felt something spray on my neck and it was as if everything was in slow motion. Turning around, the scene behind me was like something out of a horror movie; Luke and Ryan were both behind me clutching at their throats, coughing up blood and mucous, frothing at the mouth as they coughed, tears pouring down their face as they begged me to help them, I looked at Scott beside me as he grabbed me only to see him in exactly the same state.

"The drink."

He managed to choke those words out before falling back in his seat, that's when it clicked; Verity gave me my bottle specifically so that I wouldn't get them mixed up, she, she poisoned them. Amongst the shock and fear of what was going on I hadn't noticed the car in front of me stopping, I turned the wheel as hard as I could, trying to stop myself crashing into the car in front. I hadn't realised how close the girls were behind us and sure enough I spiralled into their car; sending it off the road before my car followed too. The car tumbled a few times, hitting my head on both the roof and the steering wheel before the car finally stopped a few feet away facing the girls' car. The sound of wolves filled the air and there was a whole host of smells around us; blood was the main one, from the three men I called friends hanging dead in my car, the cucumber and lime from the drinks that had exploded, burning the skin of my friends, indicating that it was wolfsbane in their water. Why didn't they realise?

I watched in horror as some filthy rogues surrounded the girls' car. I had to get out now. I mind linked Thomas, "*The guards were poisoned; we've crashed not far from town. Hurry, there are rogues.*"

I was brought out of my thoughts when I heard Shannon screaming; I ripped the seat belt off with my extended claws before smashing my front window with tremendous force and shifting into action, I launched at the two wolves who had a hold on Shannon first; killing one and injuring the other. I obviously had the upper hand seeing as they expected me to be dead; although there were about fifteen rogues and I was on my own, even though I was incredibly outnumbered, I'd protect Shannon or die trying.

Shannon

I was stirred back to consciousness by the sound of my door being forced open; two men dragged me out of the car; I screamed in protest, my head pounding from the accident. I was sure everyone was dead. I couldn't believe it; such a lovely day ended like this. The two men forced me to my knees pulling my hair back to expose my neck.

"Get off me *now*." I tried sounding as forceful as I could but it didn't work, one of the men shifted whilst the other stood there pulling my hair still. All of a sudden there was snarling and the man behind me fell to the floor. I hesitantly glanced back to see that he was now missing a head. I screamed before jumping back on my feet. I noticed Jason's wolf Gianni pouncing and killing another rogue before he stood in a protective stance in front of me; fighting any rogue that dared to attack us. He was doing so well, until, one came at us from behind me; biting down on my arm causing me to scream in pain, this was only a distraction though. It allowed Jason to lose focus enough for a rogue to bite down hard on his leg.

"Jason, behind you!" I screamed as I noticed three wolves getting ready to pounce him at once, thankfully he was quick enough to anticipate and moved only for them to hit the ground. But this victory was short lived as another rogue anticipated his move and jumped on his back. I watched as this wolf dug its canines into his shoulder; swiftly ripping a chunk out of him.

"NOOOOOOO!"

I mustered any and all strength I had to knock the wolf off me; running as fast as I could, I pulled the other wolf off of Jason, I wanted to snap its neck but I couldn't, I'm not a wolf. I held

Gianni's large head on my lap and watched as a single tear fell from his eye, nodding at me in respect before he shifted back into Jason.

I heard the sound of more howls and paw prints around us but my only focus right now was Jason, I cradled him in my lap, tears falling from my cheek as I took my top off trying to stop the blood that was pouring from his shoulder.

"Sh-Sh-Shannon, i-i-it's pointless. I'm dying."

"No, Jase, you can't; we, we were just becoming friends, you were gonna propose. Hold on, you have to. For those babies, for Skye. Please, Jase, don't die. I can't lose you."

"I-I'm sorry for not a-a-accepting you at first, Shannon, you are kind, you—you are amazing. You are the bestest friend for Skye. P-p-promise me you'll look after her, promise me you'll help with my babies – don't let them forget me."

"They won't forget you because you're going to be there, you are not dying, Jase, I won't let you. Don't give up. Please."

I wasn't even talking at this point, I was sobbing; Jason lay there dying in my lap and there was nothing I could do, I couldn't save him, heal him – I couldn't even fight with him.

"Sh-Sh-Sh-Shannon, give Skye the ring please. I need her to know how much I tr-tr-truly love her. Y-y-y-you will always be my L-L-Luna."

I watched as he closed his eyes, his body going limp in my lap.

"NOOOOO, COME BACK, DAMN YOU! DON'T DIE! YOU CAN'T! HELLLLLP! SOMEONE PLEASE HELP!"

I pulled Jason's body closer; trying to shake him awake as I searched the clearing for someone, anyone that could help him, bring him back. But the scene before me was bloodier than I had imagined. Thomas had brought enough wolves to completely tear the rogues apart. I noticed in the distance a naked Stefan helping Jade out of the car, oh my, Jade! She looked okay but I couldn't really tell; I could see Atticus fighting another large wolf which must have been the rogue leader?

I turned my attention back to Jason, sobbing and burying my head into his chest; he hated me for so long and then gave his life to protect me, how could I ever look Skye or their babies in the eyes again knowing her mate, her life, her love, had died protecting *me*. Did she feel it? Did she know already? I cradled his body until Thomas came over to me, his warriors trying to take his body.

"No, you can't take him! He's not dead! He's not! He can't be!"

Thomas picked me up and restricted me so that they could take Jason's body away; it felt like my heart had been ripped in half watching them carry him, I hit as hard as I could at Thomas' chest, hoping that he would move so that I could get my friend back, there was still time, he couldn't be dead.

"NOOOO! He's not dead, he can't be, Thomas, let me go! Damn you!"

"I'm sorry, angel, but he's gone. He died a hero."

I broke down in his arms, if it wasn't for Thomas holding me so tightly, I think I'd have fallen to the floor; all I could do was cry, shout that he couldn't be dead, he wasn't. Thomas bundled me up into a car that a warrior had brought; I was in Thomas' lap in the back and Jade was sat to the side of him.

"They're all dead, aren't they? Wh-what happened?"

"Jason mind linked us to say there had been a crash and the men were poisoned, we came as fast as our wolves could carry us." Thomas' voice was shallow, broken. He was just as upset as I was. How could they have been poisoned? They didn't even stop for a drink when we did. The only drinks they had today were from—

"Verity." My voice was whispered and broken but Jade looked at me and I watched as the horror spread across her face; coming to the same realisation as I did.

"Wait, what about Verity?" Stefan shouted from the front of the car; I could see Jade's anger building in the same way that I could feel mine rising to the surface.

"The *only* drinks those men had today were given to them by Verity. *She* poisoned them!"

"I'll kill her," Stefan growled at Jade's words; you could see she was completely serious.

Chapter Twenty-One
The Loss of a Mate, a Brother, a Friend… a Hero

Skye

I walked slowly to the pack hospital; I can't believe how much of your energy pregnancy takes, I'd had two naps today already and it was only twelve p.m. The only reason I got up was for the hospital check-up. I had hoped that Jason would come but he wanted to make sure Luna Shannon got to town and back safely, he had really started to warm up to her which was nice seeing as in the beginning he hated her because she was human. Unfortunately, he gets his assumptions from his mother, I've never met such a horrible, power hungry woman – I know it's not nice to say about your mate's mother but she was. It's weird because her mom and dad were the loveliest Omegas you could ever meet, they would offer to babysit, cook us all snacks even when their eldest daughter Ellie turned out to be mated to Alpha Lochlann from Red Valley pack, they didn't change. They watched her move and start a life but stayed here for Lori because they felt that she needed them more. I was only three when they died but I can remember how much it hurt for everyone; not to mention the way that they died was awful – it was a house fire, no idea exactly how it started but by the time anyone noticed the fire was too big to stop. I can remember the devastation as Ellie planned their funeral; they were given such a beautiful service, the whole pack showed up with flowers, I had never known a funeral to be beautiful before this one but it was.

Going past the pack house I watched as the two cars heading to town drove past, Jason and the girls waved at me as they went past looking so excited. I couldn't blame them I wished that I was going but I had an appointment so couldn't but Jason said he'd get my dress for me which was good enough for me. He's been so doting on me lately – forcing me to rest more than I actually need to, although I'm not complaining; I usually need it. The pack hospital was only a short walk from the house but when I arrived, I was surprised to see it so full, blood and warriors everywhere; I ran into Doctor Bane as she was rushing to aid a warrior.

"Ah, Skye, there was a small rogue attack, go wait in maternity and I'll be with you as fast as I can."

I nodded at her as I carried on walking to the maternity ward; it was pretty quiet here so I decided to just find an empty bed and have a nap, Doctor Bane was going to be a little while so why not. Thankfully no one looked seriously injured downstairs and the fact she said "small" attack meant that they had already dealt with it; strange though, we hadn't seen hardly any rogues since the night Shannon was brought here.

It felt like I'd only been asleep for a second when I was shaken gently by a slightly bloody and panicked Doctor Bane.

"You worried me for a second there, Skye. Tired?"

"Yeah, sorry. I wasn't sure how long you would be and I saw this empty bed—"

"It's fine, honestly, I remember how draining pregnancy can be. Now let's check on the trouble twins, shall we? I brought the machines in here to make it easier."

She checked my blood pressure and pulse before taking a urine sample and getting her ultrasound machine out; it was honestly the best thing ever listening to their heartbeats and seeing them move on the screen, the perfect mixture of me and my amazing mate.

"Do you want to know their genders?"

I thought about it for a second; me and Jason hadn't decided yet but even if we wanted to, we should find out together, not me then him. That wouldn't be fair.

"Could you write it on a piece of paper for me please, then me and Jason can find out together?"

"That's no issue at all, Skye; you clean up and I'll print these before writing it down."

I cleaned the cold gel off my stomach before climbing down from the raised hospital bed; I could see Doctor Bane still busying herself with the printing, she always made sure we had enough copies so that Jason could give his sister a copy. He never actually said what his mother thought of the pregnancy but I felt his anger and pain whilst he went there. I'm sure she tried to hurt him because of the pressure I felt around my throat whilst he was there but he refused to tell me anything. It's always been like that with him, he's always looked up to her and wanted her approval but never really got it, something changed recently and he stopped bringing her up completely but again he wouldn't tell me why so I dropped it. Why should I risk our happiness by dragging up something that upsets him when we have our whole future ahead of us? Twins on the way, new friends, David Rye is even talking about making Jason the head warrior apprentice! Life is going to be so good from now on; I can feel it.

Doctor Bane gave me all my bits and we made another appointment for two weeks' time.

"Make sure Jason is at that appointment, you have to grow the babies, the least he can do is show up to check their progress."

I chuckled, saying goodbye as I walked to the door when

suddenly I could feel a wave of fear and panic through the mate bond; what was going on? Why was Jason scared?

"Is everything okay, Skye?" Doctor Bane was at my side; obviously concerned by the fact that I had stopped so abruptly in my tracks but I couldn't answer instead I focused on my wolf.

"Amelia? Can you feel that?"

The fear grew stronger, now accompanied by my fear, pain radiated from my head meaning Jason was hurt, he only went to town! What could have happened in that time, I tried to mind link him.

"Jason? Jason!" but he had a channel open meaning I was blocked, the block stayed up as I felt pain radiating through my body. I fell to the floor crying, the pain was unbearable yet I could feel his determination, what was going on?

"Amelia, can you link Gianni?"

I didn't get a response all I heard was her howling in pain; then I felt it myself, my heart felt like it was being pulled apart. A scream escaped my lips as Doctor Bane shouted for help, assuming the problem was with me or even the twins but it wasn't, this wasn't something she could fix, Gianni was gone. I felt the connection die; I could feel Jason's connection slowly fading too, the pain unbearable by this point and then suddenly it was gone. There was no pain, no connection, no love, nothing. My heart had been ripped out and stepped on a thousand times over; I felt empty, like I had no purpose, I sat there screaming, crying for what felt like hours. My mate, my love, my lifeline was gone; why? How? Someone ran into the room and I overheard them tell Doctor Bane the cars were here; she was needed immediately, that was all I needed to hear to rush down the stairs, Doctor Bane shouting behind me.

"Skye, don't! Grab her! You shouldn't see this!"

I ran faster than I had ever run, reaching the hospital doors, I ran to the approaching vehicles; I saw Alpha, Jade and Shannon climbing out of the one car. I ran over practically screaming in their faces.

"Where is he? Where is my prince?"

"Th-tha-that car." Shannon was covered in his blood, I could smell it, his scent all over her; he wasn't alone at least. I ran towards the car that Shannon pointed at; throwing the door open, I fell to my knees once I saw him, he was covered head to toe in blood, wounds scattered all over his body, his beautiful dark hair crimson from the blood but his face was beautiful. His face was hardly touched by all of the destruction that had occurred, he looked so peaceful; almost as if he was sleeping, I felt strong arms around me, picking me up off the ground – I looked up to see Stefan, I was surprised that he would be doing this but then I realised why and I tried my hardest to break free.

"NOOOO, LET ME GO! I CAN'T LIVE WITHOUT HIM! NO! STEFAN! JASONNNN! WAKE, PLEASE, I NEED YOU, WE NEED YOU!"

My voice was broken, all I could do was sob whilst I tried to free myself from Stefan's grip but he was a lot stronger than me – being a Beta, he would be. It hurt so much; I watched as they took my mate's body away, to the morgue below the hospital, where he would stay until his funeral. Funeral. No, he couldn't be dead; he couldn't. He promised to always be there for me, for our pups; he couldn't be dead! My fear replaced with anger, I managed to break free of Stefan's grip; obviously surprised by my sudden burst of strength, I ran as fast as I could towards the car Shannon and Alpha Thomas were stood at. I grabbed Shannon; forcing her to the floor with great force.

"What happened? Why is he dead? Why are *you* covered in his blood?"

I was only there for a second before Thomas pulled me off

her, restricting my arms so that I couldn't do anything; I screamed and threw myself, trying to get out of his grip but it was no use. I finally wore myself out, I would have fallen to my knees if it wasn't for Thomas's hold of me; he let me go, helping me gently to the ground below. I looked up at Shannon, my eyes swollen and red, my throat was so sore you'd have thought I had swallowed a cup of razors. I looked up to see Shannon on her knees in front of me taking both my hands.

"Shannon, please. What happened?"

"We don't know exactly, th-they were poisoned. We saw the car lose control and then the rogues attacked. J-J-Jason, he—he saved my life; he kept the rogues at bay until the pack arrived. I-I'm sorry, Skye. H-he only spoke of you until the end."

"We think Verity poisoned them, Skye, do you know anything?"

My mouth drooped hearing Jade say this; sure, Verity was evil but she'd never purposely hurt Jason, would she?

"No, no, no. She—she loved Jason; she wouldn't hurt him."

"Listen, we can discuss the ins and outs later; the guards are searching for Verity and Lori who will remain in the dungeon until we know what happened. For now, I want the three of you checked over." Thomas bent down, making direct eye contact as he spoke gently. "You have just gone through the hardest thing a wolf could ever go through, we will find out what happened, I promise you, but for now you need to think about the two babies growing inside you and focus on them."

I nodded at Thomas before letting him carry me inside the hospital where all this began; all I wanted to do right then was crawl up and die, but it was in this moment, the moment that I wanted to end it all that I got the reminder that I needed to push through. I felt flutters in my tummy, sending hope through my heart once more. Maybe I could get through this; for them.

Chapter Twenty-Two
Hindsight Is a Wonderful Thing

Verity

I set the four water bottles up on the worktop, making sure to use Jason's old one so that his wouldn't get mixed up with the other guards. I had the lemon and cucumber sliced neatly on the side – lemon is the only thing with a bitter enough taste to hide a small amount of wolfsbane, not that it would take a lot of it to kill a wolf, mind you, but too much and they would smell it before drinking. The idea of poisoning the guards was mine, my mother just wanted to let the rogues kill them one by one but I thought that was cruel. I made sure that they promised no harm would come to Jason; he didn't deserve any of this but he never left Shannon's side when she left the pack and we were running out of time, the Luna ceremony was tonight so it was our last chance. Once the drinks were finished, I skipped ov er to the pack house; feeling pretty proud of myself, I hoped Mother would be proud. All I'd ever wanted was for her to love me but she didn't, she loved Jason – until he found Skye that is; she wanted him to reject her but he didn't, he stood up to her and moved out. I wish I could do that. We all thought for years that Thomas would be my true mate but when he found that baboon in the forest it was obvious that I wasn't; he didn't even acknowledge me from that moment on, he just got on with his life as if I didn't exist, as if… we didn't exist. Not to mention from that moment on my mother beat me for it, as if I chose not to be his true mate! I was so deep in thought that I almost missed the cars driving off. I waved my arms and ran over to Jason's window.

"Hey, guys; I brought you some drinks to tide you over and keep you refreshed! Can't be guarding our future Luna dehydrated now, can you?"

"Erm, thanks, Ver, that's unusually kind of you." Jason grabbed the drinks, I watched him start giving them out when he went to give Scott his.

"Jase, no. I mean I bought you that water bottle when you lived at home; please use it."

"Oh, sorry, Ver. Of course, I will but we have to go."

"Okay, love ya. Bye!"

I watched as the cars drove away, when they were far enough away, I ran back to my house to pack my things. I had to meet mother in the rogue territory an hour or two away. I packed as many clothes as I knew my wolf Vicki could carry; then only packed the bare necessities like a toothbrush and paste. I walked to the edge of the forest by the house, placing the bag on the floor. I shifted as quick as I could; not even caring about the clothes that would rip as I did. Unfortunately, I have always struggled with shifting; I'm not sure why, the lowest I could get my shift to was one minute which is dangerous for a warrior. I thought that they would demote me to Omega because of it because usually only the weakest wolves couldn't shift quickly. But Thomas wouldn't allow it; he just insisted I never had guard duty or if there was an attack I was to hold back and defend the vulnerable, giving me time to shift.

Vicki ran as fast as her legs could carry her; which was pretty fast, we definitely did better in running than shifting, we slipped past the guards – I hope unnoticed but even if someone saw they would likely just assume I was going for a run which I have been doing every day for the past month or so, in preparation to run away.

I ran for what felt like minutes before I came to a small clearing where I knew some rogues were camping; they were obviously the team that was set to deal with the baboon and her guards. I had a small flicker of guilt shoot through my mind thinking of Jade and her unborn pup. I hope that they survive; I grew up with Jade and the last thing I wanted was to see her dead but unfortunately, she was a means to an end. I shifted so that I could ask the small group where I was supposed to go from here.

"Are you Clarity?"

"Uh, no, I'm Verity."

"Same thing, princess, shift back. I'm here to take you to your parents."

I went to ask him a question but he had already shifted to his wolf; my parents? Did he mean my mum? I've never met my dad? I shifted back; picking up my bag before the sound of crashing and screams could be heard behind me. I wanted to watch them kill her, I wanted to make her suffer, I wanted to make sure Jason was okay, maybe even save Jade, but the wolf had already started running in the opposite direction and I had to be as far from here as I could or Thomas would kill me. He already suspected me without actually being close to the scene. I'll go back in a few days and I'll act like I didn't know anything, comfort him during his grief and maybe then I will be good enough to be his Luna, maybe then he will see that I'm not a bad person. I love him.

I followed the rogue for about half an hour before we came across what looked like an old abandoned hospital; it was quite creepy, the walls outside were Victorian type bricks, windows broken throughout and although it looked creepy, I couldn't help but admire it, it was like a castle, the workmanship was beautiful. Walking through the front doors the first thing I noticed were the scattered beds that littered the hallway, some had blood stains but some didn't, it looked like bones were scattered on the floor but I wasn't sure, this place had obviously been abandoned in a hurry. I walked forward apprehensively when I noticed a small dolly that had been left behind; it made me sad to think of a child missing their favourite doll but I ignored it when I noticed the other wolf shifting, putting some clothes on that were by the reception desk. I shifted and followed once I had put my own clothes on.

"Would you hurry up, girl! I've never known someone to take so long, you'll get killed taking that long."

"Oh, shut up, where's my mother?"

"Not interested in seeing your father then?"

A man emerged from behind a door at the end of the hallway, his tone was cruel and abrupt.

"I don't even know my father."

"Well, you'd better follow me then."

I followed hesitantly as the man walked through the door he had come from. I couldn't lie I was curious; Mom *never* spoke about our dad and we knew better than to ask her about him. I remember once when Jason asked who he was because he had a school project, something about our family tree, she beat him until he was unconscious, we didn't dare mention it after that, it was also the day I swore to do anything to keep her happy. Jason was stronger than me, bigger than me. I couldn't survive a beating like that. As I followed him through the maze of hallways, I noticed a lot of the building had started collapsing, what remained of the floors above now scattered all over the floor beneath our feet. Some rooms had started being taken over by nature once again with trees and grass growing through the walls, floors and ceilings. It was hauntingly enchanting. We walked outside for a little bit before entering another part of the building, this area had quite a menacing feel to it, I felt so uneasy being here, graffiti littered the walls in this broken-down section of the hospital.

We were only walking a few minutes before we came to what looked like a large office; inside there was a big desk, some file cabinets and two chairs, one behind the desk which was occupied by one of the largest men I had ever seen. Standing next to him I noticed my mother. I smiled and ran towards her for a hug but she just held her hand out to stop me.

"Verity, *sit.*"

I sat in the chair in front of the desk without saying a single word, my mom wasn't kind at the best of times but you'd think after everything that had happened today, she would at least be comforting. I waited patiently for her to speak but she didn't; she didn't even look at me, the first to speak was the giant man.

"Were you followed?"

"N-n-n-no, I-I'm sure I wasn't."

I wasn't sure why I stuttered; I've never stuttered in my life, you could see my mother's distaste of my stuttering but she never said anything about it, instead the man spoke again, this time his tone was gentle.

"You have no need to fear me, daughter; after all it is you that will carry on my legacy."

"Y-y-you're my father?"

"Yes; I am king of the rogues. My warriors will bring your brother and we will make plans to attack Forest Lake within the month; their Alpha will be weak after losing his Luna, it is the best time to attack."

"N-no, you can't kill Thomas – I love him."

"Daughter, that Alpha chose a human over *you*; he does not deserve to live, you are of Alpha blood, you were destined to be a Luna, I will make sure of it."

"I-I am not of alpha blood; my mom, she's a warrior and you – you're a rogue."

"I am only a rogue because I refused to serve under my twin brother; he was born two minutes before me so they crowned him Alpha, despite me being the stronger one."

My mouth dropped as he spoke; I was of Alpha blood all this time? So was Jason! I couldn't contain my anger as I looked at my mother, she had not only terrified me my entire life but she lied to me without a care in the world! Why wasn't I mated to Thomas if I was of Alpha blood? It made even more sense for us to be together now!

"Why didn't you tell me?"

"I saw no need; I had hoped that you would be mated to Thomas but your father has pointed out to me that you clearly have a bigger destiny. We have found you a chosen mate who you will mate with and create pups with, you will not argue this or object."

I wanted to argue, I wanted to scream but, before I had a chance, a breathless, naked man broke through the door covered in blood. My father stood up, slamming his hands on the desk to grab the man's attention.

"*What is the meaning of this?*" I trembled slightly as he shouted with his Alpha voice; it was the scariest thing I had ever heard, the man that had just ran in cowered on the floor, showing his neck as a sign of submission.

"O-o-one of th-the guards, h-he was alive still. H-he fought us, trying to protect the L-Luna, he got a m-message to his p-pack, it was a m-massacre. I only just got out of there."

A shiver went down my spine as I looked at my mother; my thoughts immediately turned to Jason; he was meant to be brought here yet this guy was alone.

"What was the guard's name? Do you know?"

"I think I heard J-Jason maybe? The girl called him it."

"D-did he make it?"

"I'm not sure, Ashley got the upper hand and tore a chunk out of his sh-shoulder. But the pack arrived a few minutes later; I ran as soon as I heard them. He was injured pretty badly though; I hope he bled to death."

"*Excuse me?*" I could hear my anger bubbling to the surface, this thing hoped that my loyal, innocent big brother was dead! I jumped off my seat and grabbed him, pinning him against the wall. "*You hope that my brother is dead! Your Alpha's son?*"

I snapped his neck with ease, watching as his eyes went dull, lifeless. I let him go and watched his body slump to the ground, turning around I saw a large smile across my father's face; as usual my mother just looked angry.

"Why wasn't Jason already dead, Verity? I told you to poison *all* of her guards!"

"I-I couldn't. Jason didn't deserve to die, Mom!"

It was then that my father made his first contact with me, I heard it before I felt it; a crack as his hand met my cheek, a burning sensation coursing through my cheeks; only to be replaced by pure agony in my jaw. He had broken my jaw with just one slap; my sobs escaped before I could stop them, I watched as disgust spread across both my parents' faces.

"You will submit to me, girl, if I ever catch you shouting at your mother again I will make you suffer for it, make no mistake about that. *Sirus!*"

He sat back down in his chair watching me as a small man entered the room.

"Yuh—yes, Alpha?"

"Go and fetch Malaki from his room. Then remove this body from my office before it soils itself."

My father kept his gaze on me the entire time; watching me, studying me, it felt like he was daring me to move but I was like a deer in headlights, I couldn't move, object or anything.

"I was almost impressed by the way you killed that traitor; the fact he ran away was enough to warrant his death and you delivered it beautifully but the way you spoke to your mother. You're lucky I didn't kill you. My legacy means more to me than your death though; you will go to Malaki's room and you will not come out until you are with child."

My jaw dropped; my father didn't care about my feelings, my dignity, he just wanted me as a breeding machine to some man I didn't know. My thoughts were interrupted by a man being dragged into the room; his hands were bound with rope and chains, he looked weak, scarred, dirty – like he hadn't washed in weeks but his eyes were like blue sapphires. I couldn't look away. Amelia started howling in my head as the smell of freshly cut grass mixed with pine needles hit my nose; it was intoxicating, I wanted to go over there and grab him. Take him here and now.

"MATE," Amelia howled, trying to push me to mate with him there and then; our eyes met before his turned black, possessively.

"Malaki is an Alpha pup we stole from some pack in Ireland about seven years ago. Malaki, you will mate and mark my daughter tonight or I will kill you and find an Alpha who will."

Malaki growled at this which only made my father angrier; he jumped straight out of his chair, he punched Malaki so hard that he hit the floor unconscious. I rushed to his side trying to act like I wasn't as hurt as I was so that my father wouldn't realise that we were true mates; we needed to escape, get back to the pack and warn everyone, apologise and beg for forgiveness, make sure that Jason was okay. If I wanted to get out of here alive, I would need to be strong, my mate needed to be strong.

"Take them to their cell now."

The small man called Sirus dragged Malaki along the floor; I felt awful watching it but what could I do? They had to think I wasn't okay with this, my jaw was healing but it was still broken; I couldn't object if I wanted to. I thought about the way I was towards Shannon as I followed Sirus; I was awful, I called her names, bullied her, tried to kill her twice. When, she was forced into all of this, she didn't choose to be Luna or Thomas' mate. I wish that I could take it all back, that I could apologise; stop what was going to happen but I couldn't, I never should have listened to my mother but then if I hadn't, I wouldn't have found my true mate. I had no idea what awaited me at the pack; Jason would know that I poisoned the water, he would hate me forever. Although, it was nothing less than I deserved.

Chapter Twenty-Three
The Aftermath of Betrayal

Thomas

**Three Weeks After Jason's Death*
Atticus was running as fast as his paws could carry him; we were out on yet another scouting mission but this time the rogues we ran into weren't friendly, we had to escape them before they killed us.

"Come on, Atticus, you got this!"

I felt his speed increase, jolting us forward even more; the pack border was in sight, just one final stretch! The rogues behind me retreated, obviously knowing we were at the border and it would be suicide to come any closer. I ran straight to the pack house, shifting and changing into some clothes that I found behind a tree. I headed straight for my office before summoning Stefan using the mind link; I wasn't supposed to be out scouting but what else could I do? All I've thought about is the death of my mate and Beta's guards, we could have lost both women as well! I couldn't rest until I found Verity, no doubt her mom was involved too seeing as neither of them have been seen since. Stefan entered my office; he looked exhausted, he's taken it all about as well as I have. Shannon won't touch me; she won't look at me – heck she won't even talk to me! She moved into one of our spare bedrooms and hardly comes out, she's taking it so hard and I can't blame her, she watched his life end, she blames herself. *"If I wasn't here, if I wasn't the Luna, he'd still be alive"*

– It's the only thing I've heard from her.

"What's going on, Tom?"

"Have the scouts returned? Any word from the other packs in regards to whether they have been seen?"

"No, the scouts found absolutely no trace of her or Lori, no news from other packs either. They've disappeared completely."

"Is—is Skye ready to have the funeral?"

"No, Thomas, quite frankly neither is Shannon but we need to. We sent Luke, Scott and Ryan to the moon goddess with a hero's cremation two weeks ago. Jason needs to be there too; he needs peace, their mates understood, so should Skye."

"Stefan, their mates weren't pregnant with twins or currently living under suicide watch at the hospital! Do you really think I want to put more stress on her right now than there needs to be? She's only just started eating again."

"I know, Tom, and I get it but she needs to do it so that we can move on and make Verity pay; maybe you could visit her and try to talk to her?"

I nodded my head and watched as Stefan left the room, probably to visit Jade in the hospital, her waters broke a few days ago so she's on bedrest and antibiotics because she hasn't gone into labour. She still has a month left until the pup is due so we want her to hold on as long as she can. I sat there with my head in my hands when there was a knock at the door; I was startled but I told them to come in anyway, I was shocked to see Shannon walking through the door, she has never visited me in my office and lately she only goes as far as our kitchen if she does leave the room.

"Hi." She had a small smile when she spoke, a shyness like the first time we met; it made me smile.

"Hello, my angel. How are you feeling?"

"Tired – I wanted to have a cwtch in bed but when I got there you were already gone, I-I tried to mind link you but it was blocked."

"Oh, I'm sorry, honey, I-I stayed out all night scouting; I-I want to make Verity and Lori pay but I can't do anything stuck here."

It was as if a switch had flicked in her mind; I watched as anger coursed through her veins, bubbling to the surface, although I hated that I had obviously upset her it was nice to see her feel anything but depressed.

"So, you're telling me that we lose four warriors because of two selfish, power hungry bitches, as you say, and your first thought is to go scouting for those two same bitches? Without a second thought to me, the pack or anyone but *them*? How would you even know where to start?"

I was surprised by exactly how angry she was; but it wasn't my fault.

"I thought if I-I followed the rogues then they would—"

"*They would what, Thomas? Kill you? Then what, huh?* The pack would no longer have an alpha because he was too stupid to trust his own scouts who are trying everything they could! You don't think I want them to pay? You don't think I want to kill them for what they've done? Of course, I do! But I know it would be stupid to chase them; regardless of me being a human, if I died you would lose your mate and your Luna. How would *you* feel then, huh? Judging by the way Skye is you'd be about as useful as her!"

"How do you know about Skye?"

"Even though I've been depressed you don't think I've checked on her and Jade every single fucking day? *I'm* the whole reason they're where they are, Thomas! If I hadn't gone to that stupid lake six and a half years ago, Jason, Luke, Scott and Ryan would still be here; Verity would be your chosen mate and you'd all live happily ever after. Me? I'd live a simple life as a human without having to watch my friends die!"

"Shannon, please, my life would be nothing without you – I—Verity would never have been my chosen mate, I swear, my parents only believed in true mate matching; it's why I waited and I saved myself *for you.*"

"So why does Verity think I took you from her? Why is she trying so hard to kill me?"

"Ver-Verity and I were inseparable growing up, she was the only friend I had at one point. We bonded, we grew up together; I'm not ashamed to say I loved her, we honestly thought that we were going to be true mates when we turned eighteen but when I turned eighteen, my father, he made me go and check the border as my first Alpha duty. That's when Atticus found Clara and Emily; they both smelt like you but even when you showed up, we were confused about how we knew when you weren't eighteen. My father said because you're human we'd be able to tell from birth, Verity and her mom wouldn't accept it though, she started clinging to me, insisting that I was wrong. She didn't accept it when she turned eighteen either, even tried to mark me whilst I slept." I showed Shannon the scars on my neck, seeing the horror in her face. "I stopped her as soon as I felt it, I still have no idea how she got in. We had our own house, like everyone back then. I ignored her from that moment on and it hurt because at one point I did love her. Not a fraction to how I love you but enough. That faded eventually and I just saw how weak she was, why she'd never be Luna of my pack. She wasn't deserving of the title and never will be."

"So, she deceived her pack, killed four warriors – one who

was her brother all for… for a fantasy?"

"Yes, but I don't think she meant to kill Jason. We—we searched the car and only three bottles had wolfsbane in, the other didn't. I think she's working with rogues and she had maybe expected him to let you die or she expected the rogues not to kill him. I'm not sure but growing up – Jason was her idol, she adored him. I just can't see her being okay with his death."

"Well, I'm sorry, Thomas, but she's not the woman you loved once, she's evil and will stop at nothing until I'm dead. You need to sort your head out or you'll never be able to do what's needed."

"What's needed?"

"Verity and her mother need to suffer for their actions if you can't see that then maybe you aren't as good an Alpha as you thought."

Shannon stormed out of the room before I had time to process what she meant, she was right I know but the idea of killing one of my oldest friends hurt. I never thought she could do anything like this, ever. If she could do this, what else could she do? I hung my head in my hands, not knowing whether or not to chase after Shannon or visit Skye. I decided to see Skye first, Shannon needed time to calm down before I approached her again.

The walk to the hospital was quiet; since that horrible day everyone had been lost, not knowing what to do with themselves or where to go, we'd gone from a happy pack, going the extra mile for anyone who needed it to depressed, lost, doing the bare minimum – even for ourselves. We needed to get back to normal; find some sort of light at the end of the tunnel. We had hoped that Jade's baby would be the light and then Jason and Skye's trouble twins but even they had darkness surrounding them; there's a chance we're going to lose Jade's pup if it is born too early; if they can hold out another week – even two then the only concern is infection and the trouble twins? Well, Skye hasn't let Doctor Bane check on them since that day; she doesn't talk to anyone, look at anyone, we found her the day after Jason's death trying to drink the wolfsbane at Lori's house. Thankfully, she didn't digest enough to kill her or the twins, just knock her out for a few days. Doctor Bane kept check on her and the twins the entire time, making sure that either her or Kaitlyn was by their side until Skye woke, then they moved her to a more secure ward; assigning Nurse Hilary to her side at all times.

Jade is getting similar treatment now but she's not suicidal, thankfully. I couldn't believe how strong her and her pup were; the crash had hardly impacted her. She was saddened by the death of their guards but not nearly as traumatised as Shannon was, although I guess Jade was unconscious through most of it, she only saw the end when Stefan pulled her out of the car. Thankfully, no one had lasting injuries; we even managed to capture a rogue but he died shortly after, he was quite weak, he told us that the rogues had their own pack house that they use as a safe haven – he didn't say where but I was determined to find out.

I walked into the hospital and the atmosphere changed slightly; despite everything it was cheery in here, everyone's spirits were lifted, it was so nice to see in comparison to what we've felt for the past two weeks. Everyone bowed their heads in respect as I passed them, I smiled at everyone that I could, hopefully offering some positive reassurance as I walked towards Skye's ward.

I walked into Skye's room surprised to see that she was still asleep but then again it was only nine a.m. at the latest. Skye was always a morning person though – it was one thing many envied her for. I walked into her room slowly before I felt a grip on my arm dragging me back into the hallway.

"Alpha, what do you think you're doing?"

"I need to talk to her, Hilary."

"She is in no fit state to speak to anyone and you know that!"

I could see how angry Hilary was but it needed doing; it wasn't right that Jason's body lay rotting in the morgue below the hospital when it should be on its way up to our moon goddess where he could rest peacefully. I stood strong, about to do something I hate doing; use my Alpha authority.

"*Hilary, I order you to stand down and let me talk to Skye, you will not interrupt us, you will leave and only come in when I leave.*"

I watched as she had an inner battle with her wolf; fighting so that she wouldn't have to submit to me but ultimately her wolf won, exposing her neck to me in submission, I took one last look at her before I entered the room, walking over to a sleeping Skye. I gently patted her back until she stirred.

"Skye? It's Thomas, I need to talk to you."

"J-Jason?"

I watched as a flash of both sadness and confusion flashed across her face before she came to her senses and realised who I was.

"Oh, Thomas. You—you're here? W-why?"

"Skye, I know it still hurts but we… we need to say goodbye to him, he needs peace, Skye."

"I know, Tom, but I just can't. I can't accept that he's gone. Please. Please don't make me, I beg you."

I watched as Skye's head fell back into her pillow; drenching it in her tears, silencing her sobs. It broke my heart to see her in such a state but Jason needed a send-off, a proper one.

"Skye, I will make it a hero's funeral, there will be flowers; a bonfire pedestal and I will make it a requirement that every pack member has to attend. You are not alone; you will never be alone again! Your side of the Betas' floor is ready with a fully kitted out nursery."

"You can have the funeral and I will attend but that doesn't mean I have to accept anything; I will go back to our house alone."

"Skye, you know I won't allow that. I made sure to put everything from your house there, I swear anything you need and we will be there."

She rolled over in the bed, no longer facing me I took this as a sign that she wanted me to go now; I couldn't upset her any more, this broke my heart enough. Hilary was straight through the door as I left, looking at me in distaste as she closed the door. Skye didn't deserve any of this, neither did those babies.

Chapter Twenty-Four
The Final Goodbye

Skye

I climbed out of bed for the first time since Thomas visited me, I didn't want to but I knew that I had to, this was my final chance to say goodbye to Jason, my mate, my life, my prince. It's been hard to carry on, even with the pups kicking away inside me reassuringly, I've struggled. I just don't see how it's possible to live without him; from the moment we found out we were mates it was all about him. I only ever looked after myself for him, he was my life support, he was the only thing I could think about until the pups and since his death I'd felt an emptiness, the world seemed grey, there was no colour, no light, it was as if a grey fog clouded my vision preventing me from seeing again.

My whole perception on living has changed; every day I wake up wishing that I hadn't, wishing that me and our pups were with Jason on the other side, I've found myself wishing not only Verity but Lori dead too. Some days I wish that Shannon had died instead which breaks my heart because she has done nothing wrong but find her mate. Shannon and Thomas check in daily on me and the pups; I haven't let Doctor Bane near them since the day Jason died. I know it's wrong but I can't listen to her about their progress when he's not here to listen too. I can't find out what they are when I swore I'd find out with Jason, I still have the folded piece of paper under my pillow – I've never looked at it, it just stays there, waiting to be opened but it never will be because he isn't here.

A knock at the door pulled my attention away from the note only to see Shannon slowly entering the room with a small smile; she wore all black, obviously dressed for the funeral happening later today, the whole pack are ordered to wear black for the rest of the week except for children and babies, out of respect to Jason.

"May I come in, Skye?"

I nodded respectfully towards her; not feeling like saying much to her, I haven't really said much to anyone since I was put on the ward but it didn't matter, nothing mattered any more. I hadn't noticed that Shannon was taking a seat next to me on my bed, I also noticed for the first time she was carrying a few bags.

"Skye, I-I should have brought these to you sooner, I just didn't know the right time if I'm being completely honest – although I suppose there never is. Here, that day we went to the town, Jason picked up some baby bits, he was so excited to give them to you."

She handed me a sort of medium-sized bag with a few little teddies in it and some gorgeous white baby grows, some of the tiniest socks and booties I had ever seen were placed inside a slightly smaller bag. I started tearing up looking at the beautiful little bits he had bought for our twins, he was so thoughtful and kind, even when working he didn't stop thinking of us.

"Th-thank you, Sha—Luna."

"It's okay; I have something else to give you from him as well but, Skye, I need to know that you're ready for it. I don't want to cause you any more grief or pain, but I promised Jason that I would give it to you."

"Did he say anything before he died? I mean you were there, covered in his blood so I assumed you at least spoke."

"He loved you, Skye; you and the pups were the only thing he could think about when he was dying. He asked me to make sure I gave you this."

She handed me a small bag; I noticed my hands were shaking as I took the bag from Shannon. I could feel how nervous I was, this was a gift that Jason used some of his last few breaths to make sure I got. I looked up at Shannon in confusion but she only nodded and placed her hand attentively on my back. With shaky hands I removed the tissue paper from the bag revealing nothing but a small, red velvet box. I took the box out staring at it in confusion, it looked like an engagement box but it couldn't be, we had never discussed marriage or anything like that. In fact, being an orphan myself, he knew it was a prospect that I was uncomfortable with. I opened the box slowly, revealing the most beautiful ring I had ever seen; it was rose gold (he knew that was my favourite) in the centre there was a pink oval diamond surrounded by pure white diamonds I think they were? Maybe pearls, I'm not sure. Around the band there was the same beautiful pink diamonds that were in the centre of the ring; I just stared at it, studying it, wondering why he got me this, did he want to marry me? Is that what this was?

"H-he was going to propose, Skye, he chose it that day in town; he wanted to do it after the Luna ceremony. W-we had it all planned. He chose a tiara because you always say he's your prince so he wanted to make you his princess."

My jaw dropped as tears clouded my vision; I had no words, he was going to propose, he wanted us to get married and live happily ever after. I would have said yes too, I loved him more than I have ever loved anyone; losing him was the hardest thing I've ever had to go through. I took the ring out slowly, studying it, passing it between my fingers before noticing an engraving on the inside. It read, *"Forever and always, my love"*, I wiped the tears cascading down my cheeks before placing it slowly on my finger, I will never take it off for as long as I live. I couldn't help it as I broke down; as if realising for the first time since he died that he won't be coming back, we won't do anything else together again, he will never hold our children or know their gender, he will never be able to propose properly but today we will release him to the moon goddess and let his ashes promote new growth to the earth, his death will not be in vain at least and when we find Verity he will get justice, they all will. Me and Shannon sat there crying together for what felt like an eternity before Nurse Hilary appeared at the door with a black dress and some red roses.

"It's time to get ready, Skye."

I nodded before giving Shannon a hug and watching her leave, I put the black dress on which was quite tight over my ever-growing bump; I looked at my ring proudly before I picked up the roses and, walking up to my bed, pulling the note out from under my pillow, feeling ready, I walked out of the room to where Shannon stood. As broken as I felt, I needed to hold my head high, Jason needed to be put to rest, he deserves nothing but peace in his afterlife until I can join him and give him a massive earful for leaving us so soon. I was surprised to see how many wolves had come to the hospital and made a pathway for us; we walked forward through the crowds, everyone following behind us. Thomas joined us after a while, patting my back reassuringly. We finally reached our stadium and I noticed that there was ivy laced through the biggest bonfire I had ever seen, marigolds surrounded the base of the bonfire as well as scattered across the ground surrounding it, there were all different kinds of roses. I realised that there were words made from flowers at the base of the bonfire; one said '*Friend*', it was made entirely out of yellow roses with what looked like black roses around it, another word said '*Hero*', this one was made of the whitest, purest roses that I had ever seen in my entire life. I stopped in my tracks when I saw the final two words; '*Father*' and '*Mate*' these were made with red roses, the father had white roses as well as a few black ones but the '*Mate*' was just pure red roses, symbolising pure and passionate love which fit perfectly for us. Shannon and Thomas rubbed my back to check that I was okay; I hadn't realised that everyone stopped when I did but I just nodded and carried on walking, I couldn't believe how beautiful the stadium looked. There were tea lights everywhere with Omegas on hand to relight or replace where needed. There were tall candles being handed out too but my hands were full. I walked up to the bonfire; knowing Jason was inside it, ready to be sent up to the moon goddess with the smoke to guide him. I placed the roses against the bonfire before I stood there with my hand and head against the bonfire; wishing for one final moment that it was all a nightmare, that it would end now. I will wake up and be cwtched up with Jason, talking about our babies and our future.

"Hey, Skye. We've got some seats over here, okay?"

I nodded to Shannon who led me towards a few chairs placed carefully away from the bonfire so that it was safe but still personal. I took my seat and watched as everyone took a seat around the stadium. Once everyone took their seats I watched as Thomas made his way slowly towards me.

"Skye, would you like to speak?"

"I—uh—yeah—no—wait, I..." I couldn't speak, I had no idea what to say, tears clouded my vision as I just shook my head at Thomas; staring at the bonfire which held the only goodbye to the only love of my life. I couldn't speak. It still didn't feel real, how can he be here one minute and gone the next?

"Is it okay if I say a few words in your place, Skye?"

I nodded at Thomas, he was Alpha; it made sense for him to say something and not only that, he was one of Jason's friends, it was the reason he trusted him with Shannon so much. He walked closer to the bonfire, asking everyone to be quiet in his Alpha tone, normally I would flinch but I was too depressed to even care.

"*We have come here today to remember a true hero, he was one of our best warriors – recently made an elite but he was also one of the best friends that someone could have, he was loyal, caring and he'd honestly put anyone and everyone above himself. He died doing the most noble thing a wolf can do; protecting his Luna. It is because of this my mate, our Luna is still here. He fought the rogues until his final breath. He wasn't just an elite or a hero though, he was a mate and soon to be a father, he cared about nothing more than his mate and his children – even in his final moments he spoke only of them, they will be celebrated until the end of their days for Jason's sacrifice. He was betrayed by the only family that he had which is horrifying, he worshipped his sister and loved his mother but I want to make this clear now, any kind of betrayal like Jason and our other guards suffered will not go unpunished. I will find Lori and Verity and they will be brought to justice; I will do so for anyone who betrays our pack. We are a family; this never should have happened.*"

I couldn't help the sobs as I listened to everything that Thomas was saying, he only spoke the truth but that didn't make it any easier; he loved his family so much and, in the end, it was their selfishness that caused his demise, he was the best kind of person, he didn't deserve any of it. I had missed the rest of Thomas's speech; only looking up to see an Omega hand him a torch, obviously to light the bonfire with.

"*NOOOO!*"

My screams escaped my mouth before I could stop them; Thomas stopped in his tracks looking at me confused as I approached him, holding my hand out to take the torch.

"A-Alpha, please, m-may I?"

"Are you sure, Skye?"

"Yes, I-I need to."

Thomas nodded at me before giving me the torch and stepping away only slightly; I walked towards the bonfire slowly, everything felt numb, I had no emotions, no more tears to cry, this was it. Goodbye. I stopped at the bonfire, holding my head against the wood, placing one hand gently against it as I spoke.

"I waited for you; you know? I didn't find out our babies' gender, I wanted us to find out together – that night. Shannon, she said you were going to propose, I'm wearing the ring now, you know? I swear to you that I will never take it off, I'll look after our babies and tell them about you every single day until I meet you up there in eternity. I will love you forever and always, Jason, the way you spoke in your sleep, the way you would always shake your hair after a shower as if you were a bloody dog." I chuckled at this memory, remembering how he did it on our first date at the lake and then carried it on every time he showered to make me laugh, that's all he ever did was make me happy. "You will always be my prince but now you take your place with our goddess until we meet again, my love."

I placed the torch gently against the bonfire; watching as the fire slowly made its way around it, I placed the torch inside a small crack on the side of the bonfire. I stepped away, watching the flames dance over the bonfire, smoke slowly rising; I placed my hand in my pocket only to feel something that I had forgotten about, the note. Written in Doctor Bane's handwriting on the top it said, *"Trouble Twins Gender";* for the first time since that day, I considered opening the note and finding out but it was meaningless, I promised that we would find out together and I guess in spirit when they are born we will. I approached the bonfire slowly, aware of the growing flames and I held the note close until a flame had taken hold of it. I threw it onto the bonfire and watched as the flames engulfed the note as well as the bonfire; for the first time since that day I could smile. It felt like a weight had been lifted, for the first time since I last woke up next to Jason, I felt warm – I didn't feel cold or empty. The bonfire finally offered a light through the darkness I had sat in recently, I felt warm, the cloud finally lifting.

Chapter Twenty-Five
The Luna Ceremony

Shannon

I hated having the Luna ceremony so close to Jason's funeral but Thomas said we had already wasted enough time, not that it was wasted; we have had more than enough going on in recent weeks to justify waiting but 'it doesn't work like that' as Thomas keeps reminding me. Jade came running into the room with a few bags which was the last thing that I expected if I'm being totally honest.

"Jade? What? You should be in bed!" I ran over to Jade practically dragging her to my favourite chair.

"Last time I checked it was pack law that every single pack member had to attend! Especially the Betas!"

"Not when said Beta has been ordered to bed rest by Doctor Bane! She's going to flip her lid when she sees that you have gone."

"Come on, Shannon, let loose, have fun! It's your Luna ceremony; your best friend should be here! Bedrest or not, I refuse to stay away."

"Fine, as long as you sit down through it all okay?"

"Yes, sir!" she held her hand to her forehead as if saluting me when she spoke; I knew that there was no use in arguing it but I could at least make it look like I was, so that she would take it easy. We started getting ready together; doing our own hair and make-up, it was the first time I'd had fun since before Jason died;

it felt good. Just as we finished getting ready I heard shouting in the hallway before Thomas and Stefan forced themselves through the door.

"Hey, Shan, have you see—"

Thomas didn't finish his sentence before he was looking at Jade; they were both red and out of breath, they must have been out looking for her all this time.

"What the hell do you two think you're doing? Jade, you are supposed to be on bedrest for the sake of both you and *our baby*! Do you think this is a joke? Doctor Bane said no to attending the ceremony! Shannon, why didn't you mind link one of us?"

I had never seen Stefan so angry before, I didn't know what to say; I chose to ignore my battle with Jade but never expected one with Stefan! He's always so kind, patient, I've honestly never known him to be like this; I went to defend Jade but she spoke first, she was so calm it was weird, surely, she should be scared of Stefan too? Or at least, nervous!

"Are you saying I think our baby's safety isn't my biggest priority here, babe?"

Oh gosh; it was a trap, I watched as he went to answer her, but there was nothing he could say that wouldn't go south at this point, she's pregnant, hormonal and he just insulted her. Did I sit back and watch the fireworks or did I help?

"Obviously not if you're sat here doing your make-up."

Oh crap; I was too late! Thomas may as well start planning *his* funeral at this point.

"*I have been laid in that hospital bed for over a week now, I missed Jason's funeral yesterday for the exact same reason you want me to miss out now! Don't you ever question my priorities or you won't be one of them; I am doing my duty as not only a Beta but as a best friend right now and if you don't like it go have pups with an obedient bitch because you are not the boss of me and neither is Doctor Bane, okay?"*

I looked between them both, waiting to see if Stefan would answer back; at this point I wished that I had popcorn. I could see Thomas smirking in the corner of my eye, he was thinking the same as me.

"So, if you're both finished stressing me out, I would appreciate it if you left so we could get changed, the Luna ceremony is in an hour after all."

She pushed the two men out of the bedroom before they had the chance to object; locking the door behind them she approached the bed, lying down on it.

"Why do men just expect us to sit around and make babies all day? I'm done, I know I should be in the hospital but I'm going crazy; I need some form of normality."

"I know what you mean, Jade, but I just don't think you went the right way about all of this, you should have at least told Stefan, he's your mate. I thought that was the biggest thing ever?"

"It is, it always has been. It's just since the crash, Stefan is different, clingier, he watches over me constantly and I can't live like it. I don't even have my wolf at the moment, I feel so vulnerable and his shadowing doesn't help."

"Why don't you have your wolf at the moment? I didn't realise she could leave?" I walked over to the bed placing my hand attentively onto hers for comfort, I thought your wolf stayed with you until death? I guess there's a lot I still didn't know.

"Since the day of the crash she has put all her energy, her life-force into protecting our pup, at this point in time I may as well be human like you."

"I didn't know that your wolf could do that."

"Yeah, it's kind of like a life support in times of need; so you said when Jason passed you saw his wolf die first, right?"

I nodded, feeling my heart stop at the memory. It was what I saw most nights lately; Jason dying, the crash, I relived it every night on a continuous loop.

"Well, usually the human part of us dies first because of how strong our wolves are but J-Jason's wolf transferred whatever strength and energy he had to try and give Jason a chance; if Jason had survived, he would have been human. His wolf basically sacrificed himself for Jason."

I couldn't believe what I was hearing, what a noble thing for a wolf to do; I couldn't believe it.

"Jade, what will happen to Skye now? Would she have known he was dying?"

"Yes, I suppose you could say it's a curse in some ways. We feel everything our mate feels; I don't know if you will because of being human but Thomas will for sure. She probably would have felt everything, as did Scott, Luke and Ryan's mates. All we can hope now is that they get a second chance mate, I guess."

"A second chance mate?"

"Yes, it's rare but it does happen. Sometimes straight away, sometimes years, I'm not sure we've had one in this pack because I only moved here when I found Stefan but there definitely hasn't been one whilst I've been here. Anyway, let's get dressed, we have ten minutes."

Jade hopped off the bed, running over to my closet and grabbing the dress I chose for my Luna ceremony; it was a white dress, Thomas said it was tradition for the Luna to wear white so I didn't question it. It had spaghetti straps with a v-line bodice. It was fitted around the bodice with a corset in the back, the skirt of the dress was silk and flowy, making it easy to move in. My hair was curled and braided with white pearls cascading through it. I couldn't believe it; I looked like a princess. Even after everything that has happened I realised for the first time, this was the happiest I've been in years, after my mam left I felt so alone, dad was nowhere to be seen, I had so much to do for me and the girls that I never really had chance to breathe. If only I could go back and tell myself how much better things would get, I shed a tear as I thought about the nights I cried myself to sleep hoping to be happy again. Well, here it is. I'm finally happy.

Jade put her dress on; it was a pale pink, knee length dress that fitted her massive bump like a glove.

"You look amazing, Shan!"

Jade was squealing in excitement; typical Jade, she's always happy and excited.

"So do you! You're practically glowing."

We walked out of the bedroom where we found Thomas and Stefan sat on the settee, looking so smart. Thomas in a black suit, white shirt and black tie; Stefan wearing a deep blue suit and tie, paired with a white shirt. I stood there for a moment, staring at my drop dead gorgeous mate. He excites me like no one ever has, I want him more than I've ever wanted anyone, I will thank the moon goddess every day for giving me him. I watched their jaws drop as they notice us stood there, Stefan catwhistled but my eyes were focused on Thomas who looked like he'd just won the lottery.

"Well, don't you two scrub up well?"

"You'll catch flies if you keep your mouths open any longer."

Me and Jade chuckled at each other as we waited for the men to wake up from their shock. We decided to walk towards the door when they were finally brought back to reality.

"Wait, girls, Shannon, I want to ask you something."

I turned around, walking back to Thomas; I watched as he bent over, getting down on one knee and pulling something out of his jacket. My heart started beating a million times a minute as I realised what he was doing, my eyes started to well up and I could feel my excitement building. He was going to propose! This was the last thing I ever expected but I couldn't be happier, that is, until I realised that Jason was going to propose the night of the Luna ceremony and I know I shouldn't but I couldn't help it as I felt my heart shatter.

"Shannon, I've loved you ev—"

"Thomas, please don't. It's too much, too soon. It's disrespectful to Jason's memory as well, he was going to propose the night of the Luna ceremony."

I watched as hurt spread across his face and I couldn't help but feel guilty so I held my hand out, hoping that he would take it and he did.

"Thomas, this isn't a 'no forever'; it's just a 'not right now'. We have so many things to look forward to going forward, I don't want this one thing clouded by it, okay? I love you more than anything in this world, never doubt that."

Thomas nodded, a smile spreading across his gorgeous face. We walked down the stairs and outside, I was surprised to see that there was a red carpet illuminated by these spotlights either side of it leading into the woods.

"What's all this, Thomas?"

"It's a special night, you deserve the royal treatment."

I smiled at him before linking our arms and walking along the red carpet, we weren't walking long before we came to the meadow; the one where I first met Atticus, where me and Thomas finally mated, where he marked me. It has easily become my favourite place in the world.

There were rows of chairs as far as I could see, all centred around an arch; the arch was beautiful, there were flowers surrounding it and all over it, there were fairy lights snaked around the arch, illuminating it beautifully. There were small fire pits around the field so that everyone was warm and there was some light other than moonlight. I walked through the aisle, smiling at each pack member as I passed them, there were even some children here that would stop me for a hug or to give me a flower, I was so lucky to have been welcomed so much. I could feel myself swelling with pride as I passed each pack member, they weren't bothered by the fact that I was human anymore, they weren't bothered by the fact I had caused so much heart break in the little time I'd been here. They were just happy that I was here and that I was their Luna, I'm so excited to spend the rest of my life making their life as comfortable and happy as I can.

"Are you ready, my love? The moon is at its peak, it's now or never."

"Yes, I'm more than ready."

We approached the arch when I noticed that there was an older woman standing under it.

"Shannon, normally this ceremony is conducted by the previous Alpha and Luna but since they have passed on, it falls on the remaining wolf of the previous leaders; I'd like you to meet one of my father's Betas, Kath."

I smiled politely at the woman before me, I remember vaguely Thomas said that his parents and their next in charge were killed visiting another pack so I was surprised to see her here. I couldn't help but feel the utmost respect for the strong lady in front of me, I can't imagine how soul destroying it is to not only lose your mate but your only friends too.

"It's a pleasure to meet you, Luna, we must get on though.

You will need to accept each other first."

Thomas took my hands, looking deep into my eyes.

"I, Thomas Cannon, son of Sebastian Cannon and Florence Cannon, Alpha to Forest Lake, accept you, Shannon Rye, as my mate, my Luna, my everything."

"I, Shannon Rye, daughter of Emilia Rye, human, accept you, Thomas Cannon, as my mate, my alpha, my everything."

You could feel our bond was stronger than ever by the time I had finished, his energy coursing through my veins, it was as if I was finally complete after years of not realising how empty I was. I could feel my smile get bigger and bigger as I felt everything slot into place, it was like when I drank the potion only better, more pleasurable.

"Fab, now if I could have your attention again."

I nodded, stepping forward and taking Kath's hands as directed.

"Do you, Shannon Rye, agree to protect not only the Alpha but the pack in a time of crisis?"

"I do."

"Do you swear to put the pack and its members first, at all times, to only do what you believe is in the pack's best interest?"

"I do."

"Lastly, do you promise to be fair and neutral at all times, never letting your emotions cloud your judgement?"

"I do."

"So normally now you would both shift and Atticus would mark you but seeing as you don't have a wolf, we will have Atticus come forward alone and mark you, okay? This may hurt though."

"But Thomas has already marked me?"

"This is a different mark, I'm afraid, lovely. This has to be from his wolf alone, for it is his wolf that has the Alpha power."

She nodded at Thomas, I watched as his eyes turned black for a few seconds which I've learned is what happens as their wolves take control but then his eyes were back to brown like before.

"A-Atticus? Is that you?"

"Yes, my sweet Luna."

A grin formed across his face, it made me feel uncomfortable more than anything. He had a different aura to Thomas, it was strange. He approached me slowly, tracing his hand over where Thomas had marked me, sending sparks shooting through me straight to my core. He then stroked the other side of my neck, directly opposite to where Thomas had marked me; I watched as Thomas' face started to change, as if he was shifting but just his jaws. I didn't know he could do that! I watched in horror as his canines grew longer and he sunk his teeth into my shoulder slowly. I screamed as I could feel the pain radiating from his bite until eventually, he was in all the way, sending the most intoxicating wave of pleasure I've ever felt through my body, it felt even better than when Thomas marked me. My legs grew weak as the warmth radiated through my body, overwhelming all of my senses, it was the best thing I had ever felt, I lost my balance but luckily Atticus caught me, leaning down only to lick the blood off my neck.

"You taste so good, my little Luna, smell good too…"

I blushed, realising everyone here could probably smell my arousal from the marking, I watched as his eyes went brown again, showing me that Thomas was taking full control.

"You're glowing, my love."

"I feel amazing."

Sure enough, I looked down and I was in fact glowing, I

could feel the power radiating from me, I could feel my connection to the pack strengthening, over nine hundred different links moving into my mind at once, my head pounding. I could feel my senses heightened, I was stronger, more alert, I felt in control.

I looked up, realising for the first time that not only was Thomas crying with happiness but everyone had erupted into applause, stood up in their chairs you could hear the cheers from every pack member; happy to have a Luna finally, they didn't care that I was human, they just cared that I was finally here. I can do this; I will do this! For every single pack member here beaming proudly.

Chapter Twenty-Six
Is It a Blessing or a Curse?

Thomas

I walked hand in hand with my angel. I couldn't stop smiling the whole way; it didn't feel real, I didn't even care that she rejected my wedding proposal, she was still going to be mine forever, regardless of marriage. At one point I thought that she would reject me and I would have to take some random chosen mate, I honestly couldn't imagine anyone on my arm or running the pack by my side. She really is the only one for me.

We entered the pack house excitedly; I was in awe of how beautiful our ball room looked; our Omegas really were talented. There were bouquets of white and pink roses in a vase on each table, the chairs were covered in a white cloth with a pink ribbon tied neatly to it, there were fairy lights laced like stars across the ceiling; it really did look spectacular. I noticed Shannon gasp beside me and I couldn't help but smile.

I put my arm around her and guided her towards the front of the ballroom where we had a small stage set up with six chairs; two in the middle for the Alpha and Luna then the two on the left for Stefan and Jade – our Betas, the two on the right would have been for my Gamma Luke and his mate Charlotte but he was obviously poisoned by Verity so we have it there for Charlotte and Skye. Charlotte is still my Gamma and will be for as long as she wants to, unless she chooses to step down, but Skye, I felt that she deserved a spot up there in Jason's place.

There was a flower wall placed delicately behind us; it was Jade's idea and I loved it, hopefully Shannon did too! We sat in our seats; I hardly had a chance to say two words to Shannon before she was inundated with pack members wanting to meet her, talk to her, I was so happy that they weren't bothered by her being human – they love her as she is. I watched as her father walked over and behind the table, wrapping his arms around Shannon and giving her a fatherly hug.

"I know I'm not your biological father but I don't think even he could be prouder of you than I am; you are one of the strongest, most resilient and kindest young women I have ever met. I wish your mother was here to see what an amazing woman you have become."

"You will always be my dad, blood or not."

I could see the tears falling from David's cheeks as he embraced Shannon, when all of a sudden, the mood changed; his eyes turned black, his nostrils flared, he searched the room frantically when he stopped, confusion and horror spread across his face. I followed his line of sight as soon as he spoke. I couldn't believe what was happening.

"Mate."

David whispered as he stared at a poor heavily pregnant Skye that had finally arrived, she too had stopped in her tracks, eyes black as ebony as she looked upon David. Tears cascaded on her cheeks as she looked at him, there was no emotion in her face, at most she looked numb. David let go of Shannon and started to run for Skye, he was almost there when Stefan managed to grab him, I hadn't even thought to grab him; I was still in shock. Skye was awarded a second chance mate; but it was too soon, surely?

"Thomas, what's happening?"

I looked up only to see Shannon looking as confused as the day we told her we were wolves.

David

I walked towards the stage where the alpha always sat, I didn't make the Luna ceremony in time; I've been scouting the past week, searching for Lori and Verity, how they have managed to stay completely off the grid, I will never know! As for the safe house we keep hearing about for the rogues, I can't find that either, we've asked every pack in the country but no-one has any information to give.

I can't believe how beautiful Shannon looked tonight, she really had grown up; I remember the first day Emilia introduced us and wow, I knew instantly that she was born to be my daughter, she was the craziest toddler I had ever met, I hated the idea of her living among wolves which was when we came up with the idea of the town. Of course, I know now that she really was always destined to live among us, heck, she was going to rule over us and I honestly couldn't think of anyone I would rather tie my loyalties to. The girls were ecstatic too, they've always hated lying to her but we all knew it was for the best overall. I planned to send her to England for university so that she wouldn't have to be around the girls going through their transformation eventually but that won't be necessary now; she wanted to be our Luna, Thomas' mate, everything ended for the best.

I walked onto the stage and pulled Shannon into the tightest hug I could muster, I was so lucky to have her as a daughter; she's put up with so much and always just gotten on with it, no complaints. She deserves a happy ever after.

"I know I'm not your biological father but I don't think even he could be prouder of you than I am; you are one of the strongest, most resilient and kindest young women I have ever met. I wish your mother was here to see what an amazing woman you have become."

My vision was blurry when I spoke; it was tears of joy and sadness, I was sad because my baby girl was growing up, she was no longer that feisty, crazy two-year-old jumping around the den; she was a strong, independent and remarkable woman who was going to do wonderful things with her life.

"You will always be my dad, blood or not."

That was all I needed to let the tears turn into a waterfall, she was definitely the best woman in the world, I had no doubt. I hugged Shannon a little tighter when all of a sudden, the air grew cold, the door must have been opened because there was a gust of wind; it was likely a late comer to the party – this was to be expected but what I didn't expect was the most amazing smell to fill the air, inviting me to try it, already sending a craving through my body. My wolf was going bonkers in my mind fighting for control; the scent of mint and vanilla making my head swirl, I looked up, trying to find the owner of this intoxicating smell. It was only when my eyes met with hers, I realised how horrific this could be; it was Skye, Jason's Skye! She was my mate, I was her second chance mate, in my moment of apprehension Chase took control fully, saying only one word before running after her.

"Mate."

I honestly couldn't have wished for a better mate than Skye; she was so beautiful, although she was twelve years younger than me but age is just a number, right? That wasn't what mattered here though it was the fact that she had only just buried her first mate yesterday, the last thing I'm sure she wanted was a second chance mate! Yet, here I was unable to pull my wolf back because we'd waited twenty-four years for this moment, he wanted it so bad that he wasn't giving up without a fight and quite frankly neither was I! Whether I had to wait six months or six years, we would be together; I would worship her. Before Chase got too close, Beta Stefan had managed to grab us and pin us down, Chase was fighting it but Stefan was stronger so there was no point; he pinned me to the floor of the ballroom and I watched as Skye ran out of the ballroom, sobbing uncontrollably, I could only pray that she didn't reject me, I wouldn't let her.

Skye

"Come on, Skye, hunny, you're going to be late; you've already missed the ceremony – you can't miss the party too."

Nurse Hilary had been trying to get me out of my room for the past two hours, I know it's a requirement for every pack member to be at the ceremony but I just couldn't. Knowing that Jason was going to propose at the Luna ceremony, Shannon – she was going to help him, it still hurt. It got easier after we sent him to the moon goddess but it still hurt a lot, I stared down at my ring for the what must be one hundredth time today… I looked at Nurse Hilary and realised I wasn't going to win this argument so I stood up and walked towards the door, completely ignoring the dress that Hilary had picked up for me to wear. I only had to go, I didn't have to make an effort or want to be there, now that I was in the pack house at least it was only a case of heading down the stairs; Nurse Hilary followed me quietly like the shadow I never wanted, she's assigned to stay with me until I have the pups and feel better in myself. They still think I'll run off and kill myself. I'm not in that place any more. I can remember the pain, the emptiness, I wanted to be free from everything that was keeping me here, join Jason with the moon goddess for eternity but now; I know it's not what I need and it's not what my pups need either. I was going to live – even if just for them, I know it's what Jason would have wanted. I noticed the front doors were left open, letting in an awfully cold draft; I walked towards the big double doors for the ballroom, surprised to see them closed – they hardly ever close these doors. I opened the door, no doubt sending a draft through as I did, I looked around the room; noticing how beautiful the room looked, I think it was the prettiest it had ever looked if I'm being honest, I walked towards the stage knowing that the first thing I had to do was congratulate the new Luna – it was pack tradition after all. I started crossing the ballroom floor when a strong scent hit my nose, it was intoxicating, my wolf started howling in my head, it was the first time I'd heard from her since Jason's death.

"Mate."

This is the only thing she has said to me since Jason's death and it sent me into a state of shock, stopping where I was, searching the room until I found him, a gorgeous man stood behind Shannon, staring into his ebony eyes as he watched me, a look of both horror and confusion spreading across his face. I realised who it was; Shannon's father, Head Guard, I was his true mate all along? But, how? Does that mean Jason was always destined to die? That, that our love was nothing? How can he love me, love my children, knowing that they aren't his? What's his name? Daniel? Dylan? Dave? Damon? I'm not sure, we've not even been properly introduced, the only time I've heard about him is when Jason said he was going to train him as Head Guard and the odd occasion Shannon spoke of him. I watched as he ran towards me, I couldn't move due to the shock and my wolf taking over but I'm not sure she knew what to do either as we watched him coming closer and closer, I watched in horror as Beta Stefan tackled my mate to the floor; it was painful to watch but it was needed to help me take control and sprint out of the ballroom, straight up the stairs and back into my room on the Betas' floor.

I crawled into my bed, pulling the covers over my head, clutching my bump protectively as I cried into my pillow; not sure how to process the events of tonight, I heard the door open and expected nothing less than Hilary to walk in and check on me but the voice wasn't that of Hilary, it was Shannon's.

"Skye, may I come in?"

I couldn't bring myself to answer her, I was too emotional after the events of today; I didn't know what to say or what to do, I'm not even sure how to feel about it, I feel guilty for being happy, for being pulled to this new man when we only buried the love of my life yesterday near enough! How was this fair? Why can't I grieve properly? But now my pain, my emptiness; it's gone, I should be happy about that, I should be overjoyed to feel something other than what I have been! It feels so wrong though, it's this damn mate bond, it changes your thoughts, your feelings and I know it's not his fault but it just… it feels so wrong.

"Skye, I'm going to come in. I don't feel like you should be alone, that was such a big shock for everyone. How are you feeling?"

I wiped my eyes and slowly lifted myself out from under my sheets, sitting up next to Shannon who had placed herself on the edge of my bed, I still couldn't bring myself to say anything; I just finished wiping my tears off my already soaked face, trying to make myself presentable in front of my new Luna.

"Skye, I've heard that only the best wolves get second chance mates. You deserve one more than anyone, I know my dad – he's waited his whole life for you; he will wait until you're ready for him, I know he will."

"B-but that's the thing, L-L-Luna, I love him, the moment I smelt his scent, looked at him, I-I couldn't think of anyone or anything else and that's when it hit me how wrong it was. I said goodbye to my prince, what? Two days ago? And now I'm already in love with someone else because of that stupid mate bond! Jason deserves better than that, I've betrayed him and his memory, I don't deserve a second chance mate, your dad – even my twins deserve better."

"Skye, please tell me you don't believe that?"

"I do, Luna, so should you, so should your dad, so should everyone!"

"But, Skye, we know that's not how the moon goddess works, maybe she saw your suffering and gave you this gift because you didn't deserve the pain that you've been put through. I will never believe that, neither should you and I refuse to let anyone else believe that."

"B-but, Luna—"

"Stop with the Luna, I've told you multiple times it's Shannon, you don't have to accept him but I know that he will look after you, the trouble twins too. Please, Skye, give him a chance, you both deserve to be happy after everything."

I sat there thinking about everything that Shannon had said, knowing full well that she was right; the moon goddess wouldn't have given me a second chance mate for no reason, she wouldn't have paired us if he wasn't willing to accept us. I nodded at Shannon, I was still apprehensive but the least I could do was give him a chance to either accept or reject me.

"Okay, Shannon, but this is on my terms. I won't see him until I'm ready and tonight I am not; may I contact you when I am ready to see him?"

"Of course, Skye, I want you to be as comfortable as you can be. This is all on your terms, I will make sure that he knows to stay away until you're ready."

"Thank you, Shannon, it means a lot that you care so much. I need to sleep right now though, I would appreciate it if you would leave now, go enjoy the rest of your party."

"Okay, Skye, but know; I am here any time you need me, day or night. So is Thomas and so are any of us."

"I know, thank you. I wouldn't have survived the last few weeks without the pack."

Shannon nodded and I watched as she left the room closing the door behind her, I climbed under my sheets again, cwtching my pillow and welcoming the darkness that sleep brought me. I was glad to see the night end.

Chapter Twenty-Seven
A Shocking Revelation

Shannon

I was walking down the stairs, back to the party, my party, where I knew my dad and everyone else was waiting to hear how poor Skye was feeling, I honestly had no words; I mean it was amazing that she had gotten a second chance mate but seeing how torn up she was about it just proved it was too soon and my dad, my poor dad, he's searched for his mate for twenty-four years and now he has her, his wolf is going crazy at the fact that they have yet to mark her, make her theirs. He understands though and I know he'll understand when I tell him she wants space, he doesn't really have much of a choice though, but at least she isn't rejecting him! That's a big win for him, I'm not even sure how I would feel if Thomas died and then another wolf tried to claim me; it would feel wrong.

Walking into the ballroom I was surprised to see my dad still pinned by Stefan but also a guard holding down each of his limbs, Thomas just stood there watching.

"*What is going on in here? Let go of him!*"

I couldn't help but get angry seeing my dad in such a state, his wolf was still in control but he was visibly calmer.

"*Chase, give my father back control.*"

I watched as my dad's eyes changed back to his usual brown colour, I was surprised that he listened, wolves are quite reluctant to listen to anyone except for their Alpha. My attention was drawn away from my dad by an arm snaking its way around my shoulders, I looked up to see Thomas beaming proudly, but why?

"You used your Luna voice. That was impressive."

"My Luna voice?"

"Yeah, so you know when you're young and your mom has that one tone of voice that lets you know you're in trouble?"

"Erm, I guess."

"Well, as a Luna, you have one too and it will help with your authority over the other wolves. I wasn't sure whether you would still have one being human but you do and that's why Chase submitted to you."

"Oh."

I turned my attention back to my dad; this was a conversation that me and Thomas could have later, right now, my dad needed me. I moved out of Thomas' grasp and approached my dad, wrapping my arms around him to give him a hug that I knew he probably needed right now.

"H-how is Skye?"

"She's okay, she's at war with herself. She needs time, Dad, she's not rejecting you though, she's actually happy; which is why she's at war with herself, discovering she was mates with you removed any pain and emptiness she felt from losing Jason, she feels guilty."

"I understand, I couldn't believe it, after all this time; we have a mate. I know me and Chase lost control and it won't happen again but can we see her?"

"No, she needs time. Let her come to you, okay?"

"Okay, I-I'm going to go home, okay?"

"That's fine, we're going to end the party here anyway."

"Are you sure, my angel?" I had almost forgotten Thomas was here until he spoke. I waved goodbye to my dad and helped dismiss everyone, even the Omegas; it was nearly five a.m., they didn't deserve to be up tidying when they would be up in a few hours. Thomas told them to just come in when they were ready so that they could get as much sleep as they needed. I knew I could sleep for a week.

We walked up to our room hand in hand, I couldn't wait to get to bed it had been such a long day; I had a quick wash and changed into some comfy pjs before I climbed into bed and welcomed sleep.

I woke the next morning only to find Thomas wasn't in our bed, I had no idea where he had gone, we said we'd spend today together, just us; I could feel the hurt building as I questioned myself as to his whereabouts. I finally gave up fighting my curiosity and climbed out of bed, heading towards our living area when I saw Thomas leaving the kitchen with two plates of food, there was a whole host of smells associated with these two plates but the one that stood out most was the eggs? As soon as the smell invaded my senses a wave of nausea overcame me, sending me straight to the toilet to vomit. Bringing up everything that I had eaten last night. Thomas was by my side trying to talk to me and rub my back but I just couldn't stop being sick long enough to pay attention; when I finally finished, I got up off the floor and headed to the sink, washing the sick residue off my mouth, trying to calm my now red and puffy face, my eyes were also puffy from crying during vomiting. I brushed my teeth quickly and headed straight back to bed, there was no way I was getting up after that.

"Are you okay, babe?"

"Yeah, I'm just tired. Sorry, I'm not sure what came over me but those eggs smelt awful, were they bad?"

"Well, I mean, they smelt fine to me, I swear, but I'll definitely go throw them out now."

It wasn't long before Thomas came back with some water for me and some crackers, he climbed into bed and decided to cwtch up with me, breathing in my scent as he did.

"Do you want me to get Doctor Bane or Kaitlyn to come over and take a look at you?"

"No, Thomas, they have better stuff to do. It's likely just a bug. I'll stay in bed and sleep it off."

"Are you sure?"

"Yes, I just want to sleep." I buried my head into his chest, thankfully he had no objections towards us sleeping in bed all day, it wasn't long before I fell asleep again. My dreams were quite vivid, it was like I was living through the night Jason died again except this time it was Thomas and I kept thinking about how our baby would have to grow up without him. I would have to raise them as a wolf when realistically I had no idea what I was doing as a Luna, never mind training an Alpha.

This was my routine for the next two weeks, unable to keep anything at all down, I'd lost half a stone when I finally agreed to go see Doctor Bane.

"Alpha, Luna."

Doctor Bane nodded at us respectfully as we entered the Alpha suite, a place I hadn't been since I woke up after our mating, it was weird coming here conscious considering I usually just wake up here. I sat on the bed as Doctor Bane directed me to, for the first time ever I was able to look at the room properly. The walls were a bright white, with even brighter ceiling panels, there was a huge floor to ceiling window to the left of the bed. Royal blue curtains draped either side of the window, outside the window all you could see was the never ending forest, the light bounced off the leaves perfectly, lighting them up like green beacons. It was beautiful.

"So Alpha says that you're struggling to keep things down, Luna, is that right?"

"Yeah, it's been, I guess, two weeks since it started; I thought it was a bug but it just hasn't gone away."

"Okay, well do you mind if I take some bloods so we can run some tests, check how hydrated you are and check your iron levels."

"No, go ahead."

Doctor Bane pulled out a sterile tray prepared with tubes, cables and needles, she walked over towards me and sat next to me, placing a stretchy thing around my arm.

"This will be a sharp scratch, okay?"

I nodded, I didn't want to watch as she put the needle into my arm, I could feel myself getting queasy again at the thought. It took maybe three attempts before she found a good enough vein, they kept collapsing apparently. Although I wasn't sure what that meant.

"Shannon, you are quite dehydrated. Do you mind if I put an IV in so that we can get some fluids into you?"

"No, go ahead, whatever you think is best."

I watched as Doctor Bane prepared everything and put the IV into my arm before sitting comfortably back in the desk chair, writing some notes in her book.

"Okay, Shannon, when was your last period?"

It was as if something in my mind clicked when she asked this, I actually wasn't sure when my last period was. I had one before the rogue attack but haven't had one since, between everything that was going on it hadn't even crossed my mind.

"Oh, I don't remember, maybe the week before the rogue attack?"

"Okay, let me just get Kaitlyn in to see if she can see what's going on."

Her eyes fogged over, mind linking Kaitlyn. I looked over at Thomas who looked just as confused as me, was he thinking what I was thinking? Could I be pregnant? Or something worse? Kaitlyn came in rather flustered, dragging an ultrasound machine behind her, she stopped abruptly when she saw that we were in the room; I hadn't seen her since the day she wasn't able to read me so I wasn't sure how she felt about seeing us but her smile and respectful nod assured me she wasn't angry at least. I felt bad thinking back to that day, she looked so defeated when she couldn't get a reading from me.

"Luna, Alpha. Doctor Bane, I brought the machine for you as well, just in case."

"Thank you, Kaitlyn, that was very smart. Now, Luna, if you lie down Kaitlyn can examine you."

I lay down, exposing my stomach as I did so, I watched as Kaitlyn's hands were placed on top of my stomach, glowing as she hummed like the last time; I watched as the same mix of confusion and frustration spread across her face, which already told me that she wasn't able to read me.

"I-I couldn't do it, I'm sorry."

"It's okay, Kaitlyn, I suspected as much. That's why it's good that you brought the machine; I am curious though as to why she can't read you, I could heal you fine but as for reading you it was trickier."

"What do you mean?"

"Well," Doctor Bane was moving wires and the machine around whilst she spoke, setting it up. "When we read someone it's kind of like an X-ray machine in our mind, it doesn't allow us to see everything but can at least pinpoint some causes, so when a wolf is pregnant we don't necessarily see the baby but we can see the outline of it sort of thing, see it growing, even hear its heartbeat on some occasions whereas you, we can't read you at all. It's just… blank. This is going to be cold, okay?"

I nodded as Doctor Bane placed the cold gel on my lower stomach moving the probe around, looking for anything that could indicate pregnancy I'm guessing; the large smile that spread across her face told me what I needed to know before she had even spoke.

"Congratulations, it looks like you finally have your heir."

"So, I'm pregnant? But—but we only had sex once? I mean surely that's not right."

"Luna, with all due respect; it only takes once, and Thomas being Alpha your bodies are more inclined to be more fertile to accommodate creating an heir. Here listen, a strong heartbeat and everything looks completely healthy, you're around ten to eleven weeks which I assume would mean this is going to be a human pregnancy."

"S-so my baby won't be a wolf?"

"No, it will more than likely be a wolf. You see the wolf genes are the most dominant; that's also why Clara and Emily are wolves, your mother too went through the normal gestation for a human, I will get you some vitamins and see what anti-sickness stuff we have, okay?"

I nodded as Doctor Bane handed me a picture from the ultrasound, it looked strange, I mean it did have the outline of a baby I guess, just not as prominent. I wasn't sure how to feel; I'm not even eighteen for another week, yet here I was, eleven weeks pregnant, a Luna to a pack of wolves that I didn't know existed a few weeks ago. Why does everything keep changing? I've just gotten over the shock of werewolves, starting to get used to the idea of being a Luna but once again it's all changed and now, I'm having a baby on top of it. I looked over at Thomas to see the biggest smile spread across his face as he looked between me and the scan picture, you could see how excited he was, why didn't I feel the same? A baby is such an amazing thing, right?

"I can't believe it, babe; we're going to be parents! You're going to be such an amazing mum; I know you will! We will have to announce it straight away!"

"Uh, yeah. Of course, if that's what you want my love."

I watched as Thomas ran out of the room excitedly, probably on his way to tell Stefan like he does with everything; I've never known men to gossip until I met these two, it's cute how close they are though, I'm glad he has him. I won't ruin his excitement; I'll act excited too. I mean if I act excited enough, I'll get excited eventually, right? Right now though, all I wanted to do was cry. A baby was the last thing we needed with everything that was going on right now; Verity and Lori were still after me, I was still adjusting to being a Luna, I don't know how to be a mum on top of all that! I couldn't stop the tears as they started to fall, I know we'll get through this but right now all I felt was… hopeless.

Chapter Twenty-Eight
The Great Escape

Verity

We were forced into our room by the small man named Sirus, it was a small room with one of the smallest double beds I've ever seen. I fell to the floor beside my mate, he was so handsome but also weak, he's clearly been malnourished and beaten to keep him submissive otherwise he would be able to fight against them. I untied the rope that was cutting into his wrists, noticing the bruises and burns from it, it was laced with wolfsbane, I didn't care, I needed to get it away from him; he'd had six years of suffering, I wasn't about to let him have any more.

"M-m-mate," Malaki whispered as he rolled over to look at me, his gorgeous sapphire eyes melting my heart with just one look.

"Yes, my sweetness. Let's get you up off the floor."

I helped pull him up away from the floor and onto the small bed that had been placed there; I noticed a small bathroom to the right of the room so I walked over to it only to find no cloths, instead I ripped a section of my top off and ran it under the warm water before returning to my sweet mate, cleaning some of the dirt off his face, then his wrists and anywhere else that needed cleaning that I could see.

"I-I'm sorry, I lost interest in personal hygiene around two years ago. I'm surprised that I'm still alive if I'm honest, I thought for years my pack would find me but they never have.

My sister probably found a mate and they used them for Alpha instead, suppose it would make sense she was nearly eighteen when I was taken anyway."

"You have a sister? What's her name?"

I couldn't help but feel like I needed to know more; I wanted to know everything about his life, I knew he was from Ireland but not much more than that obviously.

"You're from Ireland, right?"

"Uh, yeah. From the Mountain Ridge pack, it's on the north side."

Mountain Ridge pack? Where have I heard that name before? There's only one pack I had ever heard of from Ireland and that was Alice's, but it couldn't be... could it?

"Malaki, what is your sister's name?"

"Alice, Alice Ridge."

I gasped at this small revelation, he didn't know all this time, he's waited for his pack and his family to come rescue him, not knowing that they were no more. I didn't even know that Alice had a brother; I don't think even Thomas knew.

"Malaki, I've met your sister."

"What? When? How?"

"Malaki... your pack is... no more. They were attacked by werewolf hunters around seven years ago, my guess is around the time you were kidnapped. My frien—alpha, Thomas, he saved her from rogues a year after your pack fell. She is Luna of Crimson Rock pack now."

"So, my parents, my friends, everyone – they're gone?"

"I'm sorry, Malaki, I'm so sorry."

I watched as my mate curled up into a ball, cradling the thin sheets I assumed were meant to be pillows; it broke my heart, he didn't deserve this, he didn't deserve any of this.

"Malaki, how old were you when you were taken?"

"Twelve."

That would make him around nineteen now, I didn't say anything else, I just crawled into the bed next to him and cwtched up, he rolled over to face me, cwtching me back, breathing in my scent whilst I breathed in his; I couldn't help but fall asleep, feeling the safest I had in a while. The irony.

The next morning I was quite literally dragged out of my bed by my long blonde hair, hitting the floor with a thud; I looked up to see it was my 'father' that was dragging me, I screamed at him, trying to free myself from his grip but nothing worked. I watched as Malaki tried to free me as well but he was pinned against the wall by two other wolves that I hadn't seen before. My father threw me to the floor, ripping some of my hair out and bruising my arm in the process, he pulled me to my knees looking at my neck, bending my neck harshly. I honestly thought he was going to snap it; he started growling and threw me back to the floor, I hit my head pretty hard but that wasn't what I was concerned about, it was the dangerous man stood over me.

"*Why haven't you mated and marked yet? I told you to get pregnant straight away!*"

I opened my mouth to argue but the look in his eyes told me it wasn't a good idea.

"*You will do it today or I will kill you, little Alpha, and find one that will.*"

My father and the two wolves stormed out of the room, leaving me whimpering on the floor, it wasn't long before Malaki was at my side trying to comfort me.

"You, uh, never told me your name."

"Verity."

I couldn't hold back the tears any more, I hated being

vulnerable but right now I was terrified, I couldn't lose my mate; not now, not ever! But I didn't want to force Malaki to be with me, I didn't deserve to be happy after everything that I'd done.

"Let me mark you, Verity."

"Wh-what?"

"The idea of someone else being with you makes me feel sick, I can't let you go through that. You're my mate, you're the only wolf I ever want to bear my mark."

"You, you wouldn't say that if you knew what I have done. You deserve better than me, Malaki, I'm not a good person."

"Verity, I-I don't care what you have done, it's what you do now that matters to me. Everyone can change given the chance, you wouldn't be my Luna if you weren't a good person."

"Y-your Luna?"

"Yes, I was to take over as Alpha of my pack when I turned eighteen; that makes you *my* Luna."

I hadn't even thought of that, I was destined to be a Luna; something that although I always wanted, I would never believe it. I hate that my 'parents' were the reason that we finally met, we could finally be together.

"We can't stay here, Malaki, they don't care about us, my father just wants a baby to carry on his legacy."

"The rogue, he's your father?"

Malaki stepped back at this revelation, a look of horror spread across his face; I was sure he'd reject me knowing this information, I mean why would he stay with me? I'm the exact reason that he has been held captive for the last seven years, to mate with me, assure my father's reign of terror.

"I-I only found out yesterday, my mother, she never told me or my brother who our father was just that he wasn't in our pack. But yesterday, we did something terrible and fled our pack, I regret it and if I could undo it, I really would, but I can't and I have to live with my mistakes for the rest of my life. I've wanted nothing more than to make my mother proud my entire life, wanting her to love me for as long as I can remember; I chose the wrong side in doing this, I didn't realise until it was too late though."

Malaki studied me for a moment before coming closer and picking me up off the floor, placing me on the bed, he was still weak but being around me was obviously helping him not only heal but grow stronger.

"Verity, I can see that you're not a bad person—"

"Your vision is just clouded by the mate bond, Malaki, don't be naïve."

"I'm not naïve, Verity, if you were a bad person, you wouldn't feel remorse the way you are; you were just a young girl that wanted her mother to love her. You're just as much a victim as I am in this."

"No, I—"

I tried to object but Malaki stopped me before I had the chance, placing his lips powerfully against mine, erupting a burning desire going straight to my core; the electricity between us was something I've never, ever felt. I pulled away breathless, trying to comprehend what was happening, Malaki growled at me as I did so; angry at my interruption of our near mating, something wolves are told about as soon as they can understand. His eyes were jet black, his voice hoarse as he spoke.

"What—what's wrong?"

"Malaki, are you sure you want this? Once we take this step; there is no going back."

He didn't answer me, instead his hand came up, moving my shirt away from my neck, trailing his fingers against my marking spot, starting that burning sensation in my core again, he leaned down and gently sucked on my spot, causing a moan to escape from my lips, then I felt it; his canines piercing through my skin, sending pain through me for only a second before the pain turned into the most amazing thing I've ever felt, it was pure pleasure, my whole body went limp as I recovered from the marking. Malaki licked his mark that now sat on my skin, sealing it in place, making me his Luna.

"Does that answer your question?"

He spoke with the biggest grin I've ever seen, it was beautiful to see him smile, he looked so happy; even under current circumstances. I just nodded and gave a small smile, still calming myself from the overwhelming sensation that came with the marking. He started kissing me again, only this time gentler, not as needy, I could feel his hardened member pushing against my leg so I touched it, a low growl escaped his lips. I brushed myself gently against it; feeling the need to have him inside me, I pushed his waist band down as far as I could, freeing his member.

"Please," I whispered against his lips as I pushed my bottoms down, he growled placing himself at my entrance before slowly entering me. I groaned in anticipation, wanting him to fill me completely, as if knowing my thoughts, he pushed himself into me fast and hard, taking my virginity before stopping as I cried out in pain. I couldn't believe how much it hurt but once it had eased, I nodded so that he could carry on. I could feel myself reaching my peak, wanting more of him, he thrusted more, reaching his peak too; as Vicki came forward, taking control, extending my canines and marking him mine, forever and always. He growled as he climaxed, planting his seed deep inside of me, collapsing on top of me; giving me the chance to seal my mark before he rolled over onto the bed.

"That, was, amazing."

I rolled over and cwtched into him, as we both worked to calm ourselves down, regulating our breathing, trying to cool ourselves down.

"Verity, you can't get pregnant."

"Huh?"

"We can't have a baby here, not around these rogues. It wouldn't stand a chance, we wouldn't. They'd kill us and raise the baby to be like them."

"I know, Malaki, but what can we do?"

"We have to escape."

"How?"

"I'm not sure but we'll find a way."

**Three Months Later*

"*Why aren't you pregnant yet?*"

My father threw me across the room as his men held Malaki back, it now took four men to hold him back, he's gotten stronger every day since our marking; my father has noticed too but thankfully hasn't realised we are true mates because he would surely kill Malaki if he did. He's made his men stay in with us the past four nights to make sure that we were mating but to be truthful it was the first time we've mated since our first time because we didn't want me to get pregnant. It's been tough but was worth it to know that we weren't going to bring a pup into this hell hole.

"Maybe it's the fact you've beat and tortured her at least twice a week since we mated! Maybe the moon goddess knows you shouldn't be within ten feet of an alpha pup never mind raising one!"

Malaki spat at my father in venom, I knew better than to speak out after my father broke my jaw but Malaki didn't care, they've tortured him for over seven years, what more could they do? I watched in horror as my father turned on his heel, running towards Malaki, pinning him against the wall by his throat.

"*If I were you, boy, I'd keep my trap shut or you can watch her die, it will be slow and painful. I will have another baby with my mate and that one will continue my legacy, make no mistake there will be a baby one way or another.*"

My father and his men left; Malaki ran over to me, cradling me as I cried into his arms.

"It's okay, my love, soon we will escape. I swear, if it's the last thing I do, I will get you to safety."

The next few weeks went by slowly, my father beat me daily until one day he realised that my scent had changed; he forced me into having some bloods done which only confirmed my worst fears – I was pregnant. He left us alone then, the only time we ever saw someone was when someone brought us a piece of toast at mealtimes.

"Verity, we have to get you and our baby out of here; as soon as possible."

"I know but how? We've searched every angle of this room, there are no weaknesses, no ways out; it's pointless."

"Verity, your father will leave with his group to go and raid the local town for supplies. There's only around six maybe seven rogues ever left behind and then the ones guarding the borders; if we can overpower them during lunch, we can make our way out. Do you remember the way you came in?"

"Erm, yeah, sort of."

"Then it's settled. We go tomorrow, you and our baby's

safety are my priority, okay?"

I nodded at Malaki, tears clouding my vision, knowing that tomorrow we would get out of here; or we'd die trying, anything was better than our baby having to come here though. We fell asleep together, Malaki placed his left arm around me and his right hand in a protective position on top of my stomach.

"I love you, Verity, more than I've ever loved anyone and anything."

"I love you too, Malaki, I never thought I would get a mate but when I met you; it was like nothing else has ever mattered. You are my everything."

We fell asleep in each other's arms, possibly for the last time.

The next morning, we were woken by the guards that bring in our slice of toast every morning, they threw it at us like they did every day; it was always stale so my guess is we just had a slice each from someone's leftovers. We sat up and put our clothes on that we had placed neatly beside the bed, getting dressed for the day and acting as if there was nothing special about today. We hadn't left the room since I got here, we had a functional bathroom and they brought us toast so I guess that they saw no need to let us out; we heard the sound of running, meaning the men were being called, probably to attack the town like they do once a month, it's about an hour's walk from here, I think, I'm not very familiar with this area I just know that the Crimson Rock pack is close. How they have managed to stay under their radar I'll never know, there's at least thirty rogues living here I believe; Malaki said that at least fifteen go on the town attack so we should be okay, since we marked and mated Malaki has only grown stronger. It wasn't long before the halls were quiet again, we only ever saw anyone if they brought toast or when they were watching us mate, now that I'm pregnant we're left to it.

"How are you feeling, my Luna?"

"Nervous, tired, nauseous. What if something goes wrong, Malaki? I couldn't live with myself if anything happened to you."

"My love, as long as you and our child survive, I will forever be happy."

It felt like an eternity before the guard brought our toast for dinner setting our plan into motion, Malaki hid behind the door and jumped onto the guard's back as he looked for him, snapping his neck with no trouble at all; it looked as if he was just snapping spaghetti, I grabbed his hand, dragging him out of the room and down the long hallway that we came up, back outside and into the other building we came through first, vaguely remembering the way out.

We came into contact with two more guards but thankfully Malaki was quicker and stronger than both of them. I grabbed him again, dragging him through yet another long corridor, it felt like we were running for hours, navigating the maze of hallways, I was almost sure we had gotten lost until we felt a soft breeze. This only made us more eager, pushing ourselves forward, we came to the same reception area I came in the first day, littered with even more blood and bones than the first time I was here; the smell of death was so prominent it made my eyes water as we broke through the double doors, running straight into three guards outside. They were a lot stronger than the ones inside but me and Malaki were able to take them, we didn't have much energy left though so we just needed to run now. Once we were sure they were dead we started running in the same direction I came from the day of the crash.

"Malaki, we have to shift!" I shouted as we ran, still going as fast we could but our wolves would be able to go faster.

"Verity, I can't, I've never shifted; my body, it's not strong enough yet."

"We'll have to do it on foot then."

I could feel myself getting weaker, we didn't have much energy as it was; I couldn't run for much longer, they kept us weak for this exact reason, so we couldn't escape or fight them, I'm sure the rest of them would be after us by now, we couldn't fight them, couldn't run, what could we do?

"Malaki – I-I can't go much further."

I stopped for a moment, trying to catch my breath as I rested, we were on high alert, knowing that they were sure to be close; we didn't know how many were still at the hospital after all, we only killed maybe ten or eleven.

"We have to go now, my love; I know you can do it. Not for me, not for you but for our pup."

I sighed, knowing he was right – I'd escape or at least die trying, we managed to run for a few more hours when we came to a clearing; I realised it was the same clearing that the rogues would have tried to kill Shannon in, but they failed, thankfully from what the traitor rogue said. I knew now that we weren't far from the pack, maybe an hour by wolf?

"Malaki, you should try to shift. I think we've put some distance between us and—"

My words were interrupted by the sound of sticks breaking behind us, thunderous growls erupting from the wolves around us; there were five, maybe six rogues surrounding us, Malaki stood in front of me and I couldn't help but scream as the first wolf pounced at him, canines and claws ready.

"NOOOOOO!"

Chapter Twenty-Nine
A Successful Scouting Mission

Thomas

"Do you really have to go?"

Shannon pouted her lips as I climbed out of bed ready to go with the scouts, she hadn't let me out of bed the last few days; I'm surprised she was still able to keep going but we didn't have sex for so long it wasn't surprising.

"You know I have to, babe; we still have to find Lori and Verity; I've got a bad feeling. It's been nearly four months since anyone has seen or heard anything from Verity whereas Lori keeps popping up and disappearing again. I know she betrayed the pack and her brother in the worst way possible but she wasn't always like that. I grew up with her, she was always nice and then when I told everyone about you… something changed."

"I know you care for her, Thomas, and I admire that in you, but don't let it cloud your judgement. She needs to be dealt with."

"I know, now I have to go. We're going to go to where the crash happened and see if there's any sign of rogues nearby, hopefully we can track their scent."

I walked back over to Shannon giving her a soft kiss before drawing my attention to her stomach where our baby wolf was growing inside her, I kissed her stomach and looked back at her attentively.

"I love you both so much, now rest and I'll see you when I

get back."

Placing another kiss on her forehead I left our room, heading downstairs where I knew our scouts were waiting for me; Stefan wanted to come but I told him he needed to be there for Jade and their son seeing as the little terror never sleeps. He is such an amazing dad, dotes on Theo like nothing I've ever seen but sometimes his loyalty to the pack and his position clouds his judgement; like today, he wanted to go with the scouts instead of looking after Jade and Theo but I refused to allow it, even David has taken time off now because Skye is due any day. She hasn't accepted him yet but they hardly ever leave each other's side which is great, he loves her and those babies as much as he does his own, I know Jason would be so proud.

"Alpha." The eight scouts that were coming with me stood at attention, bowing their head respectfully.

"Are we all ready to go?"

The men nodded and we walked outside together, I shifted first, followed closely by the scouts that were coming along today.

"Stay alert, vigilant and last but not least; no wolf gets left behind, no rogues escape."

I mind linked my men as Atticus ran into the forest, only looking behind to check that they were following.

"Yes, Alpha."

My men responded in unison and it made me proud; I know how well trained my men are, I will forever trust them with my life as I hope that they would me, the clearing where we killed the rogues was only around a thirty minute run so we were studying the area. Once past our borders, we were on high alert, looking for any signs of a rogue at all but nothing, it was as if they all disappeared after that day.

"Let's carry on."

We carried on running, getting closer to the clearing when I heard a blood curling scream; I recognised the voice instantly, I knew it was Verity before I had even entered the clearing.

"NOOOOO!"

Entering the clearing I was stopped in my tracks, thankfully my men didn't share my shock and just pounced on the rogues that had surrounded Verity, another two attacking a man who was bloody and wounded on the floor; hardly moving. Why wasn't Verity in wolf form and who was the man? Atticus jumped into the fight, pouncing on the back of a wolf that had his canines sunk into the man; he struggled a bit but we managed to rip a chunk out of his throat eventually, moving onto the other wolf that was a lot easier to kill. I watched as Verity ran to the man's side, screaming, cradling him in her arms.

"Don't die on me. I need you; we need you!" Verity screamed at the man she cradled, he laid there unconscious, hardly breathing; Atticus gave me back control and I shifted back to my human form. I looked at Verity, feeling nothing but pity. I have imagined finding her so many times, all the things I would do to her for trying to kill Shannon and killing four of our guards, including her brother, but right now all I felt was pity. She was thin, weak, her hair dull and drenched in blood, her once plump and colourful face was now pale and withdrawn. I noticed a mark on her neck; she found her mate, after all this time, that must be the man she cradled, dying in front of us.

"Get a car and come to the clearing now as fast as you can."

I mind linked one of the guards back at the pack, it would take about twenty minutes to get here by car, ten if he drove like a mad man – not that I'm encouraging dangerous driving but this man wouldn't make it if we tried to carry him back.

"Verity, who is he?"

I spoke softly and touched her leg reassuringly, she jumped at the contact, looking up at me terrified. I don't think she had realised it was us that had arrived, although she hadn't focused on anything other than the man in front of us.

"H-h-he's m-m-my mate, T-T-Thoma—Alpha. He can't die, he can't."

"I have someone coming with a car okay, let's put some pressure on his wounds, okay? What's his name?"

"M-M-Malaki."

"All right, Malaki, can you hear me?"

I was applying pressure to a bad wound on his arm whilst Verity applied pressure to a wound in his side, some of the scouts returned with clothes that we used to soak up some of his blood.

"Alpha, what are you doing here?"

"Looking for you."

Just as I spoke, the sound of horns erupted from on the main road; I was surprised to see Stefan and two other guards all driving cars. We lifted Malaki up and carried him up to the car, placing him gently on the back seat of the car Stefan was driving. Verity climbed in beside him, placing his head back onto her lap.

"Who is he?" Stefan mind linked me as I climbed into the front seat of his car so that we could drive.

"Verity found her mate."

"You should have just killed her and him for what they've done."

"You know that's not how we do things, what are you doing here anyway?"

"I told the guards to notify me if you needed help so they did."

"You should be looking after Jade and Theo not worrying

about me."

"I'm your Beta, it's my job to."

I cut off our mind link so that I could mind link Doctor Bane to prepare the Alpha suite, we needed as much privacy as possible dealing with this. The drive to the pack felt pretty short, you could see Malaki fading quickly so I'm sure Stefan was going slow just in the hopes that he died; as much as I can't blame him, it's not how I do things in my pack. I jumped out of the car before we had even stopped grabbing Malaki and placing him on a trolley Doctor Bane and a few nurses had brought outside ready. They rushed him straight upstairs so that they could take care of him. I watched as Stefan grabbed Verity and dragged her in the direction of the dungeons; I followed behind them, watching as Verity kicked and screamed to be with her mate. As we were close to the dungeon, we passed Skye and David, anger spreading across Skye's face as she saw Verity, trying to run after them but David held her back. Verity obviously saw Skye too because she was shouting at her, telling her to get Jason, tell him she needs him; this small exchange made me angry so I couldn't imagine how Skye felt.

Chapter Thirty
Working With the Enemy

Thomas

I watched as Stefan threw Verity onto the hard dungeon floor, she was hysterical by this point, screaming at him, not making any sense. She ran towards Stefan who pushed her straight back to the floor, this time hitting her head on the way down, kicking her aggressively. I pulled him off her and dragged him out of the room. As angry as I was over everything, never would you find me attacking a she-wolf.

"Stef! That's enough!"

"Dude, she deserves to be punished!"

"That's not how we do it and you know it!"

I shut the door and walked back in to Verity, helping her sit up against the wall, she was bleeding quite a bit, even her head was now bleeding from where Stefan pushed her back down.

"Please, Thomas, I'll tell you anything you want but don't hurt my mate. He's completely innocent in all of this, he's just a victim."

"A victim? What do you mean?"

"Malaki, he's… Alice's brother. He was taken from their pack over seven years ago—"

I stood there trying to process this information; Alice told us about her pack, she never once mentioned a brother though? So, was this the truth or not? I noticed Verity was coughing quite a bit, possibly just winded.

"No, Alice never mentioned a brother."

"Thomas, I think it was before the attack, he—he didn't even know, my father—"

"Your father?"

This news was just as surprising, even my father never knew who fathered Verity or Jason; we honestly thought they may have been half human or something, especially with how weak Verity was.

"Yes, my father. It was where me and my mother ran away to; he's a power hungry, rogue Alpha, he kidnapped Malaki in order to have us mate and mark. He wanted to make sure his legacy was assured."

"So, you're of Alpha blood too? The problem is, Verity, I don't believe you. This is all incredibly farfetched."

A rogue Alpha, a young Alpha being kidnapped conveniently around the time that werewolf hunters attacked his pack, my thoughts were interrupted by Doctor Bane who was mind linking me.

"Alpha, the boy was wounded pretty badly but he's all healed thanks to Kaitlyn, he's weak so will need time to recover."

"Thank you, Doctor Bane, could you ask Kaitlyn to come to the dungeon and heal Verity please?"

"Are you sure, Alpha?"

"Yes, I don't think she's as evil as we've allowed ourselves to believe."

I cut the mind link with Doctor Bane so that I could focus on Verity.

"Why did you poison Ryan, Scott and Luke, Ver? I've known you my entire life; I knew you struggled but to poison your fellow pack members?"

"I-I was wrong, all I ever wanted was for my mom to love

me, like she loved Jason or even herself but it didn't matter what I did, she couldn't. Even when Jason disobeyed her, choosing Skye instead of just rejecting her like she said; I thought this is it, she may actually love me now but… but she didn't. It was still Jason, she knew he would never betray the pack, betray you. He had even grown to like Shannon who mother had convinced me was the enemy, she had stolen you and I had nothing. I just wanted someone to love me like—like you love Shannon but no one ever has, that it is until Malaki was forced into my life and we found out that we were true mates; he loves me and our baby more than I could have ever imagined. I regret everything that I did, I really do; if I could – if I could go back and stop myself I would. They didn't deserve to die, not for my own selfishness, I put my faith in the wrong people and it got me nothing but beaten, watched, tortured and forced to mate. Right up until we escaped."

"Escaped? From where?"

We were interrupted by Kaitlyn knocking at the door, poking her head in shyly.

"Y-you called, Alpha?"

"Yes, can you come and heal Verity here for me please?"

"O-of course."

Kaitlyn walked over hesitantly to Verity, placing her one hand on her shoulder and her other on her stomach; I watched in awe as her hands glowed in their spots, watching some of Verity's cuts and bruises heal slowly, her hand on her stomach glowing slightly brighter as she hummed.

"I think that's everything, your baby has a very strong heartbeat too; they're going to be fine but, Alpha, I'd like Doctor Bane to give her a proper ultrasound so that we can make sure."

"My mate, is he okay?"

"He will be okay; he's resting right now. Healing takes a lot out of both the healer and the victim."

"Will—will you tell him that we are okay please?"

"Of course."

Kaitlyn walked out of the room as quiet as she entered, she really was going to be a great Doctor when Doctor Bane retired.

"Verity, what do you mean by escaped?"

"My father, he's set up base in an abandoned hospital around two, maybe three, hours from here; he kept us locked in one room, fed us toast three times a day so that we wouldn't starve. When he realised me and Malaki weren't actually mating, he had two men stay with us every night so that they knew we were actually mating; not preventing it."

"But why? I mean new mates are usually at it like rabbits anyway but why was he so obsessed with it?"

"Like I said, he wanted to assure his legacy, he wanted to be the strongest Alpha there was, take over any pack he wanted; he had hoped he could beat Malaki into submission but he couldn't so he planned to kill us and raise our baby as the new leader of his army or whatever he called it, so that when he died his vision still carried on. We fought hard not to mate because we didn't want our baby brought into that life; he never said that he'd kill us but he made it pretty obvious that he was going to. Every day he'd come in and beat me when he realised that my scent hadn't changed, he'd have his men hold Malaki back so that he could watch."

"So, how did you escape?"

"My father and about fifteen rogues go on a monthly supplies trip. They attack a town which is around half an hour away maybe. He takes around fifteen of his men with him meaning that there aren't many left at the hospital; he's lost a lot of wolves recently. We kept running, both of us too weak to shift and that's when they found us at the clearing. It was like a miracle when you found us. I thought they were going to kill us."

This was a lot to take in, I wasn't sure what to address first; the rogue Alpha, Malaki, Verity's pregnancy, this supposed hospital which is likely the safe house we were told about before.

"Verity, why should I trust anything that you're saying?"

"I know, I have no right to ask you to trust me but you should; I-I'll take you to the hospital, where they're hiding, they're planning to attack you in the next month anyway so you would have the upper hand."

"What do you want in return though?"

"Don't kill me or Malaki, I will live the rest of my life in the dungeon if I have to – I'll work hard until you all forgive me but please grant Malaki and my baby a safe place to live, they don't deserve to suffer because of my mistakes."

"I will have to talk to Shannon and Stefan, even Skye. She deserves an input on this; once I have spoken to them, I will have an answer for you."

"Thank you, Thomas."

I walked towards the door when Verity spoke again.

"Thomas, do you think you could convince Jason to see me please? I know I don't deserve it but I owe him an apology for betraying him."

I turned around to look at her; I didn't even think about whether she knew he had passed away or not, I just assumed she did. I walked back towards her, lowering myself so that I could make eye contact with her, placing my hand comfortingly on her shoulder.

"Jason died, Verity, the rogues… they practically tore him apart, he died in Shannon's arms, in that clearing. I assumed you knew."

"N-n-n-no, he, he wasn't meant to die. No, the—the rogue, he said you stopped them, he said he wasn't dead."

"I'm sorry, Verity, but he is, we had the funeral around a month ago now."

I watched as her head fell to her knees, her tears already soaking them, she was screaming as if she was in pain but she obviously wasn't, at least any more; this was a pain that couldn't be healed by Doctor Bane or Kaitlyn. My thoughts were interrupted by Doctor Bane freaking out over a mind link.

"Alpha! I've got a very distressed young man here, he's saying his mate is hurt; what are you doing to Verity?"

"Nothing, I just told her about Jason."

"Well, you had better bring her here because he's not going to settle without her. I've got Stefan and David here pinning him down."

"On our way."

"Right come on, Verity, your mate is awake."

I couldn't help but pity her as she looked up at me, quite obviously heartbroken over the news of her brother's death; they were pretty close, I always assumed it was because there was only two years between them but maybe their mother's neglect pushed them together. I mind linked Shannon asking her to meet me at the pack hospital, in the family room by the Alpha suite; we were almost there so I didn't think there was a chance of us running into her before we got there.

As we got closer I noticed poor Skye sat outside on the steps; David's arms wrapped protectively around her, I watched as Skye broke away from him, running towards Verity as fast as a heavily pregnant wolf could, punching Verity square in the face before David caught up with her.

"How could you? Your own brother!"

"I-I'm sorry! He wasn't supposed to die!"

"Well, he did and it's all your fault!"

I had to interrupt, none of this was good for Skye or the babies; she was supposed to be at home resting, not here fighting. I pulled Verity away and looked at David.

"David, take her home please. We don't want her and the babies stressed more than they already are, now do we?"

"Yes—uh, no, Alpha, come on, my love."

"Your love? He's been dead what? Three months and you've already moved on? You didn't deserve him!"

I watched Skye as she ran away, no doubt upset by what Verity just said. I dragged her into the hospital, fed up of all this drama already, I took her straight to the Alpha suite where Stefan and Doctor Bane were waiting. I pushed her into the room, losing patience, watching as she ran over to the man in the bed; both embracing and observing each other.

"Stefan, watch them. I need to make a phone call."

I walked straight to the family room; thankfully Shannon wasn't here yet, I picked up the phone and dialled the only person who could give me some sort of clarification.

Dial tone

"Alpha Kye's office."

"Kye? I need to speak to Alice now."

"Who is this?"

"Thomas, now get her."

"Okay, she's coming, what's going on?"

"Only she can answer me."

There was a bit of shuffling and talking before finally Alice took the phone.

"Thomas, what's going on?"

"I have a question that only you can answer; it's important.

Do you have a brother?"

There was a clattering against the phone, followed by talking and finally I heard Alice against the phone again.

"H-how did you—"

"Alice, is he young? Was he kidnapped? Before your pack was attacked?"

"Y-yes, Malaki was taken the day before our pack was attacked, w-we assumed for a ransom after we couldn't track him so—so we were going to wait for the ransom and pay whatever we needed to. I-I assumed he had been killed by his captors; he'd be about nineteen now; he was going to be our next Alpha."

"Alice, he's here."

The phone went quiet for a moment before I heard a commotion and Kye returned to the phone.

"Thomas, we're coming, we're bringing the babies too."

The phone line went dead; I mind linked a few Omegas to prepare my spare rooms because we had guests arriving soon and they would be staying with us on our floor, just as I finished talking to the Omegas, I heard the door open. I turned around only to come face to face with my beautiful mate who looked worried.

"What's going on, babe?"

Chapter Thirty-One
Facing My Insecurities

Shannon

The atmosphere in the hospital was quite hostile; everyone seemed to be whispering, running around trying to keep busy. I made my way up to the family room slowly, I've only been here once during Jade's labour so it wasn't too hard to find. Pushing through the door I was surprised to see that Thomas was on the phone, I don't think I've ever seen him use the phone outside of his office; he prefers to talk via mind link or face to face.

"What's going on, babe?"

I watched as his frown changed into the beautiful smile that I love so much, he walked over to me, wrapping his arms around me and pressing his lips forcefully to mine; igniting a fire inside of me, he pulled away almost as quickly as he approached.

"We found her, Shan."

"Verity?"

I walked over to a chair placed near the phone as he nodded; I wasn't sure that my legs could hold me with how weak they felt, Thomas followed closely behind.

"D-did you kill her?"

"No, Shan, I couldn't."

I could feel myself getting angrier, struggling to contain it much longer; I found myself almost screaming at him.

"You *couldn't*! What do you mean you *couldn't?* She orchestrated the death of four guards to kill *me*! Yet you couldn't kill her?"

"Angel, when we found her, her and her mate, they were being attacked by the rogues. They had escaped, the rogues held her captive and forced her to be with whomever they chose, her mate; he's an alpha from Ireland."

"Ireland? Like—"

"Yes, like Alice. He is her brother, angel, and Verity is carrying his baby, I can't kill her."

This was a lot of information to process, he kept talking, filling in this and that about today's events but my head was swimming by this point; Thomas kneeled in front of me, forcing me to make eye contact with him.

"My love, I genuinely believe that Verity is remorseful. She wants to help us take down the rogues, she'll take us to their safe house, we can end this."

"Thomas, do you really trust that this isn't a trap?"

"Yes, my love, she wants us to grant Malaki and their baby a place here, where they can be safe and happy. Verity will live in the dungeon if we say so."

"D-does Alice know?"

"Yes, they're on their way. She—she thought he was dead."

This small fact broke my heart, the idea of thinking everyone you had loved was dead and then finding out your brother is still alive; she must be so happy.

"Why isn't he dead? I mean her entire pack was slaughtered, right?"

"Alice said he was taken the day before the pack was attacked, they thought it was for ransom which is why she thought they had killed him when her pack fell but he was held captive and neglected all these years; all to mate with Verity and assure her father's legacy."

"Thomas, this is crazy."

"I know but at the moment we have no choice but to trust Verity unfortunately."

"I'd like to see her and her mate."

"Angel, are you sure?"

I thought about this for a moment because I really wasn't sure, on one hand I'm very obviously angry over the whole situation but then on the other she was almost killed by rogues trying to escape whatever hell she was forced to endure by her own father; we already knew how rotten her mother was but to have such an awful father as well, it's no wonder she's done what she has.

"Yes, I'm sure."

I stood up, no longer feeling weak or scared by the news of Verity arriving; I walked towards the Alpha suite hand in hand with Thomas, preparing myself to face the woman who had tried to kill me twice, even if Thomas didn't know about the first time… I did and that was enough. I took one last deep breath before entering the Alpha suite, I refused to show any signs of nerves or fear, she will not beat me; I am a Luna now, not just some weak human that she can push around, *I am a Luna.*

Walking in I was surprised to see Stefan stood awkwardly by the door with a face like thunder. He looked at me nervously, asking me if I was okay through a mind link but I just smiled reassuringly back at him. I was okay, my nerves gone; this woman didn't bother me any more. I turned my attention towards the scrawny man in the bed, he was young looking; I think Thomas said he was nineteen? He was clearly malnourished; the rogues had obviously only fed him enough to keep him alive in the last seven years, rather than giving him proper food.

"Stefan, could you please get our guests some proper food

from the kitchen please?"

"Guests?"

Stefan looked at me in shock, obviously not sure what to say about my sudden act of kindness but I planned to stand my ground.

"Yes, guests. I would rather not refer to them as prisoners when young Malaki here has done nothing to deserve such a title."

I watched as Stefan stormed out of the room, obviously not happy about the job he'd been given but it's tough; I wasn't going to let them starve on my watch. I was able to finally bring myself to look upon Verity who was sat in the chair quietly next to her mate. I wanted to be angry and I wanted to hate her but all I felt was pity. This once beautiful, confident wolf was nothing more than skin and bone; her face was pale and withdrawn, her clothes and hair were filthy, covered in dried blood and dirt, how anyone could leave them like this I will never know. I once envied the woman sat in the chair, wished I could be like her, beautiful, confident; even just a wolf like Thomas deserved but looking at her now you could see, the wolf that I felt insecure about, the one I thought deserved to be Luna more… she was gone, this was a new Verity.

"Doctor Bane, could you go and grab the ultrasound machine so that you can check on the baby, please? Ask one of the nurses to get these two a change of clothes as well, please."

"Yes, Luna."

Doctor Bane left the room in a hurry, probably eager to get away from the tension that was building amongst the four of us.

"Luna, may—may I speak?"

"You may, Verity."

I walked over to a chair at the nurse's desk, turning it to face them both before sitting down. I remained calm and neutral whilst looking at them, I couldn't allow them to know how sorry I truly felt for them.

"I-I'm sorry, for everything. I know that I can never make up for what I did to you, or Luke, or Ryan, or Scott… or even Jason but know that it will forever be the biggest regret of my life. If I could go back, I would, one hundred times over, I would never have listened to my mother or hunted for her approval, her love. I know you probably hate me and want nothing more than to rip my head off, here and now—"

Malaki growled at Verity's last sentence, obviously feeling very protective of her and their growing pup; which is only natural for a wolf, especially an Alpha.

"Being honest, Verity, I don't hate you. Thomas told me what you went through in the time your father held you captive. I think you've suffered enough in the time it took for you to escape; if you help Thomas find the safe house so that we can end this I will consider allowing you stay, you will be demoted to Omega and will have jobs as such, could you agree to that?"

"That's better than I could have ever hoped for, Luna, thank you so much. I'd be honoured to help you take down the rogues and my father."

"Malaki, we have spoken with Alice. She is on her way; we will bring her straight here as soon as she gets here, okay?"

We were interrupted by a nurse and Doctor Bane coming through the door with their hands full, I smiled at both before turning our attention to Verity and Malaki.

"You will stay here until you are well enough to travel, Verity, there will be a guard positioned outside the door at all times. We're going to leave you guys to get comfortable ready for our return with Alpha Kye and Luna Alice."

"Yes, Luna," they both said in unison, I followed Thomas out of the room feeling quite proud of myself, we didn't get far down the corridor before Thomas had picked me up, almost crushing me as he twirled me around.

"You did amazing in there, my little Luna, I'm so proud of you!"

"I only did what was needed, I do truly believe that they've both suffered enough; you told me to always be fair and that's what I'm doing."

I have no idea where we go from here, in terms of attacking the rogues but I have faith that Thomas already has a plan ready; we carried on walking until we were close to the pack house, Alice and Kye would be arriving soon so we wanted to make sure that the pack house was ready for them.

Chapter Thirty-Two
Back From the Dead

Alice

"Alice, honey, are the pups settled?"

I was taking a nap with the pups when Kye mind linked me, it wasn't his fault because I hadn't told him that I was gonna nap but it didn't stop me getting any less annoyed to be honest.

"Mhmm, yeah, babe, why?"

"I've got Thomas on the phone; he needs to talk to you – it sounds urgent."

"I'll be there now."

I jumped out of bed and rushed to his office, thankfully only a few rooms away so I could still hear the triplets if needs be. Walking into the room, Kye looked at me amusingly, smirking as if there was a joke that I couldn't understand.

"What?"

"You were sleeping, weren't you?"

"Maybe, now give me the phone."

I had to fight him for the phone, he kept holding it out of reach but I got it in the end.

"Thomas, what's going on?"

"I have a question that only you can answer; it's important. Do you have a brother?"

I couldn't help the shock as I dropped the phone, I mean how could he know this? I never told anyone about my brother, in fact I was pretty sure whoever took him had killed him all those years ago. He was taken the day before the attack, we had no time to save him, or even pay a ransom, nothing. Kye was at my side picking up the phone for me.

"Honey, are you okay?"

I couldn't answer him I just took the phone out of his hand, needing answers.

"H-how did you—"

"Alice, is he young? Was he kidnapped? Before your pack was attacked?"

I stayed quiet a moment, still in shock that Thomas knew about him, my head buzzing with different theories as to why Thomas was asking these questions but only one made sense; he had found my brother.

"Y-yes, Malaki was taken the day before the pack was attacked, w-we assumed for a ransom after we couldn't track him so—so we were going to wait for the ransom and pay whatever we needed. I-I assumed he had been killed by his captors; he'd be about nineteen now, he was going to be our next Alpha."

"Alice, he's here."

I dropped the phone running to my bedroom and packing some things, Kye followed after me confused, shouting after me but I ignored him; I had to go, Malaki, he's the only family I have now, he's back – back from the dead, my heart was broken and swelling all at once. I was stopped for a moment by Kye grabbing me, forcing me to make eye contact.

"Honey, tell me what's wrong?"

"M-my brother, I thought he was dead, Thomas has him, we, we have to go there. Now."

Kye nodded before returning to his office, I carried on packing our things; it's crazy the amount of stuff you need when you have babies, I swear they could fill an adult suitcase alone. I could see my vision clouding as my emotions took hold of me, I fell to the ground sobbing; although screaming was more of a fit, all the pain and emotion I felt years ago at the loss of my family flooding my mind, taking control of me. I felt sparks erupting all around me as Kye embraced me, making me feel safe and warm; allowing me to completely fall apart in his arms.

"It's okay, honey, you aren't alone."

It was nearly two hours before we were completely ready to go, I was already exhausted from all the crying that I'd done since the phone call, I just couldn't believe it, it was as if he was back from the dead.

"Honey, Aisling is going to use a spell to teleport us there, okay?"

"Is that safe? What about the pups?"

Aisling apparated into the room, she does this quite frequently and it always scares me.

"It's actually completely safe, you already have a binding to Shannon and Thomas so I plan to use that and send you directly there. You will need to be touching what you wish to take though, if you leave the pups in their car-seats they will be fine; I've already contacted Shannon and Thomas to make sure that they're somewhere private."

I nodded, sitting down by my pups holding onto some of our bags at the same time, I closed my eyes as Aisling began chanting. I could feel tingling all over, it was like pins and needles through every inch of my body. My stomach was queasy, it felt as if I had just done back-to-back loopty loops on a roller coaster. I had a pounding headache and a dry mouth but it wasn't long before I heard a gasp. I felt the ground below my bottom before I opened my eyes, the room was bright, it was not helping my already pounding headache as I surveyed the area; my eyes falling upon Shannon and Thomas making me smile before checking on each of my pups. They were perfect, not a single hair out of place. Thomas walked over, offering me a hand to help me up but as he did, I could feel my lunch resurfacing, which it did… all over poor Thomas.

"I-I'm so sorry, Thomas, teleportation is never kind to me."

"It's fine, you guys get yourselves settled, cleaned up, and then we will go and see Malaki, okay?"

I nodded before following Kye and Shannon to our room; I was surprised to see how big it was and that they had managed to set up three beautiful cots in the short time that we gave them. I set the pups down in them so that they could get some rest whilst me and Kye tidied ourselves up.

"How are you feeling, honey?"

"I'm okay."

"Don't lie to mate!" my wolf Annabeth shouted back at me.

"Well, what do you propose I do? Tell him how terrified I am because I've not seen my brother in over seven years? How guilty I feel because we didn't look for him all this time?"

"It's not our fault, Alice, we were captured ourselves, we assumed he was killed. We grieved for him."

"We still should have tried!"

My conversation was interrupted by Kye placing his hand on my shoulder.

"Arguing with Annabeth?"

"Yeah, I swear she argues with me more than she talks."

"Well, whatever it is I'm sure you'll work it out. You usually do, let's go."

We put the triplets in the triple stroller that we had teleported with us. We usually carried them around but they were too big for that now, not to mention with Teddy's shifting we wouldn't want to get hurt, he didn't shift as much but it was still pretty unpredictable so we liked to be safe. We wheeled the pram into the lounge where Thomas and Shannon were waiting for us.

"Are you guys ready?"

I could feel the nerves building as I thought about what we were doing; we were seeing my brother, who, for the past seven years I assumed was killed, he was all the family I had now aside from Kye and the pups obviously.

"Yes."

My legs felt like lead as I forced every step I took towards the pack hospital, my stomach doing somersaults; although I wasn't sure if it was nerves or from the teleportation.

"Thomas, how did he get here?"

"We found him when scouting for Verity, they were in pretty bad shape."

"Verity, as in the one who killed four of your pack members then fled?"

"The very same."

"What do you mean by 'they', Thomas?"

"Verity was with him, they're mates, Alice."

"What? No! He-he deserves better!"

"Alice, it is not our place to judge mates, I'm sure the moon goddess paired them for a reason, wait until you speak to him."

I stayed quiet the rest of the way, trying to control my emotions before they got the better of me. I couldn't even remember the last time I saw Malaki, our last words. I couldn't even remember what he looked like; he was twelve when he was taken so I had no doubt that he had changed a lot. The walk felt like a lifetime but it wasn't long before we were standing outside the Alpha suite in the hospital, just staring at the door, unable to bring myself to open it.

"Alice, let me and Thomas take the pups to the family room, it's only down the corridor. You need this time, just you and Kye. No interruptions."

"A-are you sure?"

"Yes, of course."

I moved away from the stroller so that Shannon and Thomas could take it. I watched as they walked down the corridor, getting further and further away. They were the only people to have them other than Aisling and her mate, it was a weird feeling but I had no concerns, I know Shannon and Thomas will care for them fully one day; I was sad at first thinking that they would have no other family but now, with Malaki, at least they're not going to be alone. I turned my attention back to the door, my hands visibly shaking as I reached for the door handle, my nausea returning as I walked into the room. I scanned the room quickly before my eyes rested on a small man laid in the bed, a blonde woman asleep against him. You could see how thin and malnourished he was, but under that I could see his long ebony hair was just like I remembered my father having all those years ago, although my father's was streaked with grey due to old age. He had a similar bone structure to my mother, they always said he was a good mix of them both. I watched as he opened his eyes, those beautiful blue sapphire eyes. I fell to my knees, unable to control my emotions any longer as years of pain, grief and mourning came flooding to the surface. I hadn't realised until this moment exactly how hard I had suppressed the memories of my past, the memories that I had found too hard to live with. Kye's arms were around me, trying to calm me as I sobbed uncontrollably on the hard, cold floor.

"A-Alice? Is—is that really you?"

I looked up to see Malaki, my younger brother, peering down at me from his hospital bed, concern spreading across his face as he watched me cry on the floor.

"I-I thought you were dead, I'm so sorry."

I jumped up off the floor and ran to his side, wrapping him up in the biggest hug I could muster, he struggled under my grip before I let him go, forgetting what he'd just gone through.

"It wasn't your fault, chimp, you didn't know… Verity, she—she told me about the pack, how we lost everything, the rogues, how Thomas saved you. He's a good guy, isn't he?"

"Thomas is a very good guy, where have you been? Who took you?"

"It was rogues too, they kept me until I was of age to mate and mark Verity."

"Wait, what? So, you aren't true mates?"

"We actually are, we had to hide it though. Her father only wanted our baby, he wanted to keep us weak and being true mates, we were just getting stronger. Although, the damage was already done, Doctor Bane said that the years of malnourishment and abuse during a time when my body needed to prepare for its shift has done its damage. I may never be able to shift."

"What? But you're an Alpha! Your wolf, is he still there?"

"Damon is, yes, but even he isn't sure if my body will ever be strong enough to shift. He thinks that I could die if I try to shift and he won't allow that."

I sat there shocked, not really sure what to say, our wolf is part of us, I couldn't imagine never being able to shift into Annabeth.

"That's because not shifting is dangerous, eventually his wolf will grow weak and just… die."

"No, Annabeth, there must be another way."

"With his true mate, he may now stand a chance but he won't have long. Maybe three years at the most."

I couldn't believe what Annabeth was telling me, I didn't think it was possible for your wolf to die; I just assumed that you always died together, without his wolf he would just be human, he could never be an Alpha.

"We'll find a way, Malaki; you don't deserve this."

"I'm already getting stronger with Verity around me, I'm sure I'll be fine. Hey, maybe once I'm healed me and Verity could live at your pack, our pups could grow up together!"

I smiled at the thought of us all growing old at our pack, our pups growing up as best friends; it was the cutest thought but that's all it was, a thought. My pack will fall. When, I don't know, but I don't want him to suffer through that too, he's suffered enough. I couldn't tell him any of this though, only a few people know what is to come, no one deserves what will happen but it needs to, if it doesn't, the supernatural world will cease to exist.

"We will see what the future holds, don't forget Verity has family here."

I looked over at the young blonde next to him, I have only ever met Verity on a few occasions but even I could see that she was a shadow of her former self. There was a knock at the door, interrupting my thoughts, I watched as Thomas walked into the room, taking another seat next to Verity, tapping her lightly on the shoulder to wake her.

"Where are the pups, Thomas?"

"Shannon has them."

"Wait, but—"

Suddenly alarmed by the idea of Shannon having the pups on her own, mainly because of Teddy's shifting, Thomas obviously understood my stress because he held his hand out interrupting me.

"She's with Stefan and Jade, so she has plenty of help. We need to discuss our next steps, we have to attack the rogues now, before they attack us."

Chapter Thirty-Three
Preparing for Battle

Thomas

I walked back to the Alpha suite, I knew they needed their reunion but we also needed to make a plan. I was hoping that Kye would also send some men to help in the fight. Verity said that the rogues had lost a lot of men during their recent attacks but I had no doubt that there were wolves willing to aid them in their time of need so I wanted to be prepared. I knocked on the door, giving them a chance to finish up whatever moment they were having so that I could talk to them. Walking in, I could tell Alice had been crying, her face was red, her eyes puffy, it even looked like Kye had been crying too, he was sat at the nurse's desk facing them – obviously trying to give them space but also be close just in case he was needed. Alice watched me as I walked in, glancing behind me as I walked towards an empty chair by Verity who was fast asleep. I know that she probably needed it but I needed her awake more, unfortunately. I tapped her shoulder, hard enough that she'd feel it but hopefully gentle enough to not hurt her. She woke pretty quickly, looking around at us all, confused and dazed from just waking up. Alice was the first to speak to us all.

"Where are the pups, Thomas?"

"Shannon has them."

I watched as concern and maybe fear spread across her face, I'm not sure why she was concerned though, it's not like Shannon wasn't going to possibly care for them one day anyway. They're just babies, not like they can kill – ah, Teddy's shifting.

"She's with Stefan and Jade, so she has plenty of help. We need to discuss our next steps; we have to attack the rogues before they attack us."

"What do you mean before they attack us?"

"Verity said that he was already planning to attack my pack but he's a rogue alpha who wants nothing but power. I wouldn't put it past him to go after every pack in the country, so we need to end it. I'm assuming he's the same leader behind the attacks when Shannon was nearly killed too."

Kye looked at me with alarm, obviously concerned for not only the safety of his pack but his family too.

"I will stand by your side, Thomas; you have our allegiance."

"Thank you, Kye, Verity said he didn't have many men now but I wouldn't be surprised if he too has allegiances that we aren't aware of."

"That's true, never underestimate our enemy."

I nodded at Kye before turning my attention to the woman sat next to me.

"Verity, we will wait until you are strong enough to lead us there but when we get there, I need you ready to either fight or r—"

I was interrupted by a growl erupting from the small man in the bed, staring at me in disgust, anger radiating from him as he spoke to me; his eyes almost as dark as his ebony locks.

"She is not going anywhere near there."

"It's okay, Mal—"

"*No*, yours and our pup's safety is my only priority."

"Malaki, I will do all I can to stop her getting hurt but she's the best chance we have at finding their home."

"Malaki, let me do this. Everything that's happened, it's my fault."

I sat there listening patiently, when I realised…

"Verity, it's not all your fault; yeah, you made the worst mistake a wolf can make but you aren't responsible for their selfishness or their actions leading up to recent events. They have tortured you like they have Malaki, don't blame yourself for their actions."

Verity stared at me with her mouth open, surprised by what I had said, it was all true, she was just as much a victim in her parents' wrong doings as us, she didn't ask for any of this; they forced it onto her.

We all sat there quietly for a moment, not knowing where to go from here or what to say, it was Malaki that spoke first.

"Then I will go too."

"With all due respect, Malaki, you would only slow us down. You're too vulnerable and weak to come with us as well."

"But—"

"No buts, Malaki, Thomas and Kye will be there to protect me. If it comes to it, I will shift and come straight back."

"Shifting is dangerous whilst pregnant, you know that, Ver."

"This whole plan is dangerous, if I can't shift so that Vicki can help us escape them, I'll die regardless. We both know no rogue could outrun Vicki."

I pursed my lips as I thought about how right she was, she may be the slowest shifter I've ever met but I've never met a faster wolf than Vicki, it was one of the only things I had to back me up when arguing with my father over keeping her as a warrior.

"So, what's the plan?"

Kye looked at me curiously, eager to know what our thoughts were? What we were going to do, how we were going to attack.

"So, having Verity does put us at a great advantage because we know that she can lead us there; I'm not sure whether they will consider her to side with us or maybe they will hope we killed her ourselves. I think that we are at a greater advantage to travel at night, attacking them early morning, we'd have the element of surprise on our side I hope. This will be our only chance to go after them."

"How many warriors do you propose we take, Thomas?"

"I can't see us needing more than one hundred warriors and even then, I think we're pushing it, you said they only had maybe thirty left right, Verity?"

"Yes, before we escaped, we killed around ten maybe, then the six you killed but I wouldn't put it past my father to already have allies on their way, preparing for battle."

"Thomas, maybe we should have warriors ready on standby, I could have at least fifty warriors waiting ready to aid us."

"That sounds good, I will talk to Doctor Bane about coming as well."

"Is that wise? We all know she's not as strong as she was now that Kaitlyn is of age, she could get hurt, or worse, killed."

"Well, what do you propose we do, Kye? We need a back-up plan; I do not intend on losing anyone during this battle."

"Well, what if Aisling was to go? As long as their mates were here, they could be teleported straight to Doctor Bane if necessary. Not to mention Aisling is strong enough to protect herself."

"That's not a bad idea, Alice, but if Aisling dies… wouldn't any spell she's cast be broken?"

I had to ask, thinking about the pups' guardian spell, we needed to guarantee it would still be in place regardless; if that meant Aisling not coming then so be it.

"Erm, we had this discussion before when she first came to the pack and helped with some boundary spells, if it's a spell where only her magic is used then yes, the spell would be broken. But if there were other factors like a potion or ritual and her magic only activated it then it wouldn't be broken because her magic was only used as an activator, the potion or ritual could draw magic from the earth if needed."

"That's good to know, can you go ask her if she's willing to be there for us then please?"

"I will go contact her now."

I watched as Alice walked out of the room, heading to phone Aisling who was waiting back at their pack; the idea of anyone getting hurt scared me to my core but unfortunately, it was what has to be done right now.

"Kye, go make preparations. We leave at midnight tomorrow, when the moon is at its peak. I pray the moon goddess favours us all."

Kye nodded before leaving the room.

"Thomas, you said when Verity was strong enough! Why did you lie?"

I looked at Malaki, obviously terrified for the welfare of his mate and pup.

"I know, Malaki, but I realised we don't have the time to waste, we need to attack before they get the chance to attack us. Rest tonight, tomorrow we leave. With Aisling coming she can teleport Verity straight back here so she won't have to shift or run back. Alice teleported whilst pregnant with the pups, it's completely safe, I swear. No harm will come to Verity, you have my word."

"Thomas, it's okay. Go be with Shannon; I would like some time with Malaki before we go."

I nodded at both people before leaving the hospital room, I opened my mind-link to address the entire pack.

"I would like all warriors and elites except for those on patrol to meet me in the ballroom in ten minutes precisely. Stefan, meet me there now."

I practically ran to the pack house, I needed to speak to Stefan before we were to address the warriors and elites. Stefan was there waiting ready, along with Shannon, Jade, Alice and Kye.

"Well, I didn't expect everyone to be here."

"This is all of our fight, Thomas, we wanted to support you when you speak to everyone."

Shannon never failed to impress me lately, she had grown into her Luna role so well, you'd think she was raised for this entirely.

"Okay, my angel, Stefan—"

"Before you say anything, Thomas, I need you to know. I am *your Beta*, you are not doing this without me, you are not only my Alpha! You're my best friend, my brother; I couldn't live with myself if something happened to you and I wasn't there to protect you."

I couldn't help but well up with the way Stefan spoke, it meant the world to know he felt so highly of me after everything we've been through.

"I'm glad you think so because I'd trust you with my life."

Stefan walked towards me and gave me a hug, he was never really a hugger but this time it felt right, it was comforting. We were interrupted by Alice clearing her throat.

"Aisling is on her way; she is travelling by car so that she can conserve her energy ready for tomorrow. How will you be getting there tomorrow?"

"I will have two warriors drive Aisling and Verity to the clearing after we have left, we will walk in human form from there, shifting when close to the hospital. At least thirty wolves will stay shifted at all times just as a precaution."

They all nodded, understanding that it all had to be done; there was shuffling behind us as the wolves filed in one by one. We moved to the stage, Alice and Jade staying at the back with the pups so that they could settle them quicker. I walked to the front of the stage, Shannon was holding my hand whilst Stefan and Kye stood either side of us.

"*As most of you will know, we had a successful scouting mission today. We found Verity, the woman who was responsible for four of our pack members' deaths but what you won't know, what any of us couldn't have known is that she too has suffered tremendously for nearly five months now; being tortured and beaten by her own father. The very same man that kidnapped her mate, Luna Alice of Crimson Rock's brother, seven years ago before her whole pack was massacred. This could also be the same man that orchestrated the rogue attacks that nearly killed our Luna. What we didn't know is that he was planning to attack us again, he was planning to kill us all, he's on a mission for power after not being able to get it at his own pack. We will be leaving at midnight tomorrow, when the moon has reached its peak and we will attack his hideaway. I need warriors to come with us and fight him, not for me, not for yourselves but for the future of our pack. Some of us may not come home but I will be damned if I do not do my best to get each and every one of you back here alive. So, who will fight with us tomorrow?*"

There was silence for a moment, you could see the fear spreading across their faces, I know I could just have told them who was coming but I thought they needed to decide their own destiny. I would rather not force them to do something that they're not comfortable with especially when it could cost them their lives; we are equal members in this pack, even if I am the Alpha there would not be a pack without them. I needed them to remember that. I scanned the crowd, searching the faces, looking for any sign of a decision. I watched as George, Kaitlyn's mate, stepped forward, pushing through the crowd, getting down on one knee in front of us.

"I will fight for my pack."

I nodded respectfully towards him. "Thank you, George."

I watched as more pack members came forward, following George's lead and it wasn't long before more pack members were kneeling than standing. I swelled with pride, I was so lucky to have such honourable warriors who were willing to put their life on the line for their pack.

"*Thank you, each and every one of you, I am so honoured to have not only the best warriors but the most loyal. Those who remain will see David Rye, our head warrior, immediately. I thank you for your loyalty too. Our patrols will need to be doubled from this moment forward, for the safety of our pack, our family. I'm sorry that I can't prepare you for what we will find but we do not know ourselves. Take this time now to be with your loved ones and say goodbye, your mates will need to be here in the ballroom for the time that we are gone. We will have a witch with us who will teleport the wounded here for healing, she will use the mate bond as a link to send you directly here, those of you without a mate, use a close friend, a family member, anyone that you could use as an anchor to bring you here. Enjoy tonight and we will see you all here tomorrow at eleven p.m.*"

I watched as every warrior and elite there nodded, walking out the door with a look of dread. We all knew that there was a chance some of us would not come back but the reality of it was so much harder. I turned around; watching Stefan cwtch up to Jade and their pup, Kye and Alice cwtching with their pups. I moved my attention to Shannon who stood there smiling sweetly at me, I couldn't help but think about how good a mother she was going to be, the fact that there was a chance that I may not even be able to meet our pup if things went wrong tomorrow. The weight that I suddenly felt knowing that I could be unintentionally sentencing not only myself but my warriors, my friends, all to their deaths. Shannon put her arms around me, looking up at me with her beautiful eyes.

"Trust me, everything will be fine, Thomas."

Chapter Thirty-Four
Going to Battle

Shannon

I woke this morning feeling anxious, knowing what tonight could bring for the whole pack, we could lose everything, everyone we have ever loved, all because of two power hungry lunatics. I rolled over, hoping to have a morning snuggle with Thomas when I realised, he wasn't there, I climbed out of bed and searched the room; noticing that the balcony door was ajar. I pulled my robe on and walked towards it. The air was crisp outside, you could see the amber glow of the rising sun illuminating the trees in front, it really was beautiful, the birds were singing their morning chorus to help start the day, as if that was the only reason the sun was rising today.

"It's beautiful, isn't it?"

I jumped, startled slightly, I hadn't even noticed Thomas sat in a chair facing outwards, watching the sunrise.

"It is, how long have you been out here?"

"Not long, I couldn't sleep and decided I wanted to enjoy some peace before the destruction we will face tonight."

"Tom, stop thinking so negatively. You will win, I bet they haven't prepared for any of this, I bet you'll get there tonight, outnumber and kill them all. Then you'll come home and laugh about how dramatic you were being."

"Shannon, if you truly believe that then you're more naive than I thought. He's attacked us multiple times now, he kidnapped an Alpha for Goddess' sake! He probably has multiple fail safes in case something should happen, he beat his own daughter and forced her to get pregnant. He's unstable and power hungry."

"Tom—"

"No, there's a chance that I may not come home tonight, angel, and I need you to be ready for that. If that happens then you must lead the pack, until our child is old enough to do so instead."

I stood there in shock, trying to process what he was telling me, was there really a chance that he wasn't coming home? Or worse yet, was there a chance that I would have to lead the pack on my own? Thomas got up from his chair and wrapped his arms around me, breathing in my scent as he did so. I could feel my eyes filling with tears as I contemplated what could come of tonight, my heart breaking over what we could lose.

"I'm sorry, angel, I just, I want you to look at it realistically. Shall we go cwtch up in bed?"

I nodded and walked back to our bed with him, still not sure what to feel or even say at this point, the silence between us was deafening. I fell asleep on his chest, the warmth from his touch making me feel safe, secure; I couldn't imagine never feeling this again, it wasn't right. I took so long to want him and accept him, now he could be gone just like that.

We woke a few hours later, we showered and changed before heading downstairs, the atmosphere was heavy compared to what it usually was, no one was smiling, we all just looked at each other with pity; we had to keep busy, keep working.

"Doctor Bane, what equipment will you need here in an emergency to treat the wounded tonight?"

"Well, I'll need lots of bandages, gauzes, antiseptic—"

"How many Omegas do you need to help bring everything over to the ballroom?"

"Around fifteen, Luna."

"Right, I'll get some over to you, I will also get a team to run into town and get as many camping beds etc. as we can ready for treating, okay?"

"That sounds perfect, Luna."

I mind linked as many Omegas as I could assigning their jobs before I headed to the ballroom myself to help clear tables and chairs into the storage rooms.

I lined a few tables up on the stage, placing water bottles and snacks on the top, with more packs of bottles under the tables so that we didn't run out. Jade and Theo showed up to see what I was up to, it wasn't long before Jade too was helping set everything up. We even had a few cots set up in the next room for the mates that had to be here but had little ones like Jade and Alice. Any children that needed to stay had been given the room across the way from the ballroom. Clara and Emily were helping some of the wolves turn it into a big sleepover room, we had even bought a big projector screen to put in so that they could watch movies, snacks were being given as well for the children, we were also preparing meals but it was a case of eat when you can.

It was nearly three o'clock before we had all finished setting up, we were all on high alert, anxious over the events to come. I noticed Thomas and Stefan over in the corner, probably discussing strategies for tonight when they should be resting. I walked over to them slowly, their eyes falling on me as I got closer.

"You two should get some rest before tonight."

"No, it's okay we want to help."

"You will, by resting. We need to know that you're both well rested for the night you've got ahead of you, now go before I use my Luna voice on you."

The men nodded; Thomas placed a kiss on my forehead before they both left for their beds. I noticed Jade sat on a mat by the stage, breastfeeding Theo, I grabbed a bottle of water for her and walked straight over.

"I thought you might be thirsty."

"Thanks, I am pretty parched."

I handed her the bottle and watched as she drank half of it in one go, making me giggle for the first time today.

"Jade, how are you so calm?"

"What do you mean?"

"Well, I feel like I'm going to break at any moment whereas you, you're cool and collected, like always."

"Trust me, I'm not as calm as I look, I'm terrified. The idea of losing Stefan is killing me inside, I feel like I'm going to throw up constantly but I know in the end, it's pointless to stress. Right now, there is nothing that we can do unfortunately."

"We, we could call it off – stop them going."

"But then it only brings the fight to our door, where we have a hell of a lot more to lose. This man, he's out for blood, he doesn't care whose. We have too many vulnerable wolves to put their lives at risk like that."

I sat there for a moment, thinking about everything Jade was saying; ultimately, I knew she was right, although, if the fight was to come to us, we could defend ourselves, no doubt there but we'd backed into a corner, no escape.

"What if Thomas dies? I mean I can't—"

"Then we'd have the best and first lone human Luna to lead us."

"The pack wouldn't accept it, Jade; you know that."

“Shannon, everyone loves you, if it came to it, we would all follow you happily. I have zero doubts at all. Not only that, they wouldn’t have a choice.”

“Jade, you’re honestly the bestest friend I could have ever asked for. I love you.”

“I love you too, Shan, I’m going nowhere so don’t you worry, you will always have me.”

I smiled at Jade before looking down at little Theo who had finally gotten off her boob, he was so adorable, those little chubby cheeks and bright blue eyes. It made me think about if I had a little girl, would they be mates? Would they be the future of our pack? I’m sure that he would be Beta regardless just because Stefan was Beta, although I know Thomas said Stefan’s parents were warriors not Beta, his father’s Beta never had children so Thomas was free to choose his own Beta.

It was nearly eleven o’clock and everyone was arriving in the ballroom, the children were overtired, some asleep, others excited to watch the men shift and head off to battle. The older ones understood though. It was hard seeing them cry as they said goodbye to their fathers or their mothers. Watching couples hold each other tightly, knowing it could be the last time, Thomas and I walked up to the stage. Thomas spoke first.

“*I know how hard this must be for everyone, not just mates, but children, parents, brothers, sisters, friends, in one way or another everyone in this room is connected. We are not just a pack, we are a family, today will forever be known as the day we fought for our pack, our family, I am honoured to be fighting by each and every one of you. Thank you to those that are staying behind, those who will be protecting our pack here. I’d like to introduce you to someone, Aisling, come here please.*” I watched as a woman walked up onto the stage, I hadn’t actually met her yet, I wasn't even aware that she had arrived. "*This here is Aisling, she is a witch who lives with our allies at Crimson Rock, Alpha Kye here asked for her help today, she graciously accepted. I want you all to show her the same respect that you would show us of superior ranks because Aisling will be the one who plays a major part in our survival tonight.*"

I watched as everyone clapped and cheered for Aisling, you could see how grateful they were to have her and their fear somewhat relieved even if it was just a little bit, I walked forward ready to say my part.

"*I know this is a daunting time for us all but please know that you are not alone, the pack house is open to everyone who wants to stay tonight. It's during times of crisis a family will either pull together or push apart, I want us all to pull together like the strong wolves that you are. Remember this as a day of unity, not separation.*"

I looked at Thomas who was looking at the clock on the wall, fifteen minutes to twelve.

"It's time, angel."

We took the lead and walked outside, standing in the clearing in front of the pack house.

"Thomas, I'm scared. I don't want to lose you; I don't want our baby to lose you either."

"I know, my angel, but whatever happens, know that I have never loved anyone or anything as much as I love you and our baby, you will forever be my Luna."

"You will always be my Alpha."

We pressed our foreheads together before we shared one final passionate kiss, tears soaking our cheeks as we cried into each other, ignoring the people around us also crying as they said their final goodbyes.

Thomas

I stood there for a moment just holding my sweet mate, breathing her scent in for what could be the final time; I was scared, I wouldn't admit it but I was terrified. The idea of losing so many, never seeing my mate again, never meeting my first child; I never wanted this, I never wanted a fight, or anything that was coming tonight, all I wanted for my pack was for them to be happy. I pulled away from Shannon, taking just a few seconds to frame her beauty in my mind, whatever happened I would never forget her.

"We have to go now."

"I know."

Hearing how broken her voice was killed me, she knew just as well as I did that some of us may not be coming home alive again. We'd had to accept it and move on. This had to happen and we had to win if we were to have any hopes of a future here. I gave her one final kiss on her forehead before stepping away and walking to the forest, Stefan and Kye either side of me. I shifted first, running into the forest, listening proudly as I heard my pack members shifting too, following our lead as Atticus ran through the woods.

"You're a good Alpha, Thomas, I hope you realise that."

"Thank you, Atticus, you have been the best wolf that I could have ever had, I'm glad that we were made together. Together until the end?"

"Until the end, Thomas."

The rest of the run was silent, when we arrived at the clearing where the crash happened it was eerily quiet. Some warriors ran off to check the area surrounding, making sure that there were no surprises. Verity and Aisling arrived shortly after us, you could see Verity's nerves bubbling to the surface, practically shaking as she walked towards us. Atticus gave me control, allowing me to shift into my human form so that I could talk to them.

"Aisling, the first sign of trouble you send Verity back, are we clear?"

"Yes, Alpha."

"Thank you."

I turned around to talk to my warriors who were stood there waiting for my instructions.

"*You may shift to human form if that is what you wish, we will take a break here before we carry on. You must all be vigilant, from here forward we are in their territory. Do not expect them to be surprised, we are not sure whether or not they would know that we would come, whether they expected us so soon I do not know, I want to thank you all again; I am honoured to have such loyal warriors.*"

I watched as some wolves shifted to human form but the majority allowed their wolves to stay in control. Stefan and Kye shifted to human form as I approached them.

"Kye, any word from your warriors?"

"They are on their way, we managed to spare around seventy, I'm sorry we could not spare any more but our pack will need protection too."

"It's fine, I understand. Some is better than none. I contacted Alpha Lochlann for warriors as a back-up too so they are on their way. We sent the coordinates of this clearing and told them to track us from here, I did contact Alpha Richard but I heard nothing back."

"That's weird, Richard is usually good when it comes to communicating with the packs."

"Yes, well there isn't much that I can do now."

We sat down on the cold grass, discussing strategies in terms of our attack when we heard a howl from a wolf not very far, it was obviously not one of ours though because they were ordered to stay silent. We shifted into our wolves and stalked forward through the forest, following Verity's lead.

We didn't walk very far into the forest when we found another clearing, this one much larger though. I almost didn't see the army of wolves on the other side of the field, a large man stood in front of them all, with a woman by his side; she looked like Lori but they were too far away for me to know for definite.

"*I see you are returning my daughter to me, young Alpha, how kind of you. Although it won't spare you your life.*"

I shifted to my human form so that I could speak to this large man myself, Stefan questioned me via the mind link but I assured him that I knew what I was doing.

"*Verity is not yours to claim, she wishes to remain with my pack and that is what she will do.*"

The man in front of me just chuckled menacingly. I looked over at Verity, signalling to Aisling to send her back; it was sooner than I had imagined but I promised Malaki that I would protect her so this was what I had to do. I watched as she disappeared where she stood, the last thing I saw was a small smile on her lips. The laughing stopped, I looked over at the large man only to see pure anger radiating from him.

"*What have you done?*"

"*I sent her to be where she belongs, with her true mate!*"

I was surprised to see the woman step forward; her mouth opened in shock.

"What do you mean true mate, Thomas? She's mated and marked to that alpha brat."

Kye growled as she called Malaki a brat, obviously feeling protective of his new found brother-in-law which was actually quite nice to see.

"*Ah yes, Malaki is Verity's true—*"

I watched as Lori stepped forward, her jaw hung open in shock at the news of Verity being Malaki's mate.

"That's how they escaped? She was destined to be a Luna all along?"

"*I knew I should have killed him, the moment I watched his pack get massacred! He's been nothing but an inconvenience all this time!*"

Kye shifted to human form beside me, making me jump as he did, I could feel his anger growing as well as mine, he spoke before I had a chance to say anything.

"*What do you mean watched his pack get massacred?*"

"*Ah, little Alpha. I orchestrated the whole thing, you see, the Alpha, Llewelyn, was a friend of mine growing up. He welcomed me with open arms, thinking it was just a catch up, he was telling me about all the ways he ran his pack, his defences, everything. He had some really good ideas if I'm honest and if he hadn't told me, those werewolf hunters never would have been able to break through their barriers, killing each and every one of them. The only thing that I asked was that they gave me a chance to get the boy so that I could bring him here, with us, ready to impregnate my daughter when the time came. I took that boy as he walked home from school, they didn't see it coming; we drugged him with wolfsbane to keep him docile and then I watched from the border as the hunters attacked. I watched them kill everyone. Even my oldest friend... it was nothing, I thought that I would feel even a little sad but no, it was inevitable after all.*"

I stood there in horror, watching as the evil grin spread

across this horrible man's misshapen face, the fact that he could betray someone so close to him was pure evil. I hadn't even noticed Stefan and a few other men having to hold Kye back, the rogue Alpha laughing at his anger.

"*So, you mean to tell me that you betrayed your oldest friend, all for the sake of getting Verity pregnant?*"

"*Young Alpha, so naive. Everything I do is because I'm thinking of the future, building an army to destroy all others. I told your father the exact same thing last year before I killed him.*"

I could feel my anger rising uncontrollably at the thought of my father dying, this wolf thinking he had the right to claim himself as my father's murderer.

"*You, you didn't kill my father, he, he was killed by—*"

"*Rogues! Are you thick boy? I actually didn't want to kill him, he was impressive. I went to my brother's pack to fight for my rightful place as Alpha. Frederick, however, wouldn't accept my challenge for the title, he knew that he could never win a fight with me so we killed them all, most begged for their life, others begged us to let them live and some were even willing to fight for our cause. We did show mercy to those that wanted to join. Your father, however, he refused to beg, he wasn't even scared when he knew he was facing his doom. I gave him a choice; he could side with me, give me his pack willingly to strengthen my army, or die. He refused, said that his son would eventually do what he couldn't, that you, you, could beat me. I guess we'll just have to show him how wrong he was, won't we, young Alpha?*"

I couldn't contain mine or Atticus' rage any longer, we shifted, charging ahead with my warriors following closely behind. I watched as his wolves jumped in front of him. He retreated into the forest behind him with Lori; what kind of coward does that? I would have to kill every wolf there to get to him, and I would. Atticus howled as we grew closer to them.

"Kill them all, stay safe."

Atticus jumped onto a rogue, clawing its back as it bucked, trying to throw us off. We managed to rip a clean chunk out of its throat before moving onto another, this one was smaller, ripping its throat out was easy. I could no longer see the rogue alpha but I knew he wouldn't go far. The adrenaline pumping through my veins as Atticus dodged wolf after wolf, we saw Stefan being cornered by three wolves, one about to lunge. So we forced ourselves forward, going as fast as we could, barrelling into one of them but not in time before the other two had already pounced on him. I killed the one I had jumped before helping Stefan with his two, he was bleeding pretty badly.

"Do you need to go back?"

"No, I'm good for a few rounds."

I couldn't help but chuckle as he pranced into action, killing a few wolves on his way into battle, I could feel myself stumble as I felt mind links severing, this meant that we were losing wolves.

"AISLINGGGG!"

She had managed a spell to connect her and Kye via our mind link for only a few more hours, I've never been more grateful to have a witch on our side. I searched the field only to find her surrounded by about fifteen wolves, using her power to protect herself which is obviously why she wasn't able to teleport the wounded to get help.

"WE NEED PROTECTION AROUND AISLING! NOWWWWW!"

We ran towards Aisling only to be tackled by a wolf on my way taking a chunk out of our side. Atticus howled in pain before attacking the wolf back, biting hard on its neck until it went limp in our jaws. It was only a second before another wolf had pounced on our back, trying to bite at my throat. Atticus managed to throw the wolf off to the side, clamping its leg with its jaw, feeling the bone completely shatter under his teeth. He pinned the wolf to the already bloodstained grass, ripping his head clean off. We were able to look back up at Aisling, seeing that the rogues around her were being attacked by our own wolves meaning that she was finally able to start sending wolves back to the pack. I didn't need to look to know that some were just bodies, I could feel the grief and the loss through our link. The pain radiating from the wolves that had lost their mates, family members, friends. But I couldn't focus on that right now; I looked towards the forest only to see more rogues joining the battle, which wasn't good. We were losing numbers quickly here after already being outnumbered, at this point it would be a miracle if we won. I ran towards the army of new rogues with Kye and Stefan once again at my side.

"What are we doing?" Stefan shouted apprehensively as we ran towards the newcomers.

"We're fighting for our pack, until the end."

"If we die, we die together."

"It's been an honour to fight by your side, lads," Kye spoke highly through our mind link, we all shared one final look before we spoke in unison via our mind link.

"For our family."

We jumped into action, attacking the rogues that had just joined the fight, looking back for only a second to see my men getting covered by both sets of rogues; in this second, a rogue took advantage, pinning me to the ground, snapping at me as I struggled under his grip, this was it, I looked around to see Kye and Stefan in similar positions, Aisling once again surrounded, unable to help anyone as she fought to protect herself. It was over, we'd lost. I couldn't help but think of Shannon and our baby, back at our pack, waiting for me to come home, going through her pregnancy without me, having our baby without me; raising our daughter alone... that is if the rogues didn't go after them next. No, I couldn't let that happen, we would end this, *today.*

Suddenly, there was a chorus of howls around us, distracting the rogues long enough for me, Stefan and Kye to get the upper hand, killing the ones that held us down, springing into action as our back-up arrived; Kye's warriors joining in with the fight, protecting their Alpha, attacking one rogue after another.

"YESSSSS."

My remaining warriors shouted in unison via the mind link, relieved at the help we were receiving, knowing that without it we would surely be dead. I turned around and finally made eye contact with the rogue Alpha, watching as he pushed Lori into the ground before shifting and running into the forest.

I ran after him without a care in the world, leaving the battle behind me, knowing one thing for sure; I had to be the one to kill him. I finally caught up to him, he stopped outside what looked like an abandoned castle, this must be their hideaway, he shifted in front of me but I stayed in my wolf form.

"*You really think you can beat me, young Alpha? Well as we speak, hunters are finishing up at Alpha Richard's pack and they will be coming for yours soon, so even with my death your pack will forever be doomed.*"

"He's lying, Thomas, as long as Shannon is Luna and your baby survives, the pack will survive."

"I know, Atticus, let's kill him."

Atticus growled before running at the man, watching as he

changed into his wolf, although he was an Alpha, I was surprised to see he had a grey wolf, he said he was an Alpha, Alphas always had black wolves, his was nowhere near as large as Atticus but he was powerful; he managed to dodge my attack, using his claw to scratch at my face, blood dripping from it as I lunged again, managing to land on his back, taking a chunk out of his shoulder. It wasn't long before he threw me off and we began circling each other. I was weaker than he was right now, I had been fighting for who knows how long now whereas he hadn't joined in on any of the fight, if I was going to win this, I needed a strategy, the sun was rising above the trees but all it did was create shadows.

"Thomas, where are you?" Stefan shouted through the mind link but I didn't have a chance to respond before the rogue alpha attacked us, pinning us down to the ground. We managed to grip his leg with our jaw, struggling for a bit before finally knocking him down to the floor. We threw ourselves at him, snarling as we tried to rip his throat out, we snarled and fought on the floor for a moment when we finally got the upper hand.

"*TRISTANNNNN!*"

There were footsteps behind us as Lori broke through the forest screaming, almost stealing the rogue alpha's attention; it was only for a second but it was long enough for me to rip his throat out completely, listening with satisfaction as Lori screamed in distress watching her 'Tristan' shift back into his human body, completely lifeless. Atticus stood there for a moment, watching with satisfaction, knowing that this deranged, power-hungry man couldn't hurt anyone else again, his reign of terror was over. We turned around, watching as Lori shifted, running at us, her wolf practically foaming at the mouth; they were that angry. She didn't get very far before Stefan's wolf had jumped on her back, ripping her throat out in one swift move.

"Thank you," I mind linked him, relieved to know that he had my back.

"No worries, you know I have your back." I looked at Stefan with nothing but respect, knowing that he truly did always have my back.

"It's over, we won. They're all dead." Kye mind linked us. I couldn't help but collapse to the ground beneath me, exhausted and in pain but overall relieved; we thought we were losing, we thought we'd all die but we beat them, we won. We were going home.

Me and Stefan carried the two bodies through the woods to the clearing where the warriors of three packs were already stacking them. I was surprised to see Alpha Lochlann and his Beta Oscar here; I threw the body on the floor before embracing them both in a hug.

"Thank you, you saved our asses."

"If something had happened to you, we couldn't look at our pack the same knowing that we didn't do everything we could to help. You're not just an ally, Thomas, you're a friend."

I couldn't help but smile as Lochlann spoke, it was true, we were all really close and always helped in times of crisis. I just never expected them to put their own lives on the line for a battle that wasn't theirs.

Once we had finished stacking the bodies, Aisling used her magic to start a fire instantly. We all collapsed on the field, watching as the bodies of the rogues turned to ash, the smoke delivering them to the moon goddess who would ultimately decide their fate. I couldn't wait to go home.

Chapter Thirty-Five
Waiting for Answers

Shannon

The atmosphere was heavy as we all sat there waiting for a sign, any sign that they were okay, that nothing had happened although I guess that we'd realise through the mate bond if something was wrong.

Two hours had passed before anything happened, even Malaki was in the ballroom so that he could be with Alice, supporting each other and all that. Suddenly there was a slow forming mist which turned into Verity after a minute. I don't think I'll ever be tired of watching someone teleport, it was amazing. We rushed to Verity's side as she collapsed into her mate, seeking comfort; we didn't expect her back so soon.

"Verity, what happened?"

"Th-they were waiting for us, there were so many… it looked like they matched our army, maybe even exceeded it."

"What do you mean waiting for you? They couldn't have known, surely!"

"I don't know what to tell you, Shannon! I just know that there was a whole army waiting, with my father leading them!"

I stood back for a moment, tears clouding my vision as worry took over, the idea of our pack being outnumbered whilst they were out there fighting for us. Panic took over.

"Is everything completely ready? Let's make sure we're ready, get some gauzes, bandages, have ice ready! Where is the antiseptic?"

I ran around as we filled buckets with ice, making sure we had everything we needed to hand but that's when the screaming started, the pain through the mate bond taking over.

"AHHHHHHH!"

We rushed to those who were screaming before two of our men appeared by their mates, they cradled them whilst Doctor Bane and Kaitlyn rushed to their side to heal them. Luckily it was just minor injuries, no deaths right now, they were going to be okay. Another man appeared, again only injured, but his wounds were quite severe. The screaming grew louder though, I ran over to one of the women who was hysterical, holding her trying to help through the pain as she doubled over, clutching her heart.

"WHERE IS HE? NOOOOO!"

"It's—it's okay, Aisling will get him here, she will!"

That's when the screaming intensified throughout the room, they were no longer just getting injured, our wolves were dying. You could feel the bonds severing via the mind link, the woman I held pushed me off her, running out of the hall screaming before I could stop her. I had no idea what to do, the pain was something I'd never felt before and that was just through our pack link, not even a mate bond like so many in the room were being crippled by. I searched for Jade and ran to her.

"Jade, what do we do? How do we help?"

She looked up at me, her face soaked in tears, cwtching her tiny baby Theo.

"Shannon, there's nothing we can do. They were outnumbered… we… we just wait, wait for our turn to feel the pain."

"NO, I refuse to believe that. We, we can't lose! Thomas wouldn't allow it!"

"Well, Thomas is out of his depth! Face it, Shannon, we've lost!"

That was when it happened, bodies upon bodies appearing by their already hysterical mates, most not moving, they were drenched in blood, some were missing limbs, others heads, it was terrifying, the screaming grew worse. Doctor Bane rushed around, looking for someone to save, finally we heard a little bit of hope.

"HELP! HE'S ALIVE! OVER HERE!"

We rushed over to see one of the warriors alive, wounded pretty badly but Kaitlyn was already working on healing him, I recognised him as Harvey, one of our newer warriors.

"Harvey, what happened?"

"Th-they, there were too many, but, help, arrived."

Harvey's eyes closed, causing his mate to scream even more.

"Juniper, it's okay, he's just unconscious. He's healing well, okay?"

Kaitlyn was reassuring Juniper, it was then that more and more people started shouting for help, realising we had more men that were coming back. Although gravely injured; they were alive. Doctor Bane and Kaitlyn ran around healing the harshest injuries whilst the nurses ran around bandaging and caring for those with minor injuries.

The screaming eventually went silent, those who lost their mates just cradled their bodies on the cold floor, refusing to let them go. I sat with Jade and Theo, putting my arm around her, seeking comfort until I knew Thomas was okay.

"Have you felt anything from Stefan?"

"He's injured but I don't think it's anything major or he would be here, wouldn't he?"

"I guess you're right."

We sat together for a moment, surveying the ballroom when another mist formed in front of us, eventually it took the physical form of Aisling; she collapsed in front of us, I jumped forward, catching her as best as I could.

"Aisling, are you okay?"

Studying her I could see blood covering ninety per cent of her body, she looked exhausted, weak, it was weird seeing the confident witch from this evening looking so weak.

"I'm fine, it just takes a lot of energy to use as much magic as I had to tonight. They nearly killed us all, if it wasn't for the wolves who arrived late, we would have died. I-I'm sorry I couldn't save everyone. They knew what the plan was straight away and kept coming after me, I had to protect myself."

"Aisling, don't apologise. You did everything you could have, these men are alive thanks to you."

"Thank you, Luna, your daughter will be a great leader with you as her guide."

"My daughter?"

Aisling smiled at me tiredly, I watched as her body went limp, slowly turning to ashes there in my arms; I felt my vision cloud and couldn't help but sit there sobbing into the ashes that were once Aisling's body. Alice was at my side, wrapping me into a warm hug.

"It's over now, they'll be home soon."

I broke down, unable to contain my sadness any longer as I thought about everyone we had lost tonight.

Chapter Thirty-Six
Mourning Our Fallen Heroes

Thomas

I watched as the fire grew stronger, destroying every single rogue body on this field, I prayed the moon goddess made Tristan and Lori suffer for their crimes. I looked over at Aisling who looked pale and weak by this point, I walked over to her as she swayed in her spot.

"Aisling, you should teleport back to the pack, get some rest."

"But, Alpha, the rest of the bodies."

"It's okay, we will carry them back. You need rest more than any of us. Without you, I'm sure a lot more would have died. I can't thank you enough."

"It was my honour to serve under you, Thomas, you will lead the new world well."

"The new world?"

"Yes, I've seen it, Thomas. This will not be your last battle, there is a bigger one to come, one that will decide the fate of our world. You and Shannon, you are the future."

I went to question Aisling more but she had already apparated away, back to the pack for rest no doubt. When we get back, we will celebrate not only my wolves' but her courage too.

I walked over to Stefan who was talking to Lochlann's Beta Oscar.

"Hey, Oscar, do you think you and your men could help carry our wounded and deceased back please?"

"It would be an honour, Thomas. Let me discuss it with Alpha Lochlann first though, you know I can't agree to anything without his say so."

"Yes, no problem. Stefan, could I steal you for a second?"

"Of course, Alpha."

I nodded at Oscar before steering Stefan away from him.

"Stef, we have at least twenty dead here and who knows how many died back at the pack."

"I know, Tom, but like you keep saying, it's what needed to be done."

"We must try and contact Alpha Richard's pack too, if what the Alpha said was true there could be a lot of dead wolves to put to rest."

"I will send some scouts, Thomas, my men are okay, hardly any casualties. I can send a group of twenty now."

Kye made me jump, he had a habit of sneaking up on people, I don't know how he's able to be so quiet.

"Are you sure, Kye? They did just battle an army of rogues?"

"Yes, I'm sure. Have you seen Aisling? I wanted to make sure that she was okay, she used a lot of magic tonight."

"I sent her back to the pack to rest, Kye, she looked exhausted."

"Well, I'm glad she listened, let me rally my men."

I watched as Kye ran off across the field, his men grouping around him for a few moments before heading east towards Alpha Richard's pack, I had a bad feeling about it. I'm pretty sure that if what the Alpha said was true that they would be too late.

We worked together, finding ways to carry the wounded gently, even searching through the abandoned hospital for stretchers and, sadly, body bags. It was surprisingly well stocked but my guess is they never needed this sort of stuff because they were used to killing; if a rogue gets injured, they usually just kill them so that they aren't slowing them down. It was brutal but necessary in their eyes.

The walk back to the pack was long and exhausting, we managed to find clothes in the hospital too so at least we weren't walking naked through the woods. Out of nearly three hundred wolves, thanks to our alliance, only eighty of us were left standing, trying to carry the bodies of our fallen wolves home. Carrying those who were alive but unable to walk; it was the hardest thing I'd done in my life. By the time we reached the meadow by the house the sun had risen, leaving a warm, beautiful glow of light over us, reminding us that even during our darkest of days there is always a light at the end of it.

"*We will place our dead gently here; it will give their widows and family a chance to say goodbye today before we put them to rest tonight.*"

"*Yes, Alpha.*"

I watched as all of our fallen wolves were laid peacefully in the meadow, the flowers and grass cascading around them. Once we knew that they were all laid peacefully we headed to the pack house where we knew everyone would be waiting. Kaitlyn and Doctor Bane would be able to look everyone over, healing those that needed it.

We walked back to the pack house slowly, it was as if our feet were made of lead as we struggled to force ourselves forward. Upon entering, the smell of blood was prominent, the atmosphere extremely heavy. In the ballroom everyone's heads hung low, bodies placed delicately at the edge of the room. It was Shannon that noticed us first, screaming in excitement as she ran towards me. I picked her up, spinning her around in a circle before placing my lips hungrily on her lips, it was like ecstasy, it was exactly what I needed to help bring me back to earth after everything in the last twenty-four hours. I noticed Shannon had started sobbing uncontrollably as I held her in my arms.

"Th-Thomas, I-I thought you were dead."

I chuckled half-heartedly, hoping to ease her sadness.

"There is no way I'm going anywhere until I've met our baby and made you my wife."

She smirked at me, looking up at me through her beautiful full lashes, with those mesmerising sky blue eyes.

"Our *daughter.*"

"What do you mean? I thought you couldn't tell yet?"

"It's something Aisling said before she—"

"Before she what?"

"She's gone, Thomas. She passed shortly after apparating here."

I fell to the floor overcome with grief, suddenly realising why she looked so exhausted, so frail, she used every ounce of her life force for this battle. I-I asked her to, I didn't think that she would die, I didn't know witches could die from overuse of magic.

"Thomas, it's not your fault. I know how you think but don't blame yourself, okay?"

I nodded, knowing that she was right, we all knew the risks we were making by joining the fight; yet we did it anyway. I got up off the floor, brushing myself as I pushed past my pack members who were all reuniting, comforting each other. I stood at the front of the stage, ready to address the pack.

"*We will move all of the bodies to the meadow, take your time today to say a proper goodbye; we will mourn together at the loss of our fellow pack members but they deserve to be welcomed by our moon goddess sooner rather than later. They deserve peace. Could anyone who is able to, help move our dead from here please and place them respectfully in the meadow. Thank you.*"

I climbed down from the stage, approaching the bodies on the right as Shannon chased after me.

"Thomas, what was that?"

"What was what, my angel?"

"That sorry ass excuse of a speech you made then!"

"Excuse me?"

"This is a time where you need to remind the pack about unity, love and strength. Not just *we're burning the bodies tonight who wants to help move them?* Our members lost their mates, their siblings, some lost children and parents, where is your compassion? Where is the love?"

"I know, Shan, but right now it's what needs to be done."

I watched as Shannon stomped her feet, grunting in anger before storming out of the ballroom, Jade and Alice chasing after her before Stefan and Kye made their way over to me.

"She has a point, man."

"*I know she does, now help me move this body.*"

"You mean Shamus? Sure."

I looked down at the body that me and Stefan were picking up, I hadn't even thought to look at who it was or anything… I just saw it as a body, nothing more, Shamus was a loyal man, he had two beautiful daughters and a doting wife. His wife passed away because of cancer two years ago, he never met anyone else… thankfully his daughters had their own children by then but still, he was loyal to my father and loyal to me, yet I didn't even acknowledge his death.

I spent the day organising as many flowers as the local

florists could give me, having them delivered to the pack house rather than the meadow for obvious reasons. I didn't see Shannon for the rest of the day, I know I did wrong but I'm not sure anyone would know what to say after what happened today.

The day went by pretty quick, I came to the field before the rest of the pack to place a white sheet over each of our fallen soldiers. If there weren't so many bodies, I would have built a bonfire to house them but the size we'd need would likely take the whole forest with it. There were fire pits along each row of bodies, ready for the chosen member to light, usually a mate or a parent, some were brothers and sisters, some like Shamus' daughter were older children. I watched as everyone approached holding candles and flowers, walking along the sides of the bodies but standing back so that it was only family close. Shannon approached me, wrapping her arms around me and cwtching in to me, seeking comfort which I was happy to offer as best as I could. As night fell and the flames became our only light source, I felt it was appropriate to start.

"*I know that my speech earlier was both insensitive and unjust but I want each and every one of you to know that I will forever be thankful to everyone that played an active part in last night's battle. Whether you were out there fighting with us, helping wounded or patrolling the borders, we thank you so much, the wolves that fought by my side last night were some of the strongest that I have ever had the pleasure to meet. Even when we saw that we were incredibly outnumbered they still stood their ground and fought by my side, they killed as many rogues as they could before they lost their own lives. They sacrificed their own lives to ensure the future of our pack. I would also like to thank Alpha Kye's and Alpha Lochlann's warriors for their loyalty, their courage and most of all their impeccable timing because without their warriors I don't think any of us would have come home. Many of you know that we had a witch helping us in the battle. It is thanks to her that our wounded were able to get back here so quickly, but what most of you don't know is that she used every ounce of energy that she had left to do so, resulting in her death too. We have also learned that one of our alliance packs, Alpha Richard's, of Silver Valley, was attacked by werewolf hunters last night. There were no survivors. So, we will also remember them as we remember our own fallen wolves tonight, then as we move forward, we won't look back on this day and mourn; we will look back and we will celebrate the lives of our fallen heroes, the sacrifice that they made for not only our pack but the world. I am proud to call every single one of you family, let this devastation unite us not tear us apart! Let the moon goddess welcome our heroes and celebrate their sacrifice! For I will forever be indebted to them for their sacrifice!"*

I got down on one knee bowing down at the bodies in front of me, showing how thankful I was for their sacrifice and how I only felt nothing but respect for them. Shannon followed suit, holding my hand as she too bowed down in respect to our fallen heroes, their families coming forward to light their bodies, using the smoke to free them from this earth.

"Thomas, let me take control. I too would like to pay tribute to our fallen heroes."

"Of course, Atticus."

I moved to the side slightly so that Shannon wasn't going to be hurt by Atticus taking control. I felt myself shifting and merely becoming a passenger. I watched as Atticus bowed towards the bodies that were slowly turning to flames, then he lay on his belly, lifting his head to the moon. I thought he was going to howl but it sounded painful, and long – almost as if he was singing. I could feel the tears moving down his face as he cried his song to the moon, I realised that other members of the pack had also shifted around our fallen pack members, joining in with Atticus' mournful song; it was… almost beautiful.

Chapter Thirty-Seven
One Year Later

Shannon

"Oh, Thomas, will you hurry up? You take longer than me and Arielle to get ready!"

"I'm coming!"

I watched as my gorgeous mate came running into the living area, his trousers in his hand, nearly tripping over one of Arielle's toys that I had missed when tidying up.

"Why haven't you got your trousers on?"

I couldn't help but laugh as I watched him blush red, trying to put his trousers on as fast as he could, I heard Arielle stirring in her pram, today is the one year anniversary of the rogue battle, everyone was to wear anything colourful as a tribute to those we lost, after all it was thanks to them that we are all still here.

"Have you heard from Alice and Kye? Are they coming today?"

"No, angel, they have lots to do today. There's an Alpha visiting them, although it's strange I've never heard of him before today."

"Strange, are you ready now?"

"Yes, let's go."

I started pushing Arielle's pram down the corridor towards the lift, I couldn't help but stare at her, her fair skin, crystal blue eyes, she had tight, curly golden blonde hair. Today I put a floral white and blue dress on her for the occasion; I never thought I could create something as perfect as her, but I did… Thomas helped too, I guess.

Walking out of the lift, the lobby looked beautiful, there were white and red roses scattered everywhere, a red carpet leading to the meadow where we said goodbye to their bodies. We walked along the red carpet, straight to the meadow where we knew our pack members would be waiting for us; we were supposed to be there first but no, Thomas was late home from a meeting so took longer to get ready. Nothing new, I suppose.

We had chairs set up in rows in front of a stage where Thomas planned to make his speech. We walked through an aisle we had put in the middle, smiling sweetly as we passed each pack member. You could see that a lot of them had spent most of today crying which was understandable, as much as we wanted to view today positively, we still lost eighty pack members. We'd also lost thirty more since because they couldn't live without their mates. I sat down at the front next to Jade who was trying to keep Theo from running off, he doesn't stop, ever, Stefan and Jade need eyes in the back of their head with his energy. I watched as Thomas walked onto the stage nearing the front so that he could speak.

"Good afternoon, everyone, I'm honoured to be the one here, speaking on behalf of our pack. As we all know, today marks the one year anniversary of the battle that killed so many people dear to us. We all knew what could happen going into battle, what we didn't know was the pain and loss that we would suffer as the year progressed. We lost so many good people but I'd like to think that we have grown as a pack because of our loss. It pushed us together, made our bonds stronger. I am proud to call each of you a member of not only my pack, but my family, when we grieve, we grieve together. I want everyone to know that you are never

alone, even in your darkest hour, there is always someone here."

Thomas walked to the back of the stage where there was a large object hidden beneath a sheet. He hadn't told anyone what was under there, it was something organised completely by him. I watched as he pulled the sheet down, revealing what looked like a giant plaque, there were gasps through the crowd as people stared at the plaque.

"On this plaque is the name of every single pack member and their wolves that we lost because of everything last year. As werewolves we tend to honour our human side more than we do our wolves but I think especially after last year it is important to remember that we are nothing without our wolves. It will be a memorial in honour of their service to our pack. I wanted everyone to have a place that they could come to, to mourn, to visit, anything. I want future generations to look at this plaque in years to come and remember the sacrifice these wolves made for us. We will be having a park installed and a picnic area too. This won't be instantaneous, it will take time but eventually it will be beautiful. Let's not look upon this place in sadness but in pride. Come here and celebrate with them, take the time to visit them, we will never forget what they have done for us."

The members around me clapped as they looked up at Thomas, climbing out of their chairs to go and admire the plaque that Thomas had built. I watched as Jade lost her grip on Theo, him bolting across the field, faster than Jade and Stefan could keep up. I chuckled before walking over to Thomas, wrapping my arms around him, pulling him into a passionate kiss.

"It's beautiful, Thomas."

"I'm glad, I know that we normally don't have headstones or anything but I felt like we needed something to honour them properly for their sacrifice. If you look, right… over… here. I had Aisling's name made slightly bigger than the rest, I felt like she deserved it for her sacrifice."

I stood there for a moment admiring the workmanship that obviously went into it, the overall build was rock but the gold had been screwed into the giant rock, each name was carved beautifully into the gold sides. I really could imagine coming here to visit the plaque whilst taking the kids for a picnic and teaching them about the ones that sacrificed themselves. I looked around the field, imagining what it would look like when it was finished, it would be beautiful.

We all walked back to the pack house where everyone had prepared a special dish each, me and Thomas baked cupcakes, brownies and even managed some fried chicken. We wanted to do more but it was more than enough work trying to cook enough for everyone in the pack. We only managed two hundred cupcakes but I'm sure that everyone else brought enough to satisfy everyone. Walking into the ballroom I was surprised to see candles everywhere, there were photos hung on the walls and on the stage at the front. Families and friends donated them so that we could all admire the faces of our heroes that we were here to honour.

The day went better than we could have hoped, there was lots of crying which was to be expected. I looked around the room whilst Thomas cwtched Arielle, there were three people missing that had every right to be there. I left the ballroom, walking out of the pack house and heading towards a house that has always stood on its own at the edge of the forest. I knocked before entering, admiring how well the place looked now. It used to be riddled with cobwebs and spiders, it looked as if no one had ever taken care of the place but they had turned it round. It looked lovely and clean, the walls were painted, floors carpeted – it finally looked like a home.

"Verity, Malaki? Are you here?"

I heard shuffling in one of the back rooms before Verity appeared, her eyes puffy and red; obviously from crying.

"Are you okay? When I didn't see you in the ballroom or at the meadow, I got worried."

"Uhm, yes, Luna. I'm fine."

"Come on, Ver, tell me what's going on?"

"I just—I didn't think I had any right to be there with the pack, mourning and celebrating with the rest of you."

"Ver, if it wasn't for you, we'd have never known, we wouldn't have had time to prepare for battle, they… they would have come for us all."

"But, if I hadn't started the whole vendetta then Jason wouldn't be dead, neither would Luke, Scott and Ryan."

"I mean that wasn't all you, your mother played a large part in that, Ver, she poisoned you, maybe not physically but mentally. You only ever did what you thought would get her to love you, there's nothing wrong about that. Heck, you tried to kill me twice and I don't hate you."

"You—you don't?"

"No, Verity, and you shouldn't hate yourself. Now come on, where's Malaki and Jacey?"

"They left for the party about ten minutes ago."

"Well, come on. Let's join them."

Verity smiled as I linked my arm with hers, dragging her back to the party with me where Thomas and Malaki waited to greet us. Malaki has become a big part of the pack, Thomas is making him his Gamma during the next full moon and giving them the option to move into the pack house on the Gamma floor if they want to. We lost Luke's mate about a week after the battle, she just didn't wake up. Doctor Bane thinks her heart just couldn't take all the loss; it was hard and only the start of more pack members not waking up but we haven't lost anyone else in six months so it's time to start moving forward, planning ahead.

The day went by quickly, by the time ten o'clock came around I was exhausted. Arielle was asleep in her pram so I walked over to Thomas, to inform him that I was going to bed with Arielle.

"Hey, honey, we're going to head to bed now, okay?"

"Yeah, do you want me to come?"

"No, it's okay. You worked hard planning today, enjoy it."

"Okay, I love you, angel."

"I love you too."

I gave Thomas a kiss before going up to our room in the lift. I changed Arielle's nappy and placed her in a clean baby-grow before placing her gently in her cot. I walked over to the bathroom to have a quick wash and put my own pjs on, enjoying the peace that rarely happens in such a busy house. By the time I got back to my bed I could feel my eyelids drooping, ready to welcome sleep. I fell asleep as soon as my head touched my pillow.

I was woken in the early hours by what felt like something ripping through me, inside – out. I couldn't help the scream that escaped my lips, I tried to move but I couldn't, the pain was crippling me, I could feel people trying to connect with me via mind link but the pain was overwhelming me. Jade broke through my bedroom door, running straight over to me.

"Shan, what's going on?"

"Th-Thomas."

"Thomas is fine, well, he looks just like you actually. We thought someone was hurting you."

"G-g-get him here."

I winced as I looked up, trying to focus on Jade, her eyes fogged over as she mind linked Stefan; I could hear Arielle crying in between my screams of agony, contractions weren't even this bad! When Stefan finally brought Thomas in it was if there was a tornado in the room, the air grew cold, papers were blown everywhere, doors and windows blown open, the pain was easing as a mist filled the room.

"What's going on?"

I shouted but the wind was too loud for anyone to hear me, I'm sure, I concentrated as hard as I could to mind link Jade.

"GET ARIELLE OUT OF HERE!"

She looked at me and nodded before fighting against the wind to get out of the bedroom door with my daughter in her arms. I watched in awe as the wind centred itself in the middle of our room, the pain almost completely gone, I was able to climb up onto my knees, eventually sitting on the edge of the bed as I watched the mist take form of two terrified little girls and the smallest wolf I had ever seen. I gasped, it was the triplets, the spell, it worked. But that meant…